Praise for Catherine Asaro's Aronsdale novels

"Fans of fantasy romance: Run, don't walk, to the bookstore to get *Charmed Destinies*. You will not be disappointed. Truly original plots, amazing writing, and touches of humor made this anthology a wonderful read.... 'Moonglow' by Catherine Asaro is the most amazing and beautiful love story I have read this year...it took my breath away. It's a perfect balance between fantasy and romance, and I am now wondering why I took so long to read Catherine Asaro."
— *Fantasy Romance Writers*

"Asaro has created a magical world in 'Moonglow.' It will leave readers desperate to know more about these enticing characters."
— *Romantic Times BOOKreviews*

"Readers will love this epic romantic fantasy that reads like an adult fairy tale."
— *The Best Reviews* on *The Charmed Sphere*

JUL 0 7 2007

Catherine Asaro

The FIRE OPAL

LUNA™
www.LUNA-Books.com

LUNA™

First edition July 2007

THE FIRE OPAL

ISBN-13: 978-0-373-80277-7
ISBN-10:   0-373-80277-3

Acknowledgments

I would like to thank the following readers for their much-appreciated input. Their comments have made this a better book. Any mistakes that remain were introduced by pernicious imps.

For reading the manuscript and giving me the benefit of their wisdom and insights: Aly Parsons, Kate Dolan, and Angie Boytner. For their critiques on scenes, Aly's Writing Group: Aly Parsons with (in the proverbial alphabetical order) Al Carroll, John Hemry, J. G. Huckenpöler, Simcha Kuritzky, Bud Sparhawk, and Connie Warner. Special thanks to my much-appreciated editor, Stacy Boyd, and also to Mary-Theresa Hussey, Kathleen Oudit, Julie Messore, Dee Tenorio, and all the other fine people at LUNA who helped make this book possible; to Stephanie Pau-Mun Law, the artist who does my gorgeous covers; to Binnie Braunstein, for all her work and enthusiasm on my behalf; to my wonderful agent, Eleanor Wood, of Spectrum Literary Agency.

A heartfelt thanks to the shining lights in my life, my husband John Cannizzo, and my daughter Cathy, for their love.

To My Sisters,
Nina and Marianna
With love

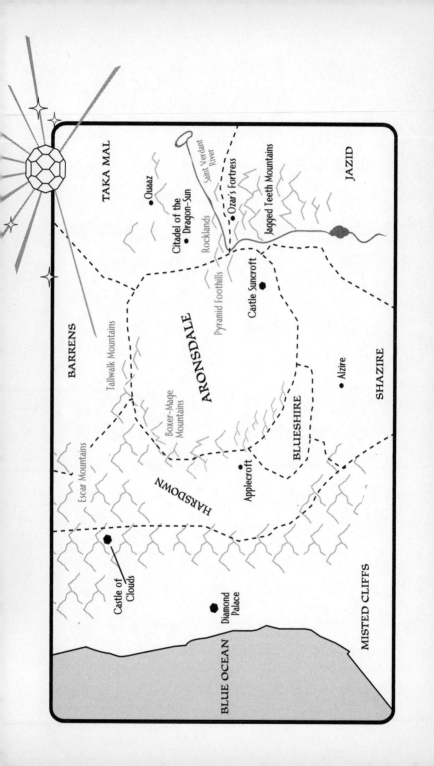

Contents

A Final Sunset

Ginger-Sun feared her own power.

She was alone inside the RayLight Chamber, a circular room two paces across with stained-glass walls. Afternoon sun hit skylights in the roof far above her, and mirrors reflected the light down to where she stood. She craved the radiance that bathed her body, for as long as it shone, she was safe from her inner darkness.

She served as a priestess for the Dragon-Sun, who blazed in the sky and lit the world. Her people worshipped the day. Her duties in the village of Sky Flames were concerned with offering comfort to her people and carrying out ceremonies in praise of the sun. She could do no magic now. She knew this to be true—for it was the middle of the day.

Her spells worked only at night.

Ginger opened her hand and stared at the fire opal on her palm. Such a dangerous gem. Her grandfather had given her the four-sided pyramid on her fifth birthday. Years ago, she had discovered it allowed her to create spells of heat and light. She had never heard of anyone with such abilities. No one knew about her power; she guarded that secret as she would her own life. It would be dangerous enough if her people suspected she could do spells; if they realized she could do them *only* at night, gods only knew how they would deal with that trespass against her calling to the dragon.

"Ginger-Sun?" a man called, using the honorific that named her as a priestess. "Come quick!"

His urgent tone jolted her. Whoever called couldn't enter here; this chamber was forbidden to all but the priestess. As she opened the door, the rumble of men talking rolled over her. The presence of so many rough voices unsettled Ginger. She felt suddenly conscious of her vulnerability; this building was a ten-minute walk from the village and she lived alone.

Ginger entered the main temple, a large room with a roof of inverted terraces high above her head. A fountain bubbled nearby, fed from the village irrigation system, and a statue of the dragon stood within it, his wings spread. Instead of fire, he breathed water. It rose into the air from his upturned head and cascaded down his body into the square basin.

Across the room, five men had gathered by the wall. They wore coarse trousers, shirts and boots encrusted with sand. The sun had weathered their faces, and heavy muscles corded their arms. Tools hung from their belts. They had shovels strapped to their backs—and massive axes.

Ginger's pulse leapt. Why did they want her? She took a breath, steeling herself. Her calling required she tend anyone who came to the temple, no matter how threatening. She walked toward them, seeking to appear calm, though sweat dampened her palms. Her bare feet made no sound on the floor. She wore the traditional garb of a priestess, a gold silk wrap that fit her snugly from neck to ankle and constrained the size of her steps.

As she reached the group, a stocky man with gnarled muscles spun around and grasped the handle of the axe sticking up over his shoulder. Ginger gulped, her gaze fixed on the blade as he pulled it above his shoulder.

Then he paused, and the clenched set of his face eased. With a start, she recognized him as Harjan, who had been a friend of her parents before they passed away. Now that she could see the others better, she realized they were miners who worked the ore flats outside the village. They kept watch over the temple, too, for her protection. The relief that washed over her was so intense, it felt visceral.

Harjan lowered his arm. "My apology for disturbing your evening, Priestess."

"Are you all right, Jan?" she asked. His pallor worried her. Behind the miners, someone was lying on a stone ledge that jutted out from the wall. A makeshift litter lay on the floor, and blood stained the men's clothes. The miners averted their gazes more than usual when she looked at them.

"Has there been an accident?" she asked.

"Not an accident," Harjan said. "This man was stabbed."

"We didn't want to bring him here, Priestess," another man said with a look of apology. "But only you can do the rites."

Ah, no. They wouldn't have come to her if the man lived; the village had another healer who treated the men. But only Ginger could give the Sunset Rites to a person whose spirit had left his body to walk among the dead.

Afraid of what she would find, she walked forward, and the miners moved aside. A large man lay on the shelf. She sat next to the body and pulled a knot of black hair off his face. The man looked in his midthirties, with a square chin and strong nose, but that was all she could see. Bruises covered his face, and deep gashes had gored his torso, his arms, even his legs. Blood soaked his clothes. She pulled away scraps of his shirt and winced as coagulated blood smeared her hand. The ragged pattern of his wounds told a gruesome tale, that he had fought hard against his assailants—and lost the battle.

"Gods," someone muttered. "Why would anyone do this?"

A tear ran down Ginger's face. "Only the Dragon-Sun can answer that." She couldn't imagine how he could burn in the sky while such a monstrous crime took place below him. "Do any of you know this man?"

"Never seen the poor bastard," another man answered. "We don't know what happened."

"I'm sorry we had to show you this," Harjan said.

She looked up at him through a mist of tears. "You were right to bring him."

"Ach, Ginger-Sun." He lifted his hand as if to lay it on her shoulder, offering comfort, but he stopped himself in time, before he touched her.

"Could you bring him to the Sunset Chamber?" Her voice trembled. If she didn't perform the rites before sundown, the man's spirit could be condemned to wander the site of his murder until his killers died.

The miners seemed relieved to take action. They lifted the body onto the litter and carried it across the temple, past the RayLight Chamber, which no longer glowed now that the sun was too low in the sky.

At the far wall, Ginger opened an arched door with a window at its apex that depicted the setting sun. The floor, walls and ceiling in the chamber beyond were bare stone in the red and ochre hues of the desert, a stark but fitting memorial to those who lost their lives in this harsh land. Here the dead received their blessing before their spirit traveled to the realms beyond.

They laid the body on a stone table that filled much of the chamber. The only light came from slits where the ceiling met the walls, and shadows were filling the room as the day aged into night. She hoped she could complete the rites in time; otherwise she would have to remain here all night with the corpse, to ensure its spirit didn't become trapped in the realm of the living.

Harjan was watching her. "We can stay."

His offer touched her, but they both knew she had to refuse. If she allowed the uninitiated to stay while she performed the rites, she risked stirring the wrath of the Dragon-Sun.

"Thank you." Her voice caught. "But it isn't necessary."

He twisted his big hands in his sleeves. "It's not right you should have to face this alone."

"I must."

"But you're so young."

She almost smiled at that. He had always been a big bear of a man with a kind heart. But she would celebrate her eighteenth year in only a few tendays, which put her two years past the age when young people were considered adults.

"I'll be fine," she told him, though she wasn't sure who she wanted to convince, Harjan or herself.

He nodded with reluctance. He and the other men bowed and quietly took their leave, closing the door behind them.

Ginger sagged against the wall. Despite her assurances, she feared being alone with the body. Her service in the temple mostly involved offering succor to the people of Sky Flames, who eked out lives in the harshly beautiful desert. She gave blessings, performed rituals to honor the sun, presided at marriages and christenings, comforted mourners, listened to those who needed to talk and tended the health of women and children. It was a calling she loved, one well suited to her. She needed to perform the Sunset Rites less often than other ceremonies, and she had never done them for someone who had suffered such a brutal death.

Ginger drew herself up, determined to do well by this man's spirit. She went to a wall niche and lit the fire-lily candles there. Their spicy scent wafted around her, and in their flickering light, the scrolled carvings on the walls seemed to ripple. As she picked up a bundle of cloths, she realized she was clenching her opal. Startled, she set it down. Then she changed her mind and took it up again. The opal gave her a sense of confidence, which right now she very much needed.

One of the candles sputtered and died, and a tendril of smoke curled in the air. She thought of doing a flame spell, then shook her head, angry at herself, and relit the candle from one still burning. In her childhood, she had discovered by accident that she could do fire spells by concentrating on the opal, but she didn't understand why it happened. She used her abilities rarely and strove to do only good with them, but deep inside she feared they were a curse.

Ginger took the bowl of water in the niche and a soap carved like a dragon. She would clean the body to give the man dignity for his trip to the spirit lands. She returned to the table and looked down at his ravaged face. Softly she said, "May you have more peace among the spirits than you had among the living."

The dead man opened his eyes.

Darz

Ginger froze. The man was staring at her with a bloodshot gaze. Her heartbeat ratcheted up, and the urge to run hit her hard. She took a shaky breath. Then she laid her palm on his neck—and felt what she hadn't seen before: a faint pulse.

"Gods above," she murmured.

"Who…?" The man's voice was barely audible.

"I am Ginger-Sun, the temple priestess in Sky Flames."

"Too young…for priestess."

"Not here." Her elderly predecessor had passed away two years ago. Ginger had been the only acolyte, so at fifteen, the age when most girls began training, she had taken on the full duties of a priestess.

She set down her supplies and went to work. Bathing him had suddenly become much more vital; she needed to tend his wounds. It flustered her to feel his skin, for no living man could touch a priestess. But the temple was too far from the village; it would take her thirty minutes to bring back the male healer, and that assumed he was home. She didn't dare leave her patient untended. She entreated the Dragon-Sun to understand; she couldn't let this man die.

Her patient closed his eyes. He breathed so shallowly, she couldn't see the rise and fall of his chest. She felt no exhalation when she held her hand in front of his mouth.

With care, she pulled away scraps of his shirt. He truly was strong, to survive after suffering such horrendous gashes in his chest and abdomen. The stab wounds must have missed his vital organs; if he had suffered internal injuries, she doubted he would still be alive. The bleeding had stopped, but she feared he had already lost too much to live.

As she treated him, the water and her cloths turned red, and she had to fetch more of both several times. It shook her deeply, for she had never treated anyone with such horrible injuries. She rolled him carefully on his side to treat his back. He also had lacerations on his cal- loused hands, as if he had grabbed the dagger of whoever was stabbing him. She flinched at the images his wounds conjured, the violence of the fight that caused them. It was no wonder they had left him for dead.

Night descended as she worked, and shadows filled the chamber. She fetched the dagger she used to shave a body during the rites, but instead she used it to slice away his trousers so she could treat his legs. She could tell little about his shredded clothes except that they had a simple cut. He lay still as she worked, never flinching, though his pain was surely terrible. Only one time, when she pressed too hard, did he lose his iron control and groan.

Her voice caught. "I truly am sorry." He probably wouldn't survive the night, but she would stay at his side to tend his life while he breathed and his spirit if he passed away.

Her opal remained where she had set it on the table, a small fiery pyramid. She could use it to create light in many ways, including symbolically, by giving comfort. Still she hesitated, agonized. She was a *sun* priestess. But the sun had gone down and power stirred within her.

Forgive me, Dragon-Sun, she thought. *I must help when I can, even if it is by the night rather than by your incomparable days.* She couldn't heal—but she could ease this man's pain.

Ginger picked up the opal, and it warmed her palm. Closing her eyes, she drew on the power she always concealed, knowing it would estrange her from her people, just as her red-gold hair and hazel eyes set her apart from everyone else, with their dark coloring. A spell grew within her. When she opened her eyes, golden light surrounded her and bathed the man. She poured the spell into him, offering it to soothe his pain.

Ginger called on her deepest resources and let the spell go on longer than she had ever tried before. She had finished tending his wounds, and this was all she had left to give him. Although he never opened his eyes, the set of his ruined face seemed to ease.

She finally sagged against the table. The opal fell out of her hand and rattled on the tabletop. As her head dropped forward, she braced her palms on the cold stone to hold herself up. The last candle sputtered, and night filled the room, waiting to stake its final claim on this man.

"I'm sorry," she said, her voice breaking. "I can do no more."

Then she crumpled to the ground.

Ginger awoke slowly, disoriented, gazing at the ceiling. The stone floor hurt her spine. She rolled onto her side and found herself staring at the base of the Sunset Table.

Her patient!

She struggled to her feet, afraid to find that he had died while she was unconscious. The man lay exactly as she had left him, his torso, arms and hands covered by bandages, and more on his legs and face. Incredibly, his eyes were moving under their lids, and his chest rose and fell more naturally than last night. An intense blend of emotions rose within her, part gratitude, part relief and part astonishment. She stroked his forehead, and he exhaled, restless in his sleep.

"Will you live, after all?" she asked. Perhaps today the Dragon-Sun would be kind.

She needed to feed him if he was to rebuild his strength. Rubbing her eyes, she walked into the main temple. It was dark except for a tinge of dawn that set the RayLight Chamber glowing faintly, as if the embers of a fire burned within it like a heart. Several redwing doves had flown inside through vents up in the roof and were cooing their dawn songs.

Ginger went to her private rooms. Sunrise mosaics tiled her parlor, rosy near the floor and shading up into the blue of a dawn sky. Lamps on fluted poles opened in glass fire-lily blossoms. A pot hung from the rafters, bright with sun-snaps. The ceiling was white, giving the room an airy feel, and light poured through the windows. A fiery glass sculpture of the Dragon-Sun sat in a niche above her bed.

Ginger exhaled, grateful to be here. These rooms were so unlike the cell where she had lived as an acolyte. She had come to the temple at an unusually young age; when she was nine, she had lost her mother to a fall in the cliffs, and her father had died a year later from the hacking-cough. Despite her brother's adamant protests, the village elders decided a boy of fifteen couldn't rear a girl child. So they sent her to the temple. She had cried in her cell every night, drowning in grief, certain the dragon had punished her by taking her family. She hoped that by devoting her life to him, she could atone for her night magic.

When Ginger had taken over as priestess five years later, her brother had entreated the elders to let her live in this suite. It drained her to toil all day and sleep on the floor in a barren cell at night. She tried to hide her exhaustion, but her brother knew. Even so, the elders denied his petition. They feared to offend the dragon by giving a child these rooms, which were among the few privileges granted a priestess. It enraged her brother, who pointed out that Ginger had all the duties, that indeed, she had done them for years. The elders remained firm: she must wait until she was sixteen to formally assume the title.

Ginger quickly washed up and brushed her hair, which fell down her back in waves. She changed into a rose-silk wrap. The wraps were exquisite, but confining; for everyday wear, she wore an old tunic and leggings so she could do her work. With a patient in the temple, though, she might have visitors and had to observe proper protocols.

In the kitchen, she prepared a tray with rose-glasses and a carafe of water. Given the man's injuries, she didn't think solid food was a good idea, so she cooked two bowls of rice-cream with brown sugar. Carrying the tray and a sheet, she went into the main temple and walked through the dawn of bird song. Inside the Sunset Chamber, the stranger was as she had left him, asleep on his back.

Ginger set her tray on the table and covered him with the sheet. Then she murmured, "Wake up. I have food."

No response.

Ginger caught her lower lip with her teeth. She had already

touched him too much. But he needed to eat. *Dragon-Sun,* she thought, *forgive my transgression.* Then she brushed her finger alongside the bandage that stretched from the outer edge of his eye down his cheek.

The man stirred, then sighed. After a moment, his lashes lifted and he stared at the ceiling. He shifted his gaze to Ginger.

"You'll be all right," she said gently. She lifted his head and tilted the glass to his mouth. At first he didn't respond, but when she ran a trickle of water between his lips, he swallowed convulsively. Although he drank with difficulty, he drained most of the glass before he sagged back. Ginger held his head, aware of him watching her with his dark, intense eyes. The swelling on his face had receded, and he looked a lot less like a corpse this morning.

"Where...?" he asked.

With apology, she said, "You are in the Sunset Chamber."

His lips quirked the barest amount, far too little to qualify as a smile, but an astonishing ghost of humor. "Not ready for my sunset...yet..." His breath wheezed and he coughed, his face contorting.

"Shhh." She laid her finger on his lips. "You must rest. Build your strength. Here." She set down the glass and offered him a spoonful of the creamy rice cereal. He even managed three swallows before he gave up.

"Can you tell me your name?" she asked.

"Darz..."

She brushed the matted hair off his forehead. "Well, Darz, you and I are alone here, and I'm not strong enough to lift you. So I'm afraid I can't move you somewhere more comfortable."

His lashes drooped closed. "This's fine...."

Catherine Asaro

After a moment, she realized he was asleep. She gently set down his head, relieved to stop breaking the taboo. Or so she told herself. Her urge to keep holding him, offering comfort, disconcerted her. She leaned on the table, more tired than she wanted to admit after having spent the night crumpled on the floor. It couldn't be any better for him on this hard table. As soon as he was strong enough for her to leave, she would run to the village for help.

She sat on the floor against the wall where she could watch Darz. She tried to eat her rice, but her head lolled forward. She brought it up with a jerk and set her bowl on the ground. Within moments, she was nodding again.

Ginger dozed, never fully asleep, always aware of her patient...

"Is anyone here?" The call resonated in the temple.

Ginger jerked awake. She jumped to her feet and hurried out of the chamber before she even fully knew what she was doing. Four miners were standing by the fountain.

"Harjan!" She couldn't run in the wrap, or even stride, but she managed a fast walk. "I'm so glad you came!"

Relief suffused his face as he and the others turned to her. "Have you been in the Sunset Chamber?" he asked.

"All night." She spoke quickly. "Can one of you go for the healer? We need a stretcher, too. We can use one of the acolyte's rooms. They're all empty, and I have no trainees. I'll get bedding from the storeroom."

"Ginger, slow down." Harjan's face crinkled with affection. "We can help you move the body, if that's what you're asking. But the healer can't do anything for him. We'll bring someone to help prepare him for burial."

"No!" She stared at him, aghast. "He lives! I thought surely his spirit would leave during the night, but it stayed. He sleeps on the table. We must move him." Another thought hit her. "Oh! If he turns over, he'll fall on the floor." She spun around and headed back to the Sunset room.

Darz had not only avoided rolling over in his sleep, he was awake when she entered the chamber. He pushed up on his elbow and stared past her, his expression hardening.

Glancing back, she saw the miners following her into the room. She went over to Darz. "It's all right. These are friends. They will move you to a more comfortable place."

Darz narrowed his eyes as Harjan came up to the table.

"You must lie down," Ginger told Darz firmly. "You could start bleeding again."

He looked as if he wanted to refuse, but his face was pale and his breathing labored. With difficulty, he eased back down. The entire time, he watched Harjan as if he expected an attack.

Harjan spoke cautiously. "I'm gratified to see that you live, Goodman..." He let the title hang like a question.

"Darz Goldstone," the man said. His voice sounded creaky, as if he wasn't ready to use it.

"Goodman Goldstone." Harjan nodded in the greeting of one villager to another.

Darz stared at him strangely, but he returned the nod as well as he could while lying on his back.

Ginger laid her hand against Darz's cheek, painfully aware of the miners watching her break the taboo. His skin felt cool. "You don't have a fever. That's good." She had feared his wounds would fester and become inflamed.

Harjan glanced at the other men. "Can you get the stretcher?" Firmly he added, "And the healer?"

Perrine and Tanner went for the litter, and the third man headed to Sky Flames for the healer. Harjan stayed with Ginger and kept a wary gaze on her patient. He was the only one of the miners she knew well, though she often saw them working in the bluffs outside the village. They sold ores to the Zanterian caravans that came by Sky Flames, or else they journeyed to the far cities themselves to find buyers. Her brother, Heath, was doing exactly that right now; otherwise, she had no doubt he would be here, too, hulking suspiciously over Darz.

Perrine and Tanner returned with the stretcher, and Darz tensed as they lifted him onto it. She wanted to assure him they wouldn't hurt him, but if he was anything like the men of Sky Flames, such words would offend his pride. So she held back.

They carried him to a cell. Darz lay completely still, his eyes closed, his face strained, and she feared they had moved him too soon. They certainly could risk nothing more. The miners had apparently understood her hurried words, for they had brought in a bed and blankets from storage, which no acolyte would have been allowed. After they set him in bed, she set a stool by the bed and sat down to check his bandages. Blood had seeped through the cloth on his torso.

The miners hovered behind her like a trio of wary hawks. She knew they didn't want to leave her alone with Darz, but the more people who crammed the room, the more it would disturb her patient. She could tend the sick and was expected to do so for women and children. Surely they realized she needed to look after Darz, as well, however uncomfortable it made them all. Nor did she feel right keeping the men away from the work that provided their livelihoods.

She spoke gently. "I thank you all for your generous help. But you needn't stay."

"It is our pleasure to help, Blessed One," Tanner said.

"We can stay," Harjan said. "It's all right."

Their solicitude both touched and flustered Ginger. She was used to looking after the temple on her own. It was grueling, and she often wished she had help, but most people in the village were struggling to support their own families.

"I don't want to keep you from your work," she said.

"It's no trouble," Tanner told her.

Harjan looked past her at Darz and frowned. "None at all."

It took some time, and many reassurances, but she finally convinced Tanner and Perrine they could go. After they left, Harjan indicated the corner. "I'll sit over there."

Ginger stood up. "I'll bring a chair."

He reached out to stop her by putting his hand on her arm. Then he realized what he was doing and dropped his hand. "My apology!" His face turned red.

"You have nothing to apologize for," she said. He hadn't touched her, after all.

"You needn't get a chair," he said. "Surely if half-grown girls can live in these cells with no soft things, I can manage for one day."

She smiled at him. "You would make a fine acolyte." When he glared, she shooed him away. "It's all right, Harjan. You don't have to stay."

"I don't mean to intrude. I'm just not easy leaving you with him."

"He can barely move," she said.

Harjan raked his hand through his unruly black hair. "All right, Ginger-Sun. But if you need us, we'll be at the bluffs."

She inclined her head. "My thanks." His concern touched her, and she did feel reassured to know they would be close.

When she was alone, Ginger watched Darz for a while. Eventually, though, she had to resume her duties, which today consisted of dull chores such as sweeping floors, dusting furniture and tending the fountain.

Darz slept soundly and roused only when the healer came. Brusque and efficient, the healer cleaned his wounds, stitched them up and gave him sky-wood tea to ease his pain. He cautioned against moving Darz and reluctantly advised Ginger to keep him in the temple until Darz recovered enough that they felt certain he would survive—if that happened.

Later, Ginger carefully woke Darz to give him water and spoonfuls of sweet rice-cream. He seemed so disoriented, and he barely ate anything before he dropped back into sleep. The only time he stirred on his own was when Tanner, one of the miners, came to check on Ginger. She wasn't sure what woke Darz that time, unless it was the clink of the tools on Tanner's belt. They sounded like weapons.

After she finished her chores, she retired to the archive room. She loved to read the scrolls, learning about her country of Taka Mal, where the Topaz Queen reigned in the ancient and splendorous city of Quaaz. Nothing ever happened in Sky Flames. It was a full day's ride to the nearest town and half a country away to any major city. But Sky Flames usually had a priestess, which was more than many such isolated settlements could claim. The women who had served here before Ginger had recorded their thoughts about the land, nature, science, even mathematics. She most enjoyed reading their historical accounts.

Ginger was working on her own history. She had little to write about in her short life, certainly no land-shaking events, but she recorded the days in the village and temple. She wrote for the pure joy of capturing beauty with words. Perhaps her scrolls might offer some future historian the same pleasure that those of past priestesses did for her.

She took an antique scroll to Darz's room and sat by his bed, reading as he slept. When she came to a fine evocation of Taka Mal, she read aloud, even knowing he couldn't hear. If beautiful words could heal, these would surely help him.

The next day was the same, except she wore leggings and a tunic. It would anger the village elders if they caught her dressed this way, but it was too hard to work otherwise. She was alone except for a patient who did nothing but sleep, and she had no appointments. It seemed absurdly impractical to toil in a tight silk wrap.

Toward midday, when even the temple became uncomfortably warm, she went to the fountain and asked the Dragon-Sun for his blessing, that she might use his bounty. Then she carried a ewer of water into Darz's room. Sweat soaked his sleep-trousers. She eased them off and removed his bandages, then bathed him with dragon soaps. She had never touched a living man, not *this* way, and her hands wanted to linger on his muscled form. She knew it was wrong, and she struggled to resist the temptation. He was powerfully built, and hairy, too, which made her blush. His beard grew fast; thick black stubble already covered his chin and cheeks. She wondered what kind of violent life he endured, for his skin had many scars much older than his wounds from this attack.

Catherine Asaro

He stirred while she cleaned him, but he didn't seem in pain and he didn't awaken. She dressed his wounds and clothed him in fresh sleep-trousers the healer had left. Then she just sat at his bedside. She truly didn't want to leave, though she had no more reason to stay. It was a while before she could make herself return to her chores.

In the evening, Ginger stood by Darz's bed, watching him sleep. "I hope you're resting better," she murmured, though he couldn't hear. "I'm sorry I had to wake you earlier to eat."

The hint of a smile touched his face as his eyes opened. "To wake up to such beauty is worth a thousand sufferings."

She jumped back. "Goodness! You're awake."

"It seems so."

"I should let you sleep," she said, mortified.

"Don't go. 'S boring. The morning...so long."

"Morning?"

"It's morning, yes?"

"No, actually, it's night."

"But those men...brought me here this morning."

She finally came in and sat on the stool so she could be closer to him. "That was two days ago."

"Gods. No wonder I'm so sore." He pushed up on his elbow. "I should get moving..."

"You must stay put," she said firmly. "You are sore, Goodsir, because you have many injuries."

His smile quirked. "Now I'm Goodsir. Your friend Harjan called me Goodman."

"You have a fine way about you," she assured him. In truth, he seemed rather rough, but her philosophy had always been to err on the side of courtesy. Goodman was the address for most people, with Goodsir reserved for those few families such as the Zanterians who had a heritage of wealth and authority. Although he didn't look Zanterian, one could never be sure.

"You're a diplomat," he said wryly. "Goodman is fine."

"Are you a merchant?" It could be why he had been out in the desert.

"Not a merchant. Soldier."

Ah. That explained his scars. The calluses on his hand were probably from wielding a sword. "Is that why you were attacked?"

"I've no idea. I had just woken up and gone to pi—" He stopped and cleared his throat. "To, uh, relieve myself."

Ginger smiled. "I've heard the word before."

He squinted at her. "One never knows what will offend a priestess."

"We're not so delicate." She hesitated. "Is the army coming here?" She had heard nothing of such events.

"No. I was on leave...before the attack."

"Do you know who attacked you?"

He shook his head. "It was dark. And they hid their faces with scarves."

The thought of masked assailants creeping up on him in the dark disturbed her. Perhaps they had been soldiers from another country. With all the recent upheavals among the settled lands, she wasn't certain who allied with whom anymore. Taka Mal had survived the war last year, but battles had destroyed much of the Rocklands, and the queen had to marry a prince from Aronsdale as part of the peace treaty. Ginger lived so far from the population centers of Taka Mal, it was hard to stay informed about the events sweeping their land.

She did know that Jazid, the country to their south, had been less fortunate than Taka Mal; it had fallen to the conquering army of the Misted Cliffs.

"Do you think it's because you're in the army?" she asked. "Maybe they were Jazid soldiers."

His brow furrowed. "Why attack me? Jazid was our ally."

She leaned forward, uneasy with her words. "We've heard rumors that minions of the Shadow Dragon have crept to the lands of the living and wander the night."

He looked more amused than worried. "Indeed."

"It's true," she assured him. "They are deadly."

"Do you mean the Shadow Dragon Assassins?"

"Is that their name?" She laced her fingers together, the sign for warding away evil. "I hope no demons come here."

"They're human, I assure you." He seemed more alert now. "Supposedly they're a covert group of assassins that served the late king of Jazid. After his death, they may have escaped into Taka Mal with several of his generals."

"Oh!" She put her hand over her cheek. "They tried to assassinate you."

He smiled slightly. "Even if they exist, which is doubtful, you ascribe far more importance to my existence than it deserves."

"You're a soldier."

"So are thousands of men." He rubbed his eyes with the heels of his bandaged hands. "Besides, I've nothing to do with the army that conquered Jazid. Hell, the Misted Cliffs tried to conquer us, too. And how would they have even known I'm in the military? I was just traveling to Taza Qu to visit family."

Ginger had to admit, her theory did sound unlikely. "Taza Qu is a long way from here." She knew little about the city besides its name. It had always sounded exotic and exciting, but also frightening, because it was the unknown. "Will your family know where to look for you?"

"I doubt it." He spoke grimly. "Whoever stabbed me didn't want to leave my body where searchers would find it. That's probably why they brought me here. To hide the corpse."

"Not very well. Our ore diggers found you."

"I was near a mine?" He tilted his head, his face puzzled. "I would have thought they'd bury me near a cemetery."

That surprised her. "The cemetery isn't far from the mine. But why bury you?"

"Camouflage. Even if my body was found—which isn't likely—who would know I wasn't from here...?"

His voice was drifting, and it worried Ginger. She plumped up his pillow. "I shouldn't keep you talking. You need rest."

His tone gentled. "I've always time to talk to a pretty girl...."

A flush heated her cheeks. Apparently he had forgotten or didn't realize he shouldn't speak that way to a priestess. She didn't answer as he closed his eyes. His breathing soon deepened into the slower rhythms of sleep.

His forbidden words unsettled Ginger. She didn't want to enjoy them. She knew it was wrong. But they gave her a tickling sensation in her throat that always came when she was nervous—or full of anticipation. She had little sense of how she appeared to other people; she wasn't allowed objects of vanity. The elders expected her to be well-groomed and provided her with brushes and soaps, but no cosmetics or mirrors. Although they had never seemed to care with her predecessor, they forbade Ginger to look at herself, which bewil-

Catherine Asaro

dered her, because Elder Tajman and Second Sentinel Spark both stared at her when they thought she didn't notice.

The only time she saw her reflection was in the fountain, which didn't offer a clear image. As much as she wanted to please the elders, she couldn't help chafing at their restrictions. She had been so young when she came to the temple, she had never known what it was like to have a man court her.

Lost in thought, she watched Darz sleep. With his bruises dark and purpled, it was hard to see his full appearance, but she didn't think he was from this part of the country. People here had intermarried for generations and had similar looks.

Ginger's grandfather had come from Aronsdale, the country west of Taka Mal. He was the reason she had exotic hair, golden-red instead of black. Her brother called it fire hair. He believed it was why she had dedicated her life to the Dragon-Sun even though she hadn't come to the temple by her own choice. She never told anyone the temple was her refuge from the dark magic. In Sky Flames, any differences could spur the townsfolk to shun a person. The strange color of her hair was bad enough; she dreaded what people would do if they discovered her night magic.

She sometimes wondered if her grandfather had suspected. She had always been curious about him. He had moved far across the settled lands to marry his lover, her grandmother. People said Ginger was like him. He had died when she was five, and by then, only a few streaks of fire remained in his silver hair. She would never forget his kindly voice or loving nature. He told her that someday she would want to go to Aronsdale. As much as she had adored him, she never understood why he believed such a thing. She had no desire to leave her home and travel to a distant land with too much fog and too many trees.

Eventually, she returned to her suite and brewed a pot of the tea that helped dull Darz's pain. She carried a tray with the tea and dinner back to his cell and set it on the floor—

A scream shattered the night.

The
Unseen

Ginger scrambled to her feet and ran out to the main temple.

No one.

Chill air breathed on her neck. She spun around, but saw no one. Turning in a circle, she looked everywhere. Across the temple, a spray of dragon-snaps gleamed on a table in the light of two candles. Shadows otherwise filled the building, and the RayLight Chamber was dark at this hour of the night. Someone could hide behind it, or if they were truly impious, within the chamber.

She folded her arms protectively around herself. That scream had been *real*. It hadn't sounded like one of fear or of pain, but something vicious. Inhuman.

"Who's here?" she called. Her voice trembled.

No answer.

"Don't go out there," a harsh voice said behind her.

With a cry, Ginger whirled around. Darz was standing in the entrance of the cell, sagging against the arch, one hand clenched on the door frame and the other crossed over his torso, holding his side where he had sustained the worst stab wounds. His face was pale and drawn.

"You mustn't get up!" She hurried over to him.

"Stay in the light. I don't— I can't—" He groaned and slid down the frame.

Ginger caught him around the waist, then glanced over her shoulder to make sure no one was creeping up on them. "I'll help you to bed."

The ghost of a smile curved his lips. "Can't argue when a beautiful woman says that."

Saints above! Again he violated the taboos. If only his forbidden words didn't sound so sweet. He draped his arm on her shoulders, and his weight almost knocked her over. His muscles were like rock. She tried to ignore how his body felt against hers. She couldn't let herself notice.

It was only a few steps to his bed, where she eased him down onto his side. "Here you are."

His eyes drooped. "Don't put your back to the door."

She straightened with a jerk, expecting to see a killer or bloody victim in the doorway. But it was empty. The only light came from the candles across the temple, and their dim glow barely reached Darz's cell.

"I should search the temple," she said uneasily. "Someone may need help."

"No!" He pushed up on his elbow. "That scream—it was familiar. Can't remember—that damn tea fogs my mind." He fell back as a cough wracked his body, huge and wrenching.

A terrible memory rushed over Ginger, from when she had been ten: her father, coughing violently, trapped in his killing deliriums. He too had kept trying to get out of bed.

He had died soon after.

Darz kept struggling to get up. She sat next to him, saying, "Please, you mustn't." Then she grasped his arm.

Darz reacted incredibly fast, throwing her facedown on the bed. He shoved her into the mattress and pinned her as if she were an enemy soldier. Her mind reeled at the illicit contact of his body against hers.

Just as suddenly, and with a mortified oath, he released her. "I'm sorry, Ginger-Sun! Don't grab me that way! I can't always control my reflexes."

Rattled and confused, she rolled over and came up against him. He leaned over her with one hand on either side of her shoulders, and she stared up at his face. They were so close, she could see individual hairs on his chin and the tiny creases in his full lips. He gazed at her as if he were hungry, and his lips parted.

Frantic, she ducked under his arm and sat up.

"Ginger…" His eyes were glazed from the pain-killing herbs. He tried to pull her back down, and the feel of his hand on her arm sent a jolt through her as if she had touched a cat after it rubbed its fur on a carpet.

"You must stop," she said, her voice shaking. As she wrested her arm away from him, she looked up—

A man stood in the doorway of the cell.

"No!" Ginger jumped off the bed. Darz lurched to his feet and pushed her behind him.

"Move back!" the man said. He had drawn a dagger, and the candlelight from the temple glinted on the long blade. His grizzled face was in shadow, and his husky frame filled the doorway. Tools hung from his digger's belt—

Digger's belt?

"Priestess, move back." He entered the room, turning so his back wasn't to the doorway. His gaze fixed on Darz. "Make her scream again, you filthy bastard, and when I'm done with you, you'll wish your would-be killers had finished the job first."

Now that Ginger could see him better, she recognized the man. It was Tanner, one of the miners who had brought Darz to her. "It wasn't me who screamed," she said. "Darz was trying to protect me. He dragged himself out of bed, half dead, to do it."

"Then who screamed?" Tanner kept his blade drawn. He gave her clothes an odd look, and she remembered she had on the tunic and leggings instead of the wrap.

"It was out there." She motioned toward the main room behind him. "But I didn't see anyone."

Tanner lowered his dagger. "Neither did I."

"Did Harjan tell you to watch the temple?"

"We've been taking turns." With apology, he added, "He says it makes you uncomfortable. I'm sorry, Ginger-Sun. But we must guard you."

She spoke quietly. "I am deeply grateful, Goodman Tanner." She took a breath. "I need to search the temple."

"You're not going out there," Darz growled.

"He's right," Tanner said, grudgingly. "I'll do the search." He frowned at Darz. "You're a soldier, yes?"

"That's right." Darz watched him as if he hadn't decided whether or not the miner was an enemy.

Tanner spoke to Ginger, his voice gentling. "If I leave you here with him, will you be all right?"

"I'll be fine. Truly."

Tanner gave Darz a hard look. "It will be safer if she stays here under your guard. But if I find out you even looked at her wrong—" He lifted the dagger.

Darz scowled at him. "I would never harm a priestess."

"See that you don't."

It was embarrassing for Ginger to realize Tanner considered a man who could barely stand up better able to protect her than she could herself. Even so. He meant well. And she had no desire to search for someone who screamed like a banshee.

Tanner left them in the cell and crossed the temple to the table with the candles. He lit another for himself, then paced along the wall until he moved out of view. Uncertain what to think, Ginger turned to Darz. He stared at her—and crumpled.

She caught him before he crashed to the floor. He was too heavy for her to hold up, but she managed to change his direction so he fell on the bed. Blood had soaked through the bandages on his chest and into her sleeve.

"Can't lie down," he said thickly. "Have to stand guard."

"I know." She nudged him onto his back.

"You shouldn't trust that man. He might be the one who screamed."

"I'm sure he isn't."

"You know him?"

"Not well, but he's always lived here." She went to the tray she had left by the wall. It held bandages, plus sticky patches the healer had given her to hold them in place.

"You don't have to do that," Darz said.

"It's no trouble." Ginger needed to do something or she would pace and worry. She set the tray on the stool and poured pale blue liquid from the glazed pot into a mug. Steam rose from the drink and curled around her cheeks, reminding her of times long ago when she had been sick and her mother brewed sky-wood tea. It could blunt the worst of Darz's pain.

She sat next to him, taking care to keep space between them. Then she offered the tea. "This will help you."

"It makes my brain muzzy," he mumbled. The steam from the mug blurred his haggard face.

"We'll take care of you," she soothed.

Although he looked as if he wanted to refuse, he took the mug. He tried bending his head forward to drink, but then he groaned and dropped back on the bed. She barely caught the mug before it splashed hot liquid over them both. Acutely self-conscious, she slid up the bed and turned so she could lift his head into her lap. The more she touched him, the more it unsettled her, but she didn't see what else to do. His shoulders stiffened against her leg, and she sensed his physical power. He drew her as if she were a moth pulled to the flame of his forbidden masculinity. Holding his head up, she tilted the mug to his mouth. As he drank, his lips moved against the mug, full and sensual.

After a few swallows, Darz let his head fall into her lap and closed his eyes. She had to fight her desire to stroke his hair. Setting the mug on the floor, she told herself she was trembling because of tonight's events. It was partly true; she balanced on a honed edge of fear. Tanner's footsteps had receded as he searched, and she could barely hear them. What if it *wasn't* him? She was as tense as a drum skin pulled too tight.

Ginger eased Darz's head onto the bed and moved back to sit at his waist. She peeled the bloodied bandages off his torso. The gashes looked terrible, even closed with the healer's neat stitches. Blood oozed from several gashes. He grunted as she cleaned and dressed the wounds, but he never complained.

After she finished, he dropped off immediately despite his attempts to stay on guard. Even asleep, he looked barbaric, with his massive size, grizzled black beard, and harsh features.

"You must be a fine warrior," she said. "Such strength and courage."

His lips curved upward. "I'm a terror in battle."

"Oh!" She put her hand on her cheek, mortified. How could a man look and sound as if he were sound asleep and yet be so alert? Perhaps it was a survival mechanism; no enemy soldier would find him defenseless in sleep.

The footsteps were growing louder, and candlelight flickered outside the cell. Ginger stood up, keeping her hands free in case she needed to defend herself. It was Tanner who appeared in the doorway, his face lit from below by the candle, his knife drawn.

"I went through the entire temple," he said as he came into the cell. "I found nothing."

"Did it look as if anyone had been here?" Ginger asked. "Anything broken? Signs of a struggle?"

"Not a thing." He held up his candle and frowned at Darz's sleeping form. "This building has several exits, though. And windows someone could climb out."

"Or into." Ginger shivered in the night's chill creeping through the stone walls. She felt cold in a way no braziers could ever warm.

Tanner spoke earnestly. "I won't leave you alone, I swear it. No one will get past me to you." He lowered the candle so it didn't shine on her face, she who could never be gazed at too long or with longing. "Please forgive my presumption, Ginger-Sun. But the three of us should stay in here until morning. It would be difficult for me to watch two places at once." Quickly he added, "I'll leave the door open."

"It's all right," she said, awkward, but grateful for his presence. "We'll need blankets. These cells get icy."

He nodded and stepped aside for her. They walked together through the main temple, Tanner holding up his candle so he could scan the area. Wax dripped into its pewter base. Ginger hated leaving Darz alone, and she increased her pace.

"Priestess," Tanner said. "Where is your wrap? Such a walk is—" He glanced at her body, then quickly looked away.

Ginger flushed and slowed down. She knew what he had meant to say. *Unseemly*. She wasn't even sure why people cared about her clothes. The loose tunic came to her knees, and she wore it with heavy leggings; together, they revealed far less of her shape than a wrap. But priestesses had always worn the ceremonial garments. In fact, in earlier centuries, the women who served the dragon had been rigorously secluded in their temples. They were brides of the Dragon-Sun, after all. It was a symbolic distinction; the justices had long ago repealed the laws that forbade a priestess to marry. But the elders adhered rigidly to tradition. No man could woo her; only the elders could choose her husband, and then only after a sign from the Dragon-Sun that he allowed and blessed the union.

Tanner stopped at the entrance of her rooms, his blush visible even in the dim candlelight. Ginger paused, uncertain what to do. It was forbidden for him to enter, of course, but it was even more forbidden for him to let her get killed while he waited outside.

"I'll just be a moment," she said. "I'll leave this door open. You can see from here into my bedroom."

He cleared his throat. "Don't be long."

She ran to her bedroom despite what he had implied about her immodest walk, yanked the covers off her bed, and hurried back out. They returned to the acolyte's cell and found Darz still asleep. He didn't look as if he had stirred.

They settled down with as much separation between them as possible, Tanner by the door, Ginger against the cold back wall. She gave him the blanket and wrapped the quilt around herself. Ill at ease, she settled in for an uncomfortable night.

The bright chirps of birds tickled Ginger's hearing as she awoke. She sat ensconced in the quilt, bleary-eyed. Light with the fresh clarity of dawn sifted into the cell from the temple. Tanner was gone, and Darz was asleep.

After a while, comprehension that she was awake seeped into her mind. Standing up, she stretched her stiff limbs. Tanner had left a note on the tray, saying he and the other miners would watch the temple. She remembered then; he could read and write, and taught children in the village when he wasn't mining.

Ginger leaned over Darz. Mercifully, no blood stained his bandages, and his forehead felt cool. She had discovered that if she cleaned wounds with water and soap, the Dragon-Sun often spared her patients the killing fevers.

Out in the main temple, with dawn lighting the windows, her fears from last night seemed overblown. She knelt on the lip of the fountain and murmured a blessing to the Dragon-Sun. Then she cupped her hands full of water. Bathing her face, she thought, *May your ride through the sky shine today, Ata-TakaMal D'Az.*

One of Ginger's duties as an acolyte had been to memorize titles for the Dragon-Sun. Most formally, he was the *Ata-TakaMal D'Az* or Dragon-Sun King. The queen of Taka Mal was *Ata-Takamal D'or*, or Dragon-Sun Princess. The late king of Jazid had been *Atajazid D'az*, or Shadow Dragon Prince. After the Misted Cliffs had conquered Jazid, some people claimed the Shadow Dragon no longer stalked the land. Ginger wasn't so optimistic. Jazid's conquerors knew nothing about the Shadow Dragon and could unknowingly release his dark forces.

Ginger shivered at her thoughts. In her suite, she changed into a red silk wrap and prepared rice for Darz. He was still asleep when she returned to his cell, so she left the bowl on the tray by his bed. She was startled to find her opal under the bandages there. In last night's excitement, she had forgotten it. She could have eased Darz's pain with a spell rather than tea, but Tanner might have seen and named her a witch. She had never harmed anyone, but that wouldn't matter; that she could do spells at all could turn people against her.

She left the cell and went to the RayLight Chamber. The light within it was faint this early in the morning, but enough to make the stained glass glow. Radiance gathered in pools of color on the floor.

"Dragon-Sun," she said. "Help me understand. I wish to serve you, not the Shadow Dragon." As much as she longed to believe the Dragon-Sun had granted her these abilities so she could bring a glow of his brightness into the shadows, she feared her power came instead from the dragon who ruled the night. Her dedication to the sun was the best way she knew to turn her powers to the day, but her calling demanded a painfully high price.

"Dragon of light, I swear my life to you. Always will you have my devotion." Tears gathered in her eyes and she wiped them away with the heel of her hand. "But I'm so lonely. Please, Great Ata-TakaMal D'Az, give me a sign I won't spend my life alone. I am honored to be your bride, truly I am. But I—I—"

Ginger stopped, afraid to offend the sun. She thought of the last priestess who had served here, elegant and slender in her wrap, with white hair curled around her face. She had told Ginger the dragon never chose a mate for her. Perhaps that was true, but Ginger thought her predecessor would never have let herself see such a sign, for she liked her independence. Had this confused yearning ever burned within her? The loneliness was crushing Ginger.

"Darz seems a good man," she said. "He's a soldier in the queen's army. So strong and brave. Is this the sign, Great Dragon? Or do I cause offense by wanting an injured man whose life is entrusted into my care?"

Nothing changed. If the dragon had an answer, either she didn't see it or he had chosen to wait. She hoped he would show tenderness. The hard life in Sky Flames left so little of that for her people, and it was why they came to her for blessings, to ease their lives. But sometimes *she* ached for warmth. Who would tend the priestess? Maybe the sun was punishing her for using a spell to help Darz in the Sunset Chamber. Had the Dragon-Sun sent a demon to frighten her? That scream last night hadn't sounded human.

Ginger shuddered. Her Aronsdale grandfather would have said demons didn't exist, that dragons of the sun and night were myths. He had to be wrong. She saw the sun in the sky every day except when he pulled a blanket of clouds over his face. He was as real as the desert breezes that whispered sensually across her skin. He was a harsh lord to serve, and maybe a possessive one who would answer her wish for companionship with severity rather than compassion. But she had to believe he was real. Otherwise, she had dedicated her life to nothing.

"Oh!" Ginger stopped in the doorway of the cell.

Darz looked up at her, a spoonful of rice-cream halfway to his mouth. He was sitting on the bed against the wall with the glazed bowl of cereal in his lap. He had pushed the bandages back from his fingers so he could hold the spoon.

He grinned at her. "This cereal is good. Did you make it?"

"Yes," she said, blushing. "I did."

"You're a good cook."

"Thank you." She loved to cook, but she rarely had anyone to do it for besides herself. "How do you feel?"

"Better." He swallowed the spoonful of cereal.

She sat on the stool by his bed. "Are you in pain?"

He paused a moment too long before saying, "I'll be fine."

She took that to mean yes, he was in pain, and he was too stoic to admit it. "Well," she said, "if you would like some sky-wood tea to wash down your breakfast, let me know."

"I'll do that." He didn't look the least interested in drinking any tea, though.

"I was wondering," she said. "You mentioned you were going to visit kin. Would you like us to send them word?" She hesitated. "Or to your wife, to let her know you're all right?"

"It isn't necessary." He ate more of the rice. "I'm not married, and I hadn't told anyone I was coming."

It pleased her far more than it should have to hear he had no wife. "So you were just traveling?"

"I do sometimes, to clear my mind." With a rueful smile, he

added, "Your temple is ideal for clearing the mind, Priestess, but I would have preferred a less drastic method of arrival."

"Aye," she murmured. She wanted to add, *I'm glad you are here,* but she bit back the inappropriate words. She felt so nervous. She had asked for a sign and found Darz awake. Could it be the sign she had hoped for? More likely, she was reading what she wanted to see into his recovery.

"Your face changes so fast," Darz said. "What troubles you? I hope I haven't too sorely disrupted your life."

"You've nothing to apologize for." She wished her moods weren't so easy for people to read. "I'm sorry your visit here had to be under such terrible circumstances."

"Ah, well. I've seen worse in battle."

"You must let your commanders know what happened, yes? So they don't think you deserted."

He set down the bowl as if he had lost his appetite. "I'm on indefinite leave. No one expects me back."

It sounded odd to Ginger, but she was too unfamiliar with the military to know if it was unusual. Maybe his attackers had tried to kill him because he had forsworn his oath to the queen. She didn't think so, though. She had no facts, just intuition, but he didn't strike her as someone who would desert.

"I wasn't discharged," he said, watching her face. "My commander has the notion that I need a rest. So it seems I'm on leave whether I want to be or not."

She wondered what had happened to him. "Did you fight in the Battle of the Rocklands? The stories we've heard are awful."

"Aye." He let out a breath. "Many men died." He looked tired. "I lost a friend and mentor I had served with for years."

"I'm sorry," she said softly.

He tried to smile, but it resembled a grimace. "Taka Mal survived. That's what matters."

Ginger wished she had better words to say. She knew so little about the war. The fighting had taken place far away, on the western border of Taka Mal with Aronsdale. They had battled the army of the Misted Cliffs, though it wasn't clear to her why.

"We heard that King Cobalt from the Misted Cliffs beheaded the Atajazid D'az Ozar," Ginger said. She shivered. "They say Cobalt the Dark is a monster, nine feet tall, a demon who slaughters his victims without mercy."

"For flaming sake," Darz grumbled. "He's only six foot seven." Then he said, "But yes, he did kill the Jazid king."

"I've heard—" She hesitated. "People say the Dragon-Sun appeared in the sky and roared flames to stop the battle."

He shrugged. "The sky lit up with what looked like a dragon."

His offhand response to such a manifestation bothered her, but she was glad for the affirmation that the dragon she served existed. "He wouldn't want his people to die fighting."

Darz rubbed his eyes with his bandaged hand. "Some say this dragon in the sky was no more than a trick of light created by the queen's consort."

"No one could do a trick that big."

"He's from Aronsdale," Darz growled, as if that explained everything and none of it good.

"You don't approve of Aronsdale?" she asked curiously. He was a veritable wealth of information. "Or the royal consort?"

"I would never speak ill of our glorious queen's consort," he said dourly. "Or our new ally, Aronsdale. Gods forbid." He leaned his head back against the wall and closed his eyes.

Guilt washed over her. Here she was, pumping him for gossip when he could barely sit up. She was about to leave when he added one last comment. "But it can't be true about these people from Aronsdale, that they make spells of light."

Ginger felt as if the ground spun beneath her. *Spells of light?* She waited until she could speak calmly. "Whatever are you talking about?"

Darz sighed, slumped against the wall. "Supposedly their queens are mages…" He opened his eyes and stared across the room. Then he eased down to the bed and lay on his back.

"Ai, I'm terrible." Ginger was appalled at herself. "I shouldn't keep you up." She leaned over him. "Would you like more tea?"

"I never drink tea," he groused. "I need ale."

She smiled. "I'm afraid I have no ale."

His lashes drooped over his eyes, dark against the pallor of his skin. "Would you read to me…as before?"

So he *had* known she was reading. "Yes, certainly."

Ginger fetched a scroll from the archive. Then she sat on the stool by his bed and read to him about life in Sky Flames a hundred years ago. But her mind was whirling with what he had said. Spells of light. Could it be she wasn't the only one who could make them? Her Aronsdale grandfather may have bequeathed her something far more complex than his fiery hair.

A disquieting thought intruded. If her spells did come from her Aronsdale heritage, from a people who didn't worship the sun, would the Dragon-Sun be angry?

What he would do, she had no idea.

Confrontation

"And if the killers return?" the Elder Sentinel demanded. "We must be ready."

Rumbles of assent rolled through the crowd in the Tender's Hall where the village held meetings. Hundreds of people filled the room, and many more stood by the walls or in aisles between the benches. Sky Flames had a population of about five hundred, and a good portion of the adults were here. Ginger stood against one wall trying to be inconspicuous. She was too agitated to sit. The stone room was designed to provide a cool refuge, but crammed with so many people, it became stifling. Oil lamps shed light, and their smoke blurred the scene, adding to her claustrophobia. She longed for the serene, spacious temple. She couldn't leave, of course; she was responsible for the man who had inspired this meeting.

The Elder Sentinel, or just Elder, stood on a platform at the front of the hall. His name was Tajman Limestone. White hair swept up from his forehead, giving his gaunt face the aspect of an avenging angel from the Spirit Lands who kept a stern eye on the living. Three others sat at a table behind him: the Flame Sentinel, a brash fellow tasked with seeing to civil order in town; the Archivist, a woman with a severe face and gray-streaked hair; and Spark, the Second Sentinel, a shorter man with a bald head and beefy arms. The Elder Sentinel, Second Sentinel, and Archivist served as elders for the village.

Personally, Ginger thought the Archivist would have made a good Second Sentinel, helping the Elder to govern. But tradition forbid such an idea. Precedent did exist for a woman in a position of authority; a queen ruled in Taka Mal. Vizarana Jade Quaazera had inherited her throne as the only child of the previous king. But here in Sky Flames, it could never happen.

The Archivist was a historian. She, too, had trained as an acolyte, but only because they kept archives in the temple, not because she intended to become a priestess. She had left the temple to assume her duties in the village long before Ginger became an acolyte. Ginger sometimes sought her out with questions about the history scrolls. Although the Archivist seemed to appreciate her interest, she never hid her disapproval of the priestess. Ginger didn't know why the elder disliked her. She treated the older woman with respect and tried to be friendly, but it didn't help. Maybe her personality grated on the somber historian; Ginger's independent ways had put off others in town. Many people expressed goodwill toward her, but at times she wondered if some would prefer a more conservative priestess. She was the only choice, however; in a village as small as theirs, it was difficult to find women willing to assume the temple duties.

"We don't know what this stranger did to provoke an attack," the

Elder was saying. "If his assailants return, one of us may be their next target. We must protect ourselves."

"The soldier should leave!" a man called.

In the packed hall, Ginger couldn't make out who shouted, but many people were nodding their agreement.

"Turn him out!" someone else yelled.

"If we turn out an injured man to die," another man said, "we are no better than the bandits who attacked him."

Bandits? Ginger blinked. Darz had never claimed such. It was a reasonable assumption, though, and more realistic than her theory about shadowy assassins who might not even exist.

More voices rose, until the room rumbled in argument. The Elder raised his hand, palm outward, and the people quieted.

"It would be wrong to turn out a dying man," Elder Tajman said. "When he is able to walk, we will send him away."

Rumbles of assent started up as people nodded in agreement. It alarmed Ginger. Being able to walk and surviving the desert were two very different matters. Darz would die if they turned him out too soon.

Ginger hadn't planned to speak. No one expected her to; it wasn't so long ago that priestesses had been rigorously confined to the temple. Public presentations made her nervous, and she gladly avoided them. But she couldn't remain silent if they intended to turn Darz out. Her pulse jumped as she stepped away from the wall. The people around her stopped talking and stepped aside with formal nods. Her bare feet whispered on the stone floor, and her wrap rustled with her small steps. The men took care not to touch her even by accident, lest the dragon smite them for sullying his devotee.

She continued past the benches, aware of everyone staring. Silence spread like the ripples from a pebble dropped into the temple fountain. The quiet washed through the crowd and up against the walls. She clutched her opal for confidence. Now, in the afternoon, it wouldn't flare with light, as could happen if agitation caused her to lose control of her night spells.

It took her a while to reach the platform. She went to the staircase on the left. As she set her foot on the lowest step, she realized the wrap was too tight for her to climb the stairs normally. She had to put one foot on a step, then the other, then repeat the process for the next step.

The crowd remained silent. Kindle Burr, the Flame Sentinel who served as the head of the village guard, rose from his chair at the table on the platform. A husky man with short hair, he was tending to a little extra weight these days. He came to the top of the stairs and watched Ginger with concern. She only had to go up a few steps, but it took eons. When she reached the top, he flexed his hand as if he wanted to offer her support. He couldn't of course; if he even just barely touched her in front of everyone, his own men would clap him in irons.

Ginger managed to incline her head to him without shaking or otherwise revealing her fear. She hoped. Elder Tajman was waiting at the front of the platform. She walked forward, and the stares of the people were like sparks against her skin.

The Elder bowed when she reached him. Although he showed respect, she knew him well enough to read the way his mouth tightened. He hadn't expected this, and he didn't like it.

He spoke in a low voice only she could hear. "You honor our meeting, Ginger-Sun."

She answered with the same formality. "I thank you for your gracious words."

"Do you wish to speak?"

She could tell he didn't want her to address the assembly. The twitch of his mouth gave him away.

"I do," she said. She had to stop herself from apologizing. She had the same right as any citizen to speak. In theory. In practice, the people expected silence from their priestess, which suited her fine, given her shyness and youth. But this had to be done, before distrust pushed them to send a man to his death.

The Elder stepped aside, offering her his place. One spot on the platform was the same as any other; his action was a symbolic acknowledgment from the town's highest authority that she had his support. She stepped forward and faced the crowd. They sat like a pond with no ripples disturbing the surface. She knew many by name; a few, like Harjan, were cherished friends. Yet now they were all strangers, for she had never come before them this way.

She took a deep breath. "I would speak on behalf of the stranger."

Gazes narrowed and people shifted in their seats.

"This man has done us no harm," Ginger said. "He is a soldier who fought bravely in the Battle of the Rocklands. He serves Queen Vizarana and, as such, he serves the Dragon-Sun, who brings life to the deserts. If we turn him away, we are turning our backs on duties tasked to us by the dragon, and by the Sunset Goddess who watches over travelers. They *guided* this man to our temple."

The weathered faces of her listeners showed the intense concentration distinctive of her people. She hoped they were hearing what she had to say. They couldn't let fear drive them to shun Darz, for if they did, they were shunning the dragon and sunset. And without those, life ended.

When nothing happened except that everyone kept staring at her, relief washed over Ginger. She wasn't sure what she had feared;

perhaps that they would explode in anger. None of them had ever raised their voices to her, but she had never before so openly broken with tradition.

Just as she was about to leave the platform, a man near the front rose to his feet. Her pulse stuttered. It was Dirk Bauxite, who built and repaired houses. He had a hard-edged view of the world, especially for those who didn't agree with him. The few times he had come to her temple for a blessing, his cold manner and avid scrutiny had frightened her. But he was also well respected in Sky Flames, a hard worker who was often willing to help others.

"Priestess," he said. "I have a question."

She couldn't refuse to answer, not if she wanted the respect of the people here. "Please ask, Goodman Bauxite."

"You speak of duty." His voice, like his name, sounded as hard as a mineral. "But what of danger? It would be a cruel task set to us by the revered dragon, should this man or his enemies kill any of us because we opened our temple to him."

It was a good question. Although she doubted Darz planned to harm anyone, she had no proof. And whoever had left him here might come back.

"I can't promise no danger exists," she admitted. "But if the dragon always smoothed our path, it would weaken us."

"You could be in danger," Dirk said. His eyes glinted.

"The soldier won't hurt me." His manner made her more uncomfortable than Darz had ever done.

"Your gentle nature is well known." Dirk moistened his lips as he stared at her. "But virtue is a poor defense against brutality."

She flushed, unsettled. He called her gentle, yet it made him angry. Or not angry exactly, but hungry somehow. "It is true, we must be careful," she said. "The Dragon-Sun has set us a trial. We must rise to that challenge."

"How can you be sure the sun sent him?" Dirk demanded. "More likely he deserted from the army, and we should send him home for punishment."

"I can't guarantee he is neither evil nor a deserter." Ginger knew she had no business contradicting such a respected citizen, someone nearly three times her age. But she plunged on. "I can say this—I have no sense either of those things is true."

The Elder spoke, and his voice carried. "Ginger-Sun, your kindness and sweet nature are well known and appreciated. But that innocence can lead you to misjudge danger."

Sweat had gathered on Ginger's palms. "I wish I could offer proof. I can't, I can only ask you to trust my judgment."

Grumbles came from the crowd. Dirk continued to stand, his gaze harsh, and she knew he wanted to escalate his confrontation. Nothing like this had happened to her before. She was certain he *wanted* to hurt her. Why? Surely not just because she spoke in public. She was out of her depth here, and she felt as if she were sinking into the sand.

When Ginger said nothing more, simply stood, waiting, Dirk frowned. He started to speak, then scowled. Finally he took his seat. The Elder stepped forward and stood with Ginger as he addressed the meeting. "If our priestess is willing to risk her own well-being, surely we can support and protect her."

The tensed set of Ginger's shoulders relaxed. He wasn't going to censure her. But she felt his disapproval; she had known him for too many years to be fooled. Too late, she realized he might feel she had shamed him with her willingness to confront this danger after he had counseled otherwise.

Hoping to defuse his anger, she spoke in a low voice. "You honor me, Elder."

Tajman studied her with a penetrating gaze. He said nothing, and she was suddenly very afraid of him. But then he inclined his head to her with respect.

Ginger took her leave of the platform, walking in the small steps forced on her by the tight wrap. In her side vision, she could see Dirk Bauxite watching her with an intensity that made hairs on her neck prickle.

Kindle, the Flame Sentinel, was hovering at the stairs, still looking as if he wanted to help. She smiled unsteadily at him, glad someone in the room didn't want to condemn her. Then she made her way down the stairs, step by excruciating step. When she reached the bottom, she saw Dirk wet his lips as he stared at her. If a person's gaze could have burned, she would have been engulfed in flame.

The meeting ended soon after, but Ginger felt no relief. She feared she had made enemies today.

Harjan took Ginger home in his cart, then joined his mining crew, which was gathering to work on a bluff not far away. Ginger felt reassured to know they would watch the temple now that she had returned.

The main temple wasn't empty. Darz was sitting on the ledge of the fountain, staring into the water. She hadn't realized he would be up and about, and she tensed, worried he could have passed out while she was gone. After the way the meeting had gone today, she was disillusioned enough to wonder if people would be relieved should he fall in the water and drown, for they would no longer have to worry about him.

He had been at the temple for five days. He looked less strange today, dressed in an old pair of trousers and a work shirt Harjan had given him. His face was easier to read now that his bruises were clearing. He seemed lost in thought. He trailed his fingers in the water, then cupped his hands and drank.

Ai! More offenses against the dragon. Perhaps she should just give up and run away to join a caravan, given how angry the Dragon-Sun would be if he was watching her today.

She came up next to Darz. "You do realize," she said, "that you just committed sacrilege."

"Ho!" He jumped to his feet and spun around, reaching across his body for his nonexistent sword, his face twisted into a snarl. If she hadn't spent the last five days feeding and cleaning him, she probably would have been terrified. After the town meeting, though, an enraged warrior paled in comparison. Either that, or she was too frightened to register the emotion.

"Goodness," she said.

"Gods almighty, woman!" he bellowed. "Never sneak up on me!"

"I did not sneak up," she said. "And don't shout at me."

Unexpectedly, he winced. "Sorry." He glanced at her feet. "Don't you wear slippers? I couldn't hear you."

She shook her head. "It is forbidden for me to wear them."

"Why the blazes for?"

"It says in the ancient scrolls. 'The chosen of the Dragon-Sun will walk softly on the soles of her feet, so as never to disturb his exalted mentations.'"

"For flaming sake," he said. "Those writings are a thousand years old. No one even knows what they mean." He gave a snort. "I'll tell you what. Your elders don't want you to wear shoes because that makes it easier to keep you penned in the temple."

She shrugged. "I've gone barefoot for years. It doesn't bother me."

"You walked all the way to town like that?"

"Harjan gave me a ride." She smiled at his annoyance. "Don't worry. If I need slippers, I use them." The elders would disapprove if they knew how often she wore what she wanted, so she didn't tell them. She couldn't completely hide it because people often came here, but she downplayed it as much as possible.

"It just all sounds so arcane," he said.

"Have you never visited a temple before?" She indicated the fountain. "This water is blessed by the Sunset Goddess and goes back out pipes to irrigate crops. We can't use it for ourselves without the proper rites." The sparkling liquid came from underground springs, the village's most valuable resource. The water source wasn't extensive enough to support more than five hundred people, but that was enough for Sky Flames. Just barely.

"I've spent little time in temples," Darz admitted. He didn't look as if he thought that situation should be rectified, but he did seem contrite about the water.

"Well, I suspect no harm was done." She blinked at him. "You certainly have a loud voice."

To her surprise, he burst out laughing, a rich sound unlike any she had heard before, robust and unaffected. "So people tell me," he said. "I must say, you're a brave one. I've had people practically jump out of their clothes when I bellowed."

"Well, then, I suspect you bellow far too much." Flustered, she added, "And I never jump out of garments."

His face reddened. "Ah. Well. I didn't mean—that is, I would never think—" He cleared his throat, obviously trying not to think whatever it was he never thought.

After a moment, he said, "That dress is gorgeous."

"Thank you," she said, self-conscious.

Darz rubbed the back of his neck. "I noticed that, uh, you don't seem to have any, well—young man who visits."

Ginger wasn't certain what he meant, that young men didn't visit the temple, or that no one in particular came to see her. She spoke carefully, aware she was skirting the limits of what was proper. "Anyone of any age may seek my blessings."

"Yes, well, I'm surprised crowds of suddenly pious young fellows aren't out here seeking them daily."

Her cheeks heated. "They go for their ten years army service when they are seventeen. Many don't come back."

"It's mandatory here for men to do ten years in the army?"

"Isn't it everywhere?"

He snorted. "It's not mandatory to do ten seconds. We're encouraged to go for one tour, and many men do, but that's five years."

It didn't surprise her. "Heath told me that, too, when he came home. He only stayed in five years. He was furious at the elders. He said they were taking advantage of me to do all the work in the temple because he wasn't here to protest."

"Who is Heath?" Darz hardly seemed to have heard the rest. "Your young man?"

She gave a startled laugh. "Goodness, no. He's my brother."

"Ah." His posture relaxed. "Didn't you have acolytes?"

"I *was* the acolyte." She shook her head. "I haven't found any girls interested in taking on those duties. It's frustrating. Everyone seems to feel I'm young enough that they don't need to worry about it."

"Your elders should send you help from the village."

In her less generous moments, similar thoughts had occurred to Ginger. She said only, "It's forbidden."

He made an exasperated noise. "No, it isn't." He stopped, then said, "Well, yes, I suppose you can't have the uninitiated mucking about a temple. But it's always possible to find help. You shouldn't have to shoulder the responsibility for this entire place alone."

"Heath does the heavy work," she assured him. "Harjan, too. Jalla, the Archivist's daughter, comes to visit, and she helps me inside."

He looked mollified. But then he said, "I know exactly why you can't get help."

She smiled, amused. "Now you are an expert on Sky Flames?"

Darz glared at her. "Don't laugh. I'm serious."

"Do tell."

He crossed his arms. "Most girls your age can't help you because they're married, with husbands more than ten years older and children. Others went with their young men to wherever the boys were stationed with the army. And that's not all I've figured out, Ginger-Sun. A stream of single men comes here to set up mining claims, don't they? Friction exists between them and the townsfolk, especially among unmarried men, because there's a shortage of women. Sometimes the newcomers carouse and cause trouble, which makes your people even more suspicious. That's why no one wants me here."

She gaped at him for a full five seconds before she found her voice. "How did you *know* all that?"

"Partially guessing," he admitted. "I've heard it happens in these mining outposts near the Jazid border. This area is rich with minerals, but it's a rough life. So you see a lot more men than women." Wryly he added, "It's no wonder your elders send all those restless young bucks off to the army."

Although Ginger had never thought about it in such terms, she knew Heath kept his friends away from her. "When my brother came back, three of his army friends came with him. They're all miners now." She gave him a rueful smile. "The only reason Heath isn't hulking around here, keeping an eye on you, is because they took a shipment of silver to J'Hiza, to negotiate with the merchants." Wistfully, she added, "You'll probably be gone by the time he returns."

To her disappointment, he said, "Probably." Then he scowled at her. "You shouldn't tell strangers that one of your main protectors is gone. Gods only know what could happen to a girl like you, alone, out here."

"But I'm not alone. The villagers protect me." She hesitated. "And I guess I don't think of you as a stranger."

His expression softened. "Thank you."

"Would you like some water? I can bring you a carafe I've prepared. It's all right to drink it if I've done the rites."

"Yes, that would be excellent."

"I will make a bargain with you," she decided.

He watched her curiously. "And what might this entail?"

"If you go back to your room to rest, I'll get the water."

"Rest!" His smile turned into a glower. "I've been resting for five days. I'm going mad. I shall be a raving lunatic soon."

She couldn't help but smile. "Soon?"

"I thought all you priestesses were the embodiment of sweetness," he grumbled.

She made shooing motions with her hands. "Go on. Go back to your room. I'll be there in a moment."

"I can't believe you talk to me this way. Me, a soldier of Her Majesty's army." When she started to tell him what she thought about that, he laughed and held up his hands, the age-old request for mercy. "I'm going!"

"I'll see you there."

Darz went off, grumbling good-naturedly, which for some reason made her feel soft inside.

As Ginger headed to her rooms, she mulled over everything that had happened. The elders would never let him remain in the temple if they saw him up and about. And he wouldn't stay put much longer. But he wasn't ready to set off in the desert. J'Hiza, the nearest town was more than a day's ride from here, and he had no supplies or horse. Moving him to town was the sensible option. If Tajman knew Darz was well enough to move, though, he would probably decide their guest was well enough to leave.

Deep in thought, she walked into her suite—

And slipped in a pool of blood.

The Trespass

Ginger's cry rang out. Confined by her wrap, she couldn't jump back or even swing her arms for balance. She fell on the stone, hitting her hip as she caught herself with her hands. In front of her, in the doorway of her parlor, a pool of blood had spread in an ugly red blotch.

Frantic, she struggled to her feet and backed away, leaving bloody footprints—until she thudded into someone.

"*No!*" She whirled around, trying to bring her arms up to defend herself, but the tight sleeves of the wrap made it impossible.

Darz. It was *Darz*. He had put up his hands to stop her from knocking him over, and now he took hold of her upper arms. "Saints, Ginger-Sun, what happened?"

"On the floor." Her arm trembled as she turned and pointed to the blood.

It suddenly hit her that he was holding her. This wasn't like when she had tended his injuries; now he deliberately put his hands on her. It was also the first time they had stood together when she wasn't supporting him, and she was acutely aware of his height, that he was taller and heavier than most men and she smaller than many women. The situation rattled her so much, she lurched back from him.

He was staring past her to her room. "Wait here," he said.

"I've taken care of this temple for years," she said, edgy with the turmoil of her thoughts. "And I've taken care of you for five days. Now that you can walk, don't treat me like I'm some helpless female you have to hide in silk wraps and bare feet." Until she said the words, she didn't realize how angry she was, not at him, but at the elders. She always held her anger inside and told herself it didn't exist.

"All right," he said. "Show me."

She was so stunned, she just stood and gaped at him. She had once—only once—spoken with such anger in the village. She had lashed out at Second Sentinel Spark when he refused to let her tend an injured miner. Her defiance had infuriated him, and she had feared he would hit her. As much as she resented it, he had that right as an elder of the village. He restrained himself, but later Elder Tajman had come to the temple and told Ginger she must spend two days in penance, meditating on her "unseemly behavior." It angered her that they punished her when she had only wanted to help someone who was suffering, and two days locked in an acolyte's cell had been dreadfully boring, but it was better than having Spark beat her.

Ginger took a deep breath and led Darz to the archway of her parlor. As he knelt to examine the blood, she stared at the streak of red her foot had left on the tiles.

He looked up at her, his face drawn. "This could be from a goat or a sheep. But we'll have to check your suite to see if anyone is inside."

His pallor worried Ginger. "You shouldn't be taking such risks when just a few days ago you were the one who was dying."

He rose to his feet, and his lips curved upward. "Don't treat me like I'm some helpless invalid you have to hide in sleep clothes and bare feet."

She gave a startled laugh. Had she really been so bold to say the like to him? "Fair enough."

He raised his hand, and for a moment, she thought he would touch her. Then he flushed and dropped his arm.

Ginger wasn't sure which bothered her more, that he had almost touched her again or that she wished he hadn't held back. Torn by her confused emotions, she walked inside, scanning the parlor. Her vases from Kuzla Quian stood half as tall as a person, but they were too thin for someone to hide behind. The chairs and divan were woven wicker that she could see through. The tables were simple affairs, enameled in blue, white and rose, with no parts that could provide a hiding place. The arch to her bedroom had no door, and its curtain of beads was tied up on either side.

"Is anything out of place?" Darz asked.

Startled, she realized he had followed her inside as if it were perfectly natural. She knew she should tell him to leave, but she was afraid to be alone.

"Everything looks normal," she said.

He went to the archway of her bedroom. The room was much like this one, except for the bed, which at the moment lacked its fluffy quilt, blankets and cushions, leaving a bare mattress on a frame reinforced with sunwood slats. Seeing Darz look at the place where she slept set her cheeks burning.

"Gods," he muttered. "You could stay here, and you've been

sleeping on the floor in my room?" He glanced at her. "I owe you even more thanks than I knew."

"It's no trouble. I slept on the floor of that cell for six years."

"Gods almighty, *why?*"

"That's what acolytes do."

"It sounds cruel to me." He motioned at her bedroom. "Does anything look out of place there?"

"Not a thing." She walked into the sunny room, sweeping her gaze over the furniture, vases, her scrolls, the walls, the dragon in its niche—

"Wait." She crossed to the head of her bed and peered at the blown-glass dragon. It was tinted like the sunrise, pink and gold with a touch of blue. But today, not all of its color came from glass.

Ginger felt sick. She sat on the bed and laid her hand over her abdomen, as if that could hold down her bile.

"What is it?" Darz came over to her. "Are you all right?"

She stared across the room at one of the windows and the sky beyond. "Look at the dragon."

He leaned past her to peer at the sculpture. "I don't see—"Then he swore loudly. "Flaming hell. That's sheer malice."

She spoke dully. "Smearing blood on a symbol of the sun is sacrilege. I'll have to destroy the statue."

"No, don't do that. It's such a beautiful work." He was standing over her, studying the sculpture, so close his arm was brushing her shoulder. Touching her. Her longing for him had brought only grief, yet even now it simmered within her, and she despised herself for it. She couldn't let herself feel. If she did, the fear and shock would be too great.

Darz lifted up the sculpture and sat next to her. "It shouldn't be hard to clean this." He used his sleeve to wipe at the blood smeared on the wings. "The glass isn't damaged."

Ginger had gone beyond dismay to a numb calm, as if that could protect her. The calm wouldn't last, though. She would soon crack open, and she didn't want Darz to see her fall apart. If he were sitting here, so close, so strong and warm, she would end up in his arms and take her transgressions beyond what the Dragon-Sun would ever forgive, if she hadn't already gone that far.

"Darz, look at me," she said.

He met her gaze. "I don't know why this is happening. I swear it."

"Someone is trying to scare me." They were succeeding extremely well. "And Darz." It amazed her how steady she sounded, because she was on the verge of breaking.

"Yes?"

"Do you have any idea how much trouble we would be in if anyone found you in my bedroom, sitting next to me on my bed, holding a desecrated ritual object?"

"Oh!" He jumped up and started to leave, but then he came back. With care, he set the dragon in its niche. "You go into the temple. I'll clean up the blood here."

She shook her head. "You can't be in my rooms."

He looked as if he wanted to argue. But he was studying her face, too, and whatever he saw kept him from protesting. He limped across the room and turned in the archway. "I'll be nearby if you need me. Just call out."

"Thank you."

"Promise me you won't destroy that lovely sculpture."

Her voice shook. "I promise."

"Take care, lovely fire opal." Then he left, before she had time to be scandalized. Except she couldn't summon outrage. She had never known the simple pleasure of a man finding her pretty. No man in Sky Flames would dare take such liberties, but she thought Darz didn't even realize what he was doing. He knew as much about temples as she did about military maneuvers, which was next to nothing.

When Ginger was alone, she pulled out her opal. The orange color could have been fire solidified into a crystal. Its banked power waited for release. Except the power wasn't in the opal; it was in *her*. She wasn't certain how she knew, for her spells never worked with any other gem. Yet she felt certain the stone unlocked something within her. But only in the cold night. It could do nothing now, offer no comfort.

The dam holding her feelings broke and tears poured down her face. The events of these past days were shattering her life. The scrolls of the Dragon-Sun taught that he protected a priestess from the flames of his power, so that if she were ever in his presence, she wouldn't burn. But what of these flames destroying her heart? Nothing shielded her from their searing pain.

After a while, Ginger wiped away the moisture on her face. She put away the opal and set about cleaning her rooms. Even after she scrubbed the floor until the tiles shone, they didn't seem clean. She cried while she washed the dragon. How could someone commit such an offense? She didn't know which would be worse, that whoever tried to murder Darz had violated the sanctum of her private rooms or that someone in the village had done this.

Darz had been here when it happened, but she knew he hadn't done it. People thought she was naive, and maybe they were right, but she trusted her instincts. They had always guided her well, and now they told her Darz was innocent. If his attackers had done this, surely they would have tried to kill him again. He had probably been sleeping in his room, so they might not have known he was here, but if that were true, she couldn't see why they would go after her.

More likely someone in the village had left the blood. After today's meeting, she knew all too well how people felt about Darz. But they had violated her room, not his. It couldn't be because she had spoken today; this had to have happened while she was gone. She had come straight home afterward and seen no one else along the way. Although it wasn't impossible for someone to have run back before her, she thought it unlikely. If what had happened here with the blood became known, her people would assume Darz had done it and drive him out into the desert to die.

Ginger stood by the bed and watched Darz sleep. He must have dropped off as soon as he lay down. He looked boyish, his great power and strength momentarily lulled. He hadn't changed his clothes, and he even had one foot on the floor. Shadows of night filled the cell, barely challenged by the candle out in the temple. Caught with an affection she shouldn't feel, she lifted his leg onto the bed and set it next to his other one.

Darz opened his eyes. "Light, Ginger-Sun…"

She straightened up. "You're awake!"

He pushed up on his elbows. "Are you all right?"

"Fine." It wasn't true; she was tired, scared, and confused. She sat on the stool by his bed. "How about you?"

He scowled darkly. "I am not fine. Someone is harassing you, and I don't like it."

Ginger knew that to most people he probably looked large and dark and menacing. But he didn't frighten her. "They must have come in while I was at the meeting."

"I was asleep." He sat up and swung his legs over the edge of the bed, only a few handspans away from her. "Has anyone ever hounded you this way before?"

"Never." She hesitated, distracted by how close he was sitting to her. "It isn't because of me, I don't think. It's you. People are scared." With apology, she added, "They want you to leave. I convinced them not to turn you out, but you shouldn't stay in the temple with me anymore."

He grimaced, pulling the stitches on the gash that snaked down his face. "I sometimes forget how provincial these isolated villages are."

Ginger bristled. "We may be small and far from Quaaz, but that doesn't make us worth any less than other places."

His face crinkled with a smile. "You should see how you blaze when you're angry."

"Don't patronize me."

"I'm not!" He glared at her. "Can a man do or say nothing around you without getting into trouble?"

"Pretty much not," she admitted.

He motioned around them. "I never know what to do in these places. It's why I avoid them."

"You mean a temple?"

"The last time I was in one, I thought the priestess was going to skewer me with my own sword."

She raised an eyebrow. "Why am I not surprised?"

His eyes glinted. "I tried to stop my cousin Lima from getting a nuptial blessing."

"You didn't like his bride?"

"Her groom." He glared as if she had invoked an offense of great proportions. "Her skinny husband who wouldn't know what to do with a sword if it jumped into his hand. What the blazes kind of man is that for Lima, eh?"

"I can think of far worse traits for a husband," she said. "For example, a man who glares and yells and interferes in the lives of his family because he doesn't think thin grooms are worthy of his kin."

She thought he would shout at her, but instead he burst out laughing. "Saint Citrine, you sound just like Lima. She does what she wants no matter what I say."

That made Ginger feel like a cat with a bowl of cream. "I think I would like her."

He regarded her warily. "I don't know if Taka Mal could survive putting the two of you together."

She smiled, relieved he had decided not to shout. "Is she happy with her skinny husband?"

"Yes, actually," he said grudgingly. "She loves him. He loves her. They have a baby. They are quite happy."

She heard what he didn't say. "But you aren't."

For a moment she thought he wouldn't answer. Then he said, "I was supposed to marry her."

No wonder he was upset. It wasn't unusual for cousins to wed, though she had heard it was less common in the cities. Here in Sky Flames, it happened all the time. She was probably related to half the people in the village.

"You must love her very much," she said.

"Well, no. I mean, yes." He glared at her. "Yes, I do. Like I would love my kin. Not as a wife. But still. It's the principle. That she would choose *him* over me." He scowled and crossed his arms.

Ah. Male pride. "Perhaps she felt no one could ever measure up to you, so she had to settle for less."

Darz gave a hearty laugh. "I very much doubt that." He lowered his arms. "So you think your people will throw me out?"

"I hope not. We need to make you less threatening." She considered his large build, bulging muscles, and scars. "Or if that won't work, at least convince them you need time to finish your recovery and arrange travel."

"Why aren't you afraid of me like the others?"

"Should I be?"

He answered in a low voice. "Yes."

He caught her off guard; she had expected him to say *Of course not.* She was suddenly aware of the dim light, how it added intimacy to their meeting, as if the shadows offered a veil to hide forbidden behavior.

Darz traced his fingertip down her cheek and across her lips. "You're so damned beautiful."

She couldn't answer. The Dragon-Sun would surely send flames to smite Darz. Except apparently the dragon was asleep or paying no attention to her inconsequential temple, because no fire appeared. Ginger knew she should push Darz back, turn him away, banish him. Instead, she sat like a deer hypnotized by the glow of a campfire in the dark. Wind keened across the sands outside, and black-wings called through the night.

Darz cupped his palm around her cheek. He had taken the bandages off his hands, and his stitches scraped her skin. A flush of heat went through her. He bent his head, and when his lips touched hers, it jolted her body like a shock of heat. She had to *stop!* If anyone walked in right now they would probably kill Darz and maybe her as well. But she wanted so much to hold him, to know at least once in her life how it felt to be kissed by a man who desired her.

Darz apparently had no fear, or else he was too innocent of temple strictures to know how badly he sinned. When he pulled her off the stool, she broke away from the kiss. He easily lifted her to sit next to him on the bed and engulfed her in his embrace, his arm muscles corded against her back, his bandaged torso pressing against her chest. He was too strong, too big, but she couldn't make herself tell him to stop. She wanted so badly to believe the Dragon-Sun wasn't punishing them because he had chosen this man for her.

Darz kissed her as if he were stranded in the dunes, parched for water, and she was the oasis. His beard scratched her cheek. She felt hot, then light-headed, then wobbly, and she never wanted it to end. He laid her beneath him on the bed—and Ginger finally came to her senses.

She jerked away her head. "No!"

He nuzzled her cheek, his body stretched out on top of her, his breath coming faster as he tried to kiss her again.

"Stop, please." She struggled, pushing at his shoulders.

He inhaled sharply. Then he pushed up on his elbows and looked down at her with heartbreaking affection. "Why, Ginger? I can tell you want me."

"This is sacrilege."

"A beautiful fire-lily should be cherished, not imprisoned here like a dead flower pressed in a book."

She stared up at him. "The dragon will punish us both."

He searched her face, and she could see details of his eyes. They weren't truly black, but dark brown with the thinnest veins of gold. His low voice rumbled as if it were a spell of desire. "Would it be so terrible if I made love to you? Surely the Dragon-Sun doesn't wish you bereft of companionship." He brushed his lips across hers. "It's a crime to isolate such a lovely girl."

"Darz, get off." She hit at his shoulders with her fists. "Now."

With a groan, he pulled away from her and sat up on the edge of the bed. Cold air filled the space where his body had been. She sat up next to him, tugging her wrap, which had slipped off her shoulders. Then she stood up, miserable, her eyes downcast.

"Priestess," he said. "Look at me."

She raised her gaze to his. "You're right," she said. "I'm so lonely here, sometimes I feel as if I'll die of it." Tears gathered in her eyes. "And if you seek to take advantage of that for your own pleasure, you are cruel beyond all measure."

She turned and walked to the archway of the room. As she reached it, Darz said, "Ginger."

She paused, one hand on the door frame as she stared across the shadowed temple. She knew if she turned, she wouldn't be able to leave. So she walked out of the cell, the floor cold against her soles as she left behind his seductive warmth.

Sand Shadow

Ginger stood on the crest of a sand dune with her tear-streaked face tilted to the heavens. Stars filled the night. The sky glittered like a black sea saturated with diamonds.

"Why is he here?" she asked, her voice muted in the immensity of the night. She was alone, far from the village, far from the temple, hidden among endless mountains of sand. "Are you punishing me for wanting another besides you?"

Now that she was away from the temptation of Darz's passion, she could think. After what had happened in the town meeting today she knew she could never marry Darz, even if he had wanted it, which she doubted. The people of Sky Flames would never sanction her union with such a stranger. She could defy their will, but then she could no longer serve as their priestess. They would turn her out, just as they wanted to turn Darz out.

He was toying with her. A naive girl alone and a bored warrior; she probably seemed like a water-peach ready to pick. But if he took her from the vine that nurtured her—her home and the temple— she would wither.

Her solitude was like a great glass sphere closing her away from life. She could see the rest of the world, but never touch it. Tradition cloistered her, and the miners guarded her. Even tonight, Tanner had been posted outside the temple and had followed her into the dunes. At least he was discreet; she hadn't seen him after she started walking.

The wind rippled her shawl around her body, over the tunic and leggings she had donned in defiance of everyone. At night, temperatures plunged. With a shiver, she pulled the shawl around her body. Then she lifted her hand out of its folds and opened her palm to the sky. The opal lay there. A glow lit its center, as if it had an ember of fire in its heart.

"What are you?" she whispered. Her focus on the gem caused the light to flare, and radiance streamed out of the pyramid. Her apprehension surged; if Tanner saw, he might condemn her.

Ginger spoke in a low voice. "Warmth!" She had discovered that single words helped focus her concentration. The light faded, and her hand grew warm.

"Soothe," she murmured.

A sense of well-being seeped through her. It didn't take away her loneliness or her grief. She wasn't even sure why she grieved; maybe for the glimpse Darz offered of a life she could never have. But her sorrow somehow became more bearable.

Perhaps it was time to tell the elders she wished to marry. They would select an acceptable husband. She could imagine the type they would pick, though, an upstanding citizen in Sky Flames, perhaps Kindle, the Flame Sentinel who had helped her up the stairs at the meeting. Or they might choose someone like Dirk Bauxite, the house-builder who had challenged her that day and watched her with that covetous hunger. Dirk frightened her, with his hard attitudes that left no room for softness. She knew the elders would consider it in her best interest to have someone take a "strong hand" with her. The dragon only knew what someone like Dirk would do if she became his wife. She grimaced and knew she would never bring up the matter with the elders.

Her focus slipped, and the opal's vestigial glow faded. Closing her hand, she took away its last sliver of light. She began the long walk home. The moonless night wasn't truly dark, not with the glitter of stars overhead. The shushing of her tread in the sand was the only sound in the vast landscape.

In fact, it was too quiet. She stopped, listening. The deep silence was unnatural. Then a black-wing cried somewhere, and with an exhale, she resumed her walk.

A figure appeared on the next dune.

Ginger went stock-still. He stood on the ridge, silhouetted against the stars. She couldn't be certain, but she thought he was staring straight at her. She was on the crest of a dune, so she would be as visible to him as he was to her.

Darz. He had come looking for her. She clung to that hope though she knew he was in no condition to wander the desert. Just limping across the temple had taxed him.

As soon as the figure started down the dune, she knew it wasn't Darz. He couldn't run in that fast, sliding gait. It didn't look like one of the miners; something about the way he was approaching, with such deliberate speed, was *wrong*.

Where was Tanner? She backed up along the ridge, then realized she had nowhere to go. The temple was to the south, exactly in line with the figure, and the village lay beyond that. No one wandered here except animals that lived in the dunes. Sand-cats rarely ranged this far east, and they were the only predators that posed a danger. Except human ones. He might mean no harm, but if his intentions were benign, why hadn't he called out or identified himself?

Ginger slid down the ridge until it hid her from the figure. She knew this desert well, for she spent many hours here meditating to the Dragon-Sun. He never answered, unless Darz was his idea of a response. It would be a cruel one, bringing more pain than anything else, but then, a sun god had neither to be comprehensible or kind.

The color of her clothes and hair were similar to the desert; in the starlight, she hoped that made it difficult to see her. Moving as fast as she could manage in sand that slipped and poured under her feet, she climbed toward a notch between two dunes. Within moments, she reached the small pass and slid down its other side. She stopped, breathing heavily, her hand pressed to her side while she scanned the ridges above her. No figure showed against the starred sky. The night darkened the valleys between the dunes, but as far as she could see, no sign of movement showed down here. No sounds came, either, except the wind. She didn't dare let herself feel safe, though. Not yet, not until she was home. Moving slowly to conserve her breath, she headed for the temple. She rounded another crest of sand—

Someone ripped the shawl from her shoulders.

The violent motion spun Ginger around, and she sprawled onto her stomach. Catching herself on her hands did no good; they sunk into the dune. She tried to cry out, but her mouth filled with sand. A hand shoved her down and someone lay on top of her, heavy and wide, covering her body.

"I saw you, whore." His breath was suffocating, thick with the smell of wine. "Kissing him."

She spit out the sand in her mouth. "Get off!" He didn't sound like any of the miners. "Who are you, spying on me?"

"You offend the sanctity of your calling." He was gripping her waist hard, and pain flared through her.

"That isn't yours to decide," she cried. "Stop touching me!"

He flipped her over and slapped her across the face. "You will not speak to me that way!"

Reeling from the blow, she clawed at his face with her opal. When he let go of her to protect himself, she grabbed a handful of sand and threw it into his eyes.

"Ai!" His yell flew across the desert.

Ginger twisted and toppled him sideways. They were on the slope of a dune, one steep enough that he fell hard and rolled down it, away from her. She scrambled to her feet and lunged into a run, slipping and scrabbling, staying below the crest so she wouldn't be visible against the sky. Usually she loved the constantly shifting sands, but now she cursed them for dragging away her speed. She couldn't tell if the stranger was following; the sand muffled footsteps. Except stranger was the wrong word. She *knew* his voice. She couldn't place it, but he was from the village. Someone wanted reason to throw out Darz, and now he had plenty, not only against Darz, but against her as well.

It was only a fifteen-minute walk from home, but it had never seemed so long. When she reached the temple, gasping for air, no miners were outside; apparently they thought Tanner was with her. She ran inside, into the barest light from the dregs of a candle on the table. She raced to her rooms and found the cutlery where she had left it, in a wedge of goldwood by her cutting board. She grabbed the largest chopping knife and spun around, half expecting to see the bulky figure behind her.

The kitchen was empty.

Ginger gulped in air. Her heart was beating so hard she thought it would burst. Alert to every noise, she returned to the table in the main temple where she put out candles every night. She was clenching her opal so hard, it cut her skin. She opened her hand, ignoring the trickle of blood, and concentrated until a flame leapt from the gem. She used the spell of fire to light candles until the table blazed with golden light.

"Ginger?" Darz asked. "What happened?"

"Ah!" She snapped her hand closed and doused the spell, so only the candlelight remained. She retreated to the other side of the table, keeping it between them. "Don't you sleep?"

"It's all I've been doing." He walked toward her, barely visible in the shadows.

"Stay back."

He stopped about fifteen paces away, at the edge of her sphere of light. "I won't trespass."

"It's a little late to decide that." Her voice cracked. "Someone spied on us. He followed me into the desert."

"Gods almighty! Are you all right?"

She laid her palm against her right cheek. It was already swelling. "I've been better."

"He hurt you!" Darz started toward her. "I'll kill—"

"Stop! Don't you see? You can't come near me. I can't stay in the same building with you. But I don't dare walk to the village. He might be out there. You can't walk to the village, either. It's too far."

Her voice was shaking. "Why would he attack me? If he wanted to discredit us, he needed only tell the Elder what he had seen."

"Maybe he's not from your village."

"He is. I'm sure."

"What did he say?"

Ashamed, she said, "He called me a whore."

"Anyone who calls you that answers to me!" In a calmer tone, he added, "That does make his motives obvious, though."

"It does?"

"To a man."

She regarded him dourly. "Well, maybe you could make them obvious to this woman."

"He saw me doing what he was forbidden to do. So he got angry. He probably wants to smash in my face."

"But I told you to stop." She felt dishonest saying it, because she hadn't wanted him to stop. But if someone had been close enough to see them, he must have heard.

He spoke quietly. "I am deeply sorry, Priestess, that my inexcusable behavior caused this trouble for you."

It was impossible to be angry when he spoke that way and looked so appealing, standing there in his sleep trousers and shirt, with hair falling into his eyes as if he were a boy instead of a formidable warrior. Of course, that was how she had landed in this mess, by finding him so appealing.

"He might be in here," she said.

He gave an angry snort. "Where the hell are those miners who are always hulking around?"

It was a good question. "I thought Tanner followed me into the dunes. But I'm sure he wasn't the one who hit me."

He limped forward, keeping his hands at his sides with his palms out, as if to show he had no weapons. She wasn't certain he even realized he was doing it; the gesture seemed automatic, the soldier seeking to make himself less imposing. But it wasn't his military skills that threatened her.

Darz stopped at the other side of the table. "If you want to search the temple, we should each take a candle. Also, I could use one of those knives, if you have another."

Ginger breathed out slowly. "I'll get it." She ran to her kitchen and grabbed another knife. When she returned to the main temple, Darz was waiting with two candles.

They searched the entire building, even the Sunset room, and they called for Tanner and Harjan. As before, with the scream and the blood, they found no trace of anyone. Ginger wanted to feel relieved, but she feared it meant the spy could hide so well, they couldn't find him even with such a thorough attempt.

Eventually she and Darz sat on the ledge of the fountain, holding their candles, and stared at each other. He asked the question first. "What now?"

"Dawn is in a few hours. Then we can go to the village." She wasn't certain he could get that far, but she had no better ideas.

"And after that?"

"I don't know." She rubbed her eyes. "It depends if the person who hit me tonight says anything."

"Why wouldn't he?" Darz asked. "He has a lot to gain."

"Gain what?" she asked angrily. "My humiliation?"

"Yes, actually. And my exile." He lifted his hand to her cheek, then realized what he was doing and set his palm on the ledge. "It won't help his case when people see that black eye he gave you."

She probed her face and winced as pain shot through her cheek. "Unless he says you did it."

"*I* did it?" His voice rose. "I'd like to give *him* one."

"Darz, don't yell."

"I'm *not* yelling," he said loudly. But he did lower his voice. "I'm speaking with resolve."

She couldn't help but smile. "Do you think you could be a little less resolved?"

"Very well. I'll try to speak better."

"Actually, you speak very well."

He squinted at her. "Why do you sound surprised?"

She gave him a look of apology. "I suppose I had some ill-conceived ideas about soldiers, that they trained with weapons and fists rather than their minds."

He tapped his temple. "A fighter needs this if he is going to stay alive."

"It's more than that." She searched for the right words. "You remind me of Elder Tajman. It's your confidence, I think. He assumes people will follow his lead. So do you."

"Why does that bother you?"

"It doesn't fit my picture of soldiers, I guess. They are trained to obey, yes?"

"I'm just like everyone else. Nothing special."

Softly she said, "I wouldn't agree with you on either of those claims."

His look gentled. "It only seems that way to you because I have some veneer from living in Quaaz."

"You live in Quaaz?"

Darz swore under his breath. "When I'm not in Taza Qu."

"You use far too many oaths," she chided. "Especially inside the house of the Dragon-Sun."

"I do believe you are trying to civilize me." He sounded intrigued. "It's a hopeless goal."

Her face warmed with a smile. "Why didn't you want me to know you live in Quaaz?"

It was a moment before he answered. Finally he said, "I command a company in the Queen's Army. That doesn't mean I'm particularly valuable, but some people might think so."

"I knew it!" She beamed at him. "You didn't seem the type to quietly take orders."

"I have to take my orders like anyone else. I just happen to give a few, too." He grinned at her. "Though I've heard it said I never do anything quietly."

"I imagine not." Her smile faded. "Surely you don't think any of my people were involved with the attempt on your life."

He stared at his reflection in the water and touched the healing gash on his face. "I don't know why those men attacked me. Maybe they were bandits. But why go after someone who had just woken up and was carrying nothing of value?"

"They might not have realized that."

"It's possible." He raised his gaze to her. "I don't want anyone here to think I might have anything worth taking."

"I don't think anyone wants to steal from you." With apology, she said, "They just want you to leave." She wanted to add, *Except me,* but she couldn't make that admission.

His face darkened. "Not until I stop whoever is tormenting you."

"Darz, it's a matter for my people to deal with." Softly she said, "But thank you."

"For what?" He made an incredulous noise. "Causing you this trouble because I was an unconscionable lout?"

"It's not your fault someone tried to kill you." She couldn't respond to the rest. It hadn't felt unconscionable, it had been delicious, but if anyone overheard her say such a thing, she would be in even more trouble.

Darz rubbed his eyes. "Even if we could risk walking to the village tonight, I doubt I could. I think I'm going to fall asleep sitting here."

"Aye. I also."

"You should sleep in the acolyte's cell tonight," he said. "It's safer. It has no windows. I'll sleep on the floor in front of its door." He indicated her knife. "I don't think you should keep that, either, not unless you know how to use it, and I don't mean to chop food."

Her grip tightened on the handle. "It's a good defense."

"It would be easy for someone to take it from you if you're half asleep. You need training for weapons like that."

"What makes you think I don't have it?"

"Do you?"

After a moment, she said, "No."

He regarded her intently. "Could you use it? Because if you can't, what you're really doing, by keeping it with you, is giving your attacker a weapon."

She stared at the glinting knife. "I can't imagine stabbing a person." She met his gaze. "But I would defend myself."

"Hide it under the mattress. Don't pull it out unless you're sure you can use it. That goes for any weapon."

"I'll remember." She wished she could say more.

In the morning they would have to deal with the aftermath of this night.

Judgement

Ginger and Darz set off for the village at dawn, soon after the dragon breathed fire into the sky. Neither of them had slept much. Darz had dark circles under his eyes, and his limp was more pronounced. In the temple, he had moved with relative ease, but he hadn't had to go far. Now he remained silent, his energy focused on their trek. For once she was glad the wrap and her bare feet constrained her steps, for it gave her a reason to walk slowly without hurting his pride.

The village up ahead was a cluster of houses built from sunstone and a few larger buildings with onion domes in the center. Several miners were hiking up the ridges north of town, toward the rock fields where they dug for ores. They had almost exhausted the surface veins and were digging shafts, but they needed a better way to excavate.

This last spring, Ginger had found an old scroll with a fanciful tale. It described how a man named Charles Carter had stumbled into Sky Flames, not from the west where most of the country lay, but from the east, across the killing deserts where no one lived. He must have been strong indeed, for he had survived the journey from the eastern coast. The scroll was less clear on where he came from before that, just that he had been shipwrecked. He didn't know how he ended up here; he claimed their small continent couldn't exist.

The man stayed the rest of his life in Sky Flames. On occasion, he traveled west through the settled lands and beyond the Misted Cliffs to the Blue Ocean. There, he would find a ship to take him home. According to the tale, the ships always came back to the shore, though he and the crew swore they never turned around. It saddened Ginger to think of the seaman stranded in a place he didn't believe existed.

She thought now of the scroll because of a substance Carter described. "Gunpowder." It exploded. The priestess who had penned his story dutifully recorded the ingredients and procedures, but she wrote as if the powder were a figment of his imagination. Although Ginger didn't see how it could work, either, she was studying it in the hopes of finding something useful. If it were more than a tale, it might help Harjan and his men dig mines. That would have to wait, though, until this turmoil settled.

"You're quiet," Darz said.

"I was thinking how people might react if word has spread about last night." She had worn her opal on a chain around her wrist, and now she touched it for luck.

"If they mistreat you, they'll have to deal with me."

She couldn't think of much that would make this worse than Darz threatening people. "I thank you for your support. But I don't think you should. It could make it look even more as if we, well—" she reddened "—you know."

"Your attacker may not have said anything."

She slanted a glance at him. "Then everyone will believe you gave me this bruise."

"For flaming sakes. I've barely been able to stand up. That's the only reason they let me stay this long, right?" When she just looked at him, he grimaced. "All right, so they won't believe me." Then he said, "I have no coins or goods to trade for a horse."

"I won't let anyone strand you in the desert." She wasn't sure how she would stop them, but there had to be a way.

"If you speak up for me," he said, "won't that make people suspicious, too?"

"It might." Disheartened, she said, "No matter what we do, we have trouble."

"I think so. People are staring at us."

She saw what he meant. They had reached the edge of Sky Flames, where villagers were coming out of their small houses to tend gardens, look after goats or fetch water. Others stood in their doorways and watched as she and Darz followed a dusty lane between the huts.

"They don't look antagonistic," Darz said. "Curious, more."

"It's a good sign." Ginger hoped she was right. If news had spread, surely she and Darz would be seeing more hostility.

As they went deeper into the village, the meandering lane became a street. They passed a girl herding a flock of tough-coated sheep, a hardy desert breed that could survive on far less water than their fluffier cousins in more hospitable climates. A gourd-tender walked by carrying his hoe, probably headed for the fields of gourds, corn, and beans, or the orange and lemon orchards. Crops never grew as large here as in wetter regions, but it was enough to feed Sky Flames.

People trickled into the streets: butchers, chicken-tenders, coppersmiths, merchants. Although she didn't know most of them well, she recognized many faces and nodded to those who greeted her. Although no one challenged them, their gazes flicked to Darz, often with distrust and suspicion.

Ginger paused at an alley behind two rows of shops. "Here."

"Is it far?" Darz's usually robust voice sounded strained.

She felt like a cretin, pushing him to walk. "Not much farther."

As they headed down the alley, memories rushed over her. These yellow-stone walls, the crack by a faded red door—it was so familiar. She had often hidden in that recessed doorway playing Seek-me. The crooked awning above it provided shade during the hottest hours of the day. Even the dusty ground, hard-packed and yellow with sand, seemed to welcome her.

The alley angled past the back of a house. She went to the door and knelt. Or she tried to kneel. The wrap kept her from bending her legs, so she had to bend over from the waist with the wrap pulled tight over her back and hips. When she ran her palms over the wall by the ground, a brick tilted under her push. She found an ornate key in the niche behind it, then replaced the brick and stood up.

Darz was leaning against the wall, watching her exertions with undisguised pleasure. His grin flashed. "Are you breaking into this house, sweet priestess?"

She raised her eyebrows at his cocky smile. "Well, my brother says I don't visit enough."

"He lives here?"

Ginger nodded as she unlocked the house. "It's where we grew up." She pushed open the door. The interior was cool and dark, but across the room, sunlight slanted through an archway that opened onto a garden within the house. A fountain in the garden spilled water out of a raised bowl into a basin.

"This is nice," Darz said.

Nice. Such a simple word for a place that held so many complicated and loving memories. "You can stay while my brother is gone. I'll ask the healer to look in on you."

He spoke quietly. "You're very generous."

She reddened, and motioned him toward the sunny archway. They walked out into the garden. Flowers grew in profusion: snaplions, rosy box blossoms, and fire-lilies. Pillars that supported balconies bordered the yard, painted red near the bottom, shading into rose, gold and then sky blue. Above them, the real sky arched, like an extension of the yard. The redstone path was smoothed by years of children running and adults walking.

"You look content," Darz said.

"I remember so much," she murmured. "Laughter and light."

His face gentled. "It's who's lived in a place that draws the memories, eh?"

"Aye."

His walk slowed as they crossed the garden. Finally he said, "Perhaps…I might lie down somewhere."

She could tell the admission cost him a great deal. Such a proud man, this commander in the Queen's Army. "You can use my brother's room."

"He won't mind?"

"Heath? No, never. He's a sweetheart."

Darz spoke dryly. "I have noticed, over the course of my life, that when a lovely young woman refers to a man as a 'sweetheart' or some such similar term, he usually turns out to be a hulking monster."

She laughed amiably. "Heath may be large, but he is never a monster. You'd like him."

Darz just grunted.

She took him under an archway and into a foyer with a high ceiling. The hall beyond ended at a room with dark red drapes and a four-poster bed. The ends of the posts were carved in figures of the Dragon-Sun with his neck arched and wings spread.

Darz barely looked around; he just went to the bed and lay on its burgundy spread, sprawled on his stomach, but favoring his wounds. With a sigh, he closed his eyes. Watching him, Ginger felt even worse about dragging him out here. She knew she should check his bandages, but she no longer dared touch him.

"I'll go for the healer," she said.

He lifted his head. "You will come back, won't you?"

She knew she should say no. But what came out was, "Yes, I will." Then she left quickly, to find a safer place than a bedroom that contained him.

As Ginger walked down the hall, a gong rang, its mellow tone echoing. Puzzled, she went to the front of the house and opened the gold door there. Tajman Limestone, the Elder Sentinel, stood outside on her doorstep with Kindle, the Flame Sentinel. Both men had unreadable expressions. The last time Ginger had seen Kindle, at the town meeting, he had seemed solicitous, even wanting to help her up the stairs, but now he was guarded. It discouraged her to think she may have lost yet another person's goodwill.

Tajman nodded formally. "Light of the morning, Priestess."

"And to you, Goodsirs." Someone must have run to tell him she was in town. Although it was natural for him to visit, he had showed up unusually fast, and it didn't bode well. Usually he would have given her time to rest and clean up after her walk from the temple.

She stepped aside, inviting them into the house. "Will you join me for tea?"

"Thank you." Tajman walked inside, his posture as stiff as his voice. Kindle followed him with a brief nod to Ginger. As he walked past her, something bothered her, but she wasn't sure what. The way he moved...?

She ushered them into the parlor, simply furnished with wicker chairs and wine-red cushions. "I'll go for the tea."

"Ginger-Sun." The Elder put up his hand. "Perhaps you shouldn't." The lines at the corners of his mouth and eyes seemed deeper.

"What's wrong?" she asked.

"We should ask you," he said. "Who hit you?"

She put her palm over the bruise on her cheek. "I don't know. It happened last night when I was walking in the dunes." Better to get it all out, so they didn't think she was hiding anything. "Someone came after me. He said he had been watching me, that I had acted improperly. When I protested, he hit me."

Kindle spoke sharply. "That's absurd."

The moment he spoke, she recognized his voice. "It was you!"

Tajman spoke sternly. "Ginger, you won't help yourself by fabricating stories against the people sent to guard you."

"I'm not," she said. "You know me better than that."

"Darz Goldstone was all over her," Kindle said.

Tajman narrowed his gaze at Ginger. "Is that true?"

A rough voice spoke behind her. "If you were spying, Flame

Sentinel, you also know she repeatedly told me to leave her alone. Or have you conveniently forgotten that?"

Ginger spun around. Darz was standing in the archway of the room, his hand braced against its side for support.

"*You.*" Kindle started toward him. "You defiled her!"

"Kindle, stop," the Elder said. "Are you going to hit a man who can barely stand on his own feet?"

"No one defiled me," Ginger said, annoyed. "I'm perfectly capable of telling someone to stop. And if you did see, Kindle, then you know he respected my wishes when I said no."

Kindle fixed her with a hard stare. "It took you too long to push him away."

Tajman was watching Kindle closely. "You didn't tell me she told him to stop. You just said they kissed."

Kindle crossed his arms. "The essence of their trespass is the same."

"Your trespass is far worse," Darz said, "to strike the priestess."

"Did you hit her?" the Elder asked Kindle.

Kindle gestured toward Darz. "It was him."

"That's not true!" Ginger said.

Darz spoke in a quiet voice, and in that moment Ginger knew, without doubt, that he was far more dangerous when he was quiet than when he was loud.

"I've dueled with men for impugning my name," Darz said. "To the death."

"You speak with disrespect," Kindle told him.

"You called me a whore," Ginger said angrily.

"Enough, all of you!" Tajman held up his hand.

She took a deep breath. "My apology, Elder Limestone."

Kindle spoke through gritted teeth. "And mine."

Ginger glanced at Darz. He met her gaze and said nothing.

The Elder spoke to Kindle. "I understand why you felt that you rather than Tanner should guard her in the desert last night. You're a sentinel." He glanced at Darz. "Maybe where you come from, men treat priestesses without respect. But not here." He considered both of them. "I see no excuse for either of you to strike a servant of the Dragon-Sun, especially since everyone seems agreed she told this man to stop touching her." Dryly he said, "And I assume neither of you plans to claim the dragon miraculously appeared and ordered you to abuse his priestess."

"I don't need any claim," Darz said. "I don't hit women."

"It's easy to lie," Kindle said, "when the only witness to the truth is a woman you dishonored."

"For saint's sake," Ginger said. "If he had dishonored me, why would I defend him?"

Kindle narrowed his gaze at her. "That's a good question."

"This arguing achieves nothing." Elder Tajman walked over to Darz. "Do you admit your trespass against the priestess?"

Even leaning against the door frame, exhausted and bandaged, Darz's presence outweighed the Elder. "I attempted," he said. "I didn't succeed."

"But you admit you tried."

Darz regarded him warily. "Yes. I do."

The Elder glanced at Kindle. "If he's lying about striking her, why wouldn't he lie about touching her?"

"I've no idea." Kindle's gaze shifted away from the Elder.

Tajman turned to face them all. "We have a difficult situation. This man admits to a trespass we cannot ignore."

"He doesn't know our ways," Ginger said.

"*Our* ways?" Kindle demanded. "The last I knew, the proscription applied everywhere, not just in Sky Flames."

"It's a stupid proscription," Darz said.

Ginger almost groaned. He wasn't helping matters.

The Elder's voice hardened. "And why is that, Goldstone?"

It startled Ginger to hear Darz called by his second name. She had grown used to thinking of him by his personal name, an intimacy that reminded her why he had to leave the temple.

"Please don't argue," she said. "Elder Limestone, I brought Darz here so he won't be in the temple. When he's well enough to travel, we can give him supplies and send him on his way."

"That's ridiculous!" Kindle said. "We reward his offense by giving him a fine house to live in and valuable supplies?"

"He has a point," Tajman said. "In ages past, the sentence for defiling a priestess was execution."

Darz's voice went quiet. "I wouldn't try it if I were you."

"No one has been executed in over a century," Ginger said. "An attempt to steal a kiss is hardly grounds for such a threat."

"Perhaps," Tajman said. "It *is* grounds for prison."

She blanched. "We don't have a prison."

"We could use the cellar under the Tender's Hall," Kindle said helpfully. His spirits were obviously picking up.

"You can't lock me in a cellar!" Darz said loudly.

Kindle rounded on him. "You admitted your trespass."

"Better that than lie." Darz's voice was rising.

"You should be locked away!" Kindle said.

"*You* hit her." Darz's face flushed with anger. "That's a hell of a lot worse than my kissing her!"

"She deserved it!" Kindle shouted.

Everyone went silent, staring at Kindle.

After a moment, the Elder spoke. "Then you did strike her."

Kindle paled as he realized what he had said. Watching Darz, Ginger suspected he had far more control over his temper than it had just appeared. He had deliberately provoked Kindle into his admission.

Kindle motioned at Darz. "He tricks us with sly words."

The Elder raised an eyebrow. "They sounded a lot hotter than sly to me." When Kindle started to respond, Tajman held up his hand. "I'm not going to lock either my Flame Sentinel or an injured soldier in a cellar. But penance must be done." He spoke sternly to Ginger. "You should have been more modest."

She didn't see what she had done that was immodest, but she couldn't deny she should have been more careful. She had never expected the constraints on her life to hurt so much. Even so. She had always known what her service to the dragon required.

The Elder looked around at them. "We will let the Dragon-Sun decide."

She wondered how he planned to do that, given how little attention the dragon seemed to be paying them. "Do you wish me to go to the RayLight Chamber and petition him?"

"No." He frowned as he sometimes did, as if everything about her dissatisfied him. Then he turned to Kindle. "For the next ten days, you will tend the temple."

Kindle squinted at him. "I know nothing of attending the Dragon-Sun."

"I didn't say the dragon. The building. Sweep the floors, repair breaks, clean the fountain, whatever else is needed."

Kindle's face turned red. "Those are a woman's chores!"

Tajman answered firmly. "They are revered tasks done in service to the sun."

Ginger almost smiled. This punishment she could live with. It would give her time to read. It also meant she would have to be around Kindle for ten days, but she didn't have to stay in the temple. She would go on many visits to town.

The Elder was watching her. "You will remain in seclusion during those ten days. You won't leave the temple for any reason. Kindle will be your guard." His gaze brushed over her wrap. "Spend your time in meditation and penance to the Dragon-Sun, and perhaps he will forgive your indiscretion."

She barely managed to bite back her protest. Ten days with Kindle underfoot sounded awful. Nor did she like that Tajman considered him an appropriate guard even after Kindle admitted to striking her. She had to remind herself Tajman could have done a lot worse, such as publicly humiliating her or ordering a physical punishment. She also recognized his impassive expression. He wasn't going to change his mind.

"And you." The Elder's voice chilled as he turned to Darz. The soldier met his gaze steadily.

"You will do the Trial of the Dragon-Sun," Tajman said. "If at the end, you are still alive, you may go on your way."

"What? No!" Ginger wanted to shake the Elder. "He's hurt. He can hardly walk. He'll freeze up there!"

"Up where?" Darz asked. "What are you talking about?"

"It's a promontory," she said. "A natural rock formation like a tower. It's called the Dragon's Claw because it looks like a claw open to the sky. The Trial of the Dragon-Sun means you stay there for ten days. Alone. With nothing more than what you can carry up with you."

"It's an excellent suggestion," Kindle said. "Let the dragon decide his punishment."

"He can hardly walk!" Ginger said. "He could barely even get up there, let alone carry food and gear."

To her unmitigated surprise, Darz laughed, that familiar deep-throated rumble. "I appreciate your championing my cause, Ginger-Sun, but I could do with a little more confidence in my survival abilities."

"You don't understand," she said. "It isn't—"

"Enough!" Tajman said. "You should look to your own piety, Ginger, instead of nay-saying my decisions."

"The Elder Sentinel governs here for a reason," Kindle told her in a sonorous voice. "His wisdom is well known."

Amazing how fast his mood changed when Darz was the one who suffered. She had enough sense, though, to keep the protest to herself. Her outbursts wouldn't help anyone.

Darz considered Tajman as if he were taking the measure of the older man. "I have a concern," he said. "Someone tried to kill me. I don't know why. It may be they intended to rob me and became enraged when they realized I had nothing to take. But I can't say for certain, and I don't want to be defenseless at the top of a mountain."

"How would they know you were up there?" Tajman asked.

"How did they know I was crossing the desert?" Darz said. "I need weapons if I'm going to stay for ten days. A sword and two daggers."

"You demand valuable items as part of your sentence?" Kindle asked. "I can't believe this."

"He has a point," Tajman said. "But we have few swords here, and I doubt their owners would part with them for a man convicted of desecrating the temple."

"He desecrated the priestess," Kindle said.

Tajman cocked an eyebrow at him. "You have a sword."

From the look Kindle gave him, Ginger suspected it would take the entire village to get that sword away from him for Darz. Tajman apparently saw the same, for he said, "No matter." He turned back to Darz. "I can provide you with a long dagger. It isn't a sword, but it comes close."

Darz nodded. "That will help."

"Then it is decided." Tajman's manner became crisp. "Kindle, you walk Ginger-Sun back to the temple. I will take Goldstone to the Claw."

"I need to gather my things first," Kindle said, "if I'm to stay with her for ten days."

"I need goods in town," Ginger added, miserable. Darz didn't seem to realize the demands of the trial. If he thought he could leave the promontory, he was mistaken. Tajman would post guards. "Goodman Goldstone needs salves and a change of bandages. My supplies are at the temple, but I can get more from the healer." She paused as she remembered something else. "The healer had planned to remove Darz's stitches in a few days. He can't if Darz is on the Claw."

"I'm sure Goldstone can manage it," Kindle said sourly.

"Actually, I probably can," Darz said.

Tajman glanced at Darz, and Ginger had the feeling he respected how Darz handled himself. In that, she warmed to the Elder. It was always that way with Tajman; one moment he could make her angry enough to clench her fists, and in another he could impress her with his judgment. He was a good leader for the village, and if she chafed under his attitudes, well, it could have been worse. She could have been dealing with Spark, the beefy Second Sentinel who had wanted to beat her for tending a wounded man.

"I'll call on the healer,"Tajman decided. To Kindle he said, "Escort Ginger to the market, then collect your things and take her back to the temple."

Unexpectedly, Kindle blushed. "It would be my honor to escort you to the market, Ginger-Sun."

She blinked at the unexpected courtesy. "Thank you." She hadn't put much credence in Darz's theory that Kindle liked her; she couldn't think of a worse way to show it than spying on her, scaring her, and hitting her. Men often bewildered her, though. Living in the temple gave her an independence she valued, but it also isolated her until she no longer remembered how to be part of the village. Or so she told herself. It was either that or admit she didn't fit in here anymore, in this place that was the only home she had ever known. She couldn't bear such a thought, so she put it away, deep in her mind where it wouldn't afflict her spirit.

8

Day Fire

Ginger didn't see Darz again that day. She and Kindle went to the Seller's Festival, a big market the village set up once every ten days. Kindle was a quiet companion, saying little and standing back while she haggled with produce-tenders. No one seemed surprised to see them together; indeed, many people gave them approving glances.

When she and Kindle did talk, she dropped hints about the blood, mentioning stains at the butcher's shop, wondering if anyone had recently slaughtered a sheep, that sort of thing. He reacted to none of it, and she was soon convinced he had nothing to do with the blood in her suite. She wondered if she had misjudged him. When he had followed her that night, he had been drinking. It didn't excuse his behavior; she would have the bruise for days as a reminder. But he had none of the submerged anger she felt from Dirk Bauxite or Second Sentinel Spark. Mostly Kindle seemed shy around her. It eased her apprehension about spending the next ten days under his watchful eyes.

In the past, Kindle had avoided her. He was fourteen years older, and she had never known him well in her childhood. After she became an acolyte, her ties with the town had receded. A mystique built up around the priestess, isolating her. It was the price she paid for having more freedom than most women.

Ginger had heard that in Quaaz, where the queen lived, women had less constrained lives. She couldn't imagine what it must be like to rule Taka Mal as a woman. Did Queen Vizarana struggle with her generals and advisors? If they wished a man on the throne, their discontent wasn't enough to stir rebellion. Far from it. The tales Ginger had heard about the queen glowed with praise. People considered her the daughter of the Dragon-Sun. Perhaps that was why it worked; most people viewed her as a priestess at the highest level, which allowed traditionalists like Tajman to think of the Dragon-Sun as the true ruler of Taka Mal. It softened his objections to a female sovereign.

Sometimes Ginger thought she should travel to a place like Quaaz where no one knew her, where she could be like anyone else. But the urge always faded when she thought of leaving home. As much as she longed to see the world, she couldn't face that much change. The prospect of the unknown had always unsettled her, especially after she had lost her parents at such a young age.

Ginger shook off her gloomy thoughts and concentrated on marketing. People usually exchanged services or goods for what they bought, but she had only her temple services to offer and they were free. So the village provided her a stipend of hexa-coins to pay for goods. Kindle carried her sacks of fruits, vegetables, cheeses and wine. She appreciated his help; lugging around the bags was exhausting. Today she only had to carry a sack with her purchase of candles, parchment, quills and ink.

On the way out of town, they stopped by Kindle's cottage. She waited in his parlor while he packed. It was a pleasant house, if a bit spare. The whitewashed walls had no adornment, but many windows let in sunshine, and red curtains billowed around the open ones. Red cushions were plumped on the wicker furniture. The room's most striking feature was a sunwood clock that hung from a scrolled bar on one wall. The timepiece had copper numerals, and it ticked. She doubted it came from Sky Flames; no one here could craft such an intricate work. He had probably bought it in Quaaz during his army days. It had a strong, masculine look and gave her an insight into him, that he liked fine, elegant works.

Kindle came out of an inner room carrying a blue sack. He had exchanged the dark trousers and red shirt of his sentinel's uniform for rough blue leggings and a blue overshirt with a rope belt like other men in the village wore. Apparently he didn't think of himself as a sentinel for this visit. She wondered if Tajman was putting them together in the hopes of encouraging a marriage. Although she had warmed to Kindle today, she had never felt attracted to him in that way. He was cordial now, but what about the next time he drank? She didn't want to think what a lifetime of that would mean.

"Are you all right?" he asked. "You look pale."

"A little tired," she said. "All this heat."

"We can take my cart." He seemed pleased to offer it.

He took her into his cactus garden and brought a wheeled cart around from the side of the house. After they loaded in their sacks, they set off walking with Kindle pushing the cart. They soon left the village behind. The desert surrounded them, and the land buckled in ripples and up-thrust crags striped by yellow rock. The bluffs were too rocky to call dunes, but in the distance, hills of sand shimmered like topaz against a parched blue sky.

"I do so love this land," Ginger said. "It's beautiful."

"It'll kill you if you aren't careful."

"It's an austere beauty," she acknowledged. "That's why it's so compelling." She stretched her arms, working out kinks from the long day. "I could write for hours about the colors, how shadows turn from yellow to red, and the hills hunch up like sleeping giants with only their shoulders above the ground."

Kindle snorted. "Such fancies are a waste of time."

Ginger deflated like a torn bulb on a water-cactus. After a moment, she said, "I like writing."

"I would think you have more important duties. Like attending the Dragon-Sun."

She frowned at him. "What do you think 'Attending the Dragon-Sun' means?"

"Cleaning his house. Tending his fountain. Meditating. Helping people." He glanced at her. "Speaking with respect."

"I always speak with respect."

"You spend so much time alone out there." He sounded as if he didn't know whether to be angry or worried. "You've forgotten how to be a woman."

She couldn't help but laugh. "How could I forget to be what I am? I'm just not the way you want me to be."

"You also talk a great deal," he grumbled.

"And if I talked about how great I thought you were, would you tell me I talk too much?"

"I didn't say—" He tilted his head as if he were confused. Then he glared at her. "You're twisting my words."

"Oh, Kindle."

He gave the cart an extra shove that toppled the sacks against one another. "You twine words around until it's all muddled. It's not right. You shouldn't do it."

Ginger didn't know how to answer such a comment. His way of looking at the world was foreign to her.

It was going to be an interesting ten days. Unfortunately.

"You've been in here all morning!" a man accused.

Ginger jumped out of her chair, and her opal skittered across the table. She spun around to see Kindle in the doorway of the room, holding a knife in one hand and a broken table leg in the other. He had been at the temple for two days, and she still wasn't used to his presence.

"What's wrong?" she asked, her heart beating fast.

"I'm fixing the leg on your damned knickknack table."

She spoke carefully. "Thank you."

"What are you doing?" he demanded. "I clean and mop, and you sit in here."

Ginger hesitated. She had been looking for references to abilities such as hers, poring over history scrolls in search of clues. She couldn't tell him about her spells, though, so she spoke another truth. "I'm working on something for the ore diggers."

Kindle came in and waved his knife at the scrolls scattered over the table. "How can crinkled parchment help a miner?" He stopped in front of her, standing too close.

She backed up. "It may help them dig mine shafts."

"Oh, Ginger."

"It's true!" She took a scroll off one chair. "This describes something called *gunpowder*."

"Powder?" He came over to her, again standing too close. "Cosmetics are for women."

"Not that kind." She slipped away and went around the table, putting it between them. Unrolling the parchment, she indicated a section of calligraphy. "This tells of a powder that explodes."

"It sounds like you made it up," he said.

She straightened up, bewildered. "Why would I do that?"

"So you can say you're working when you waste the day."

She frowned at him. "Studying isn't a waste."

He struck the table with his piece of wood, making scrolls jump and rattle. "Don't talk to me that way!"

Ginger stared at him. He had blown up the same way this morning when she had asked if he knew what was happening with Darz. She hadn't dared ask again.

"I mean no disrespect, Sentinel Burr," she said.

Kindle lowered his club. "I didn't mean to scare you. I'm just so flaming tired of housekeeping." He pointed his knife at the scroll. "What does it say?"

She offered it to him. "You can read it."

His face darkened. "I would rather you did."

It wasn't the first time he had avoided reading in her presence. She wondered if he had never learned how. It wasn't unusual in Sky Flames. That might explain why he resented her time in here. "It says to combine sulfur, saltpeter and charcoal," she explained. "Sometimes it says 'potassium nitrate.' I don't know what that means."

"Neither do I. But the others are easy to get. I've never heard of them exploding."

"Have you ever seen them mixed?" She couldn't imagine why anyone would do such a thing.

"No. But I'm sure it's happened. If it exploded, don't you think people would know?"

"I suppose." It had been her thought, too. She read to him from the scroll. "Charles told me today he doesn't understand why we haven't invented this powder." She looked at Kindle. "Charles Carter was shipwrecked here."

"Odd name, that."

Ginger liked the exotic name. "I've never heard any other like it. A priestess wrote about him a century ago." She read from the scroll. "Charles says we are isolated and get only bits of 'modern' knowledge. He sounds demented, talking about the 'British Empire.' He believes we are a lost land cursed so no one can find us, and that neither can we leave this continent. I've told him ships from our settled lands sail the wide seas and visit other lands, but he doesn't believe me. He asks when I last heard of such a ship. What can I say? We live in the desert. We have no ships. But my explanations don't convince him."

Kindle shrugged. "He probably heard that tale about a curse from someone in the village."

"Probably. It's such an old yarn." Ginger rolled up the scroll. "It's true, though, I've heard nothing in my lifetime of ships from our lands trading with others. Histories tell how they have in the past, but never today."

"I wouldn't know," Kindle said. "But I do know those powders won't explode."

"You're right," she said glumly. "I tried mixing them. Nothing happened." She paused. "I didn't do what it said with 'pressure' or heat, though."

"Why not?" he asked, more curious now than hostile.

"I don't know how." This was the first time in the past two days he had shown an interest in anything she did. She prepared their meals, but their dining was awkward and strained. If the Elder hoped to promote matrimonial bliss, it wasn't succeeding. Exploding powder seemed to appeal to him far more than domesticity.

"I don't suppose you would have time to look at it," she said, deliberately taking an offhand tone. "I know blowing things up wasn't part of your duties here."

His eyes lit up. "I could make time." He leaned over the scroll. "Tell me more of what that says."

She motioned him to a chair and sat down next to him. Then she began to read.

On the evening of Ginger's third day in seclusion, the Archivist visited with Jalla, her oldest daughter. Jalla had just apprenticed to a baker in town and wished to embark on her new craft under good auspices. So they came for a blessing.

Ginger seated them on the fountain, where a fine spray filled the air. As they settled down, she went to her rooms for her amulets. She chose two figurines, a dragon and a woman. Her opal matched the tinted glass of the figures, so she set it next to them. In the daylight, it was no more than a pretty rock.

She carried out a tray with her amulets and some cold tea. Walking to the fountain, she thought how much Jalla resembled her mother. They had the same dark hair, of course, though Jalla's wasn't streaked with gray. Jalla also had her mother's focused manner, intent on every detail. It was a trait common to adults in Sky Flames, and Jalla was a young woman of fifteen. Although Ginger admired her, she couldn't help but regret Jalla's loss of youthful exuberance.

"You look well today," Ginger said to the Archivist as she offered her the tray.

"Thank you." The historian took a mug of chilled tea.

Ginger smiled as Jalla took the other mug. "And you! You've grown again."

Jalla grinned at her, open and friendly. "Just wait until next year."

Ginger sat next to her and set the tray on the ground, then put the figurines on the ledge between herself and Jalla. After a pause, she added the opal. It gleamed against the gray stone.

Ginger touched her thumb to Jalla's brow, and the girl closed her eyes. The only sounds were the musical flow of the fountain and chirps of redwing doves on the roof.

"Jalla Bluewing," Ginger said. "May your spirit be blessed for all your days." She withdrew her hand, and Jalla opened her eyes. Ginger picked up the Sunset figurine, a woman with hair the color of dusk and a flowing dress in sunset colors. Ginger brushed the statue up Jalla's right cheek and down her left. "May the goddess bless you with wisdom, long life and insight." She touched the statue to Jalla's brow. "May she grant you healthy, happy children."

Ginger set down the figurine and picked up the dragon. Its red wings spanned her hand, and the fire-hued body glittered like her opal. Its fanged mouth was open, trumpeting to the sky. Held under its body by huge claws, the yellow orb of the sun gleamed. The stand for the figurine was colorless, so the dragon seemed to burn with a flame all its own.

Jalla watched her with curiosity. And confidence. Ginger had never felt she earned that trust, yet people came to her and the town prospered.

She turned Jalla's hands up to the ceiling and set the dragon on the girl's right palm. "May the sun favor you with strength and bring light into your days." She moved the statue to her left hand. "May he ward off evil and protect you throughout your life." Then she folded Jalla's hands around the figure. "May you always keep his spirit within you, to guide your life and your heart."

"Thank you," Jalla murmured.

Ginger opened her hands. As she set the dragon on the ledge, the opal seemed to glow more brightly. On impulse, she picked it up and pressed Jalla's hands around the stone. "May you always be joyous," she said, "and find delight in your life."

The opal flared, and yellow radiance streamed around Jalla's fingers.

"Oh!" The girl lifted her rapt gaze to Ginger. "That's lovely!"

NO. Ginger barely held in her cry. Had the sun already set? She released the spell and the light faded. As she took back the opal, she tried to smile as if this were normal. The girl seemed to glow herself.

The Archivist, however, was watching Ginger closely. As the town historian, she would know their priestesses didn't normally create yellow light.

The Archivist said nothing, however. She and Jalla stayed a while to chat, and Ginger gradually relaxed. Kindle remained in the background, repotting plants that hung from the terraces. Ginger knew her guests were aware of him, but neither mentioned the Flame Sentinel.

"I haven't had much time for my studies," the Archivist was saying. "I've been recording the ore shipments we'll send the army later this summer. It's important we keep good records to ensure we get full payment."

"Is it a problem that we don't?" Ginger asked, intrigued. This was a glimpse into the exciting world beyond Sky Flames. She grinned at the Archivist. "Surely the officers of the Queen's Army can do their sums!"

The historian spoke coolly. "Even the best number-tenders can make mistakes."

Ginger regretted making the joke. She should know by now the Archivist wouldn't laugh. Jalla was listening with a smile, though, which encouraged Ginger's spirit.

"How is that soldier you've been tending?" Jalla asked. "Is he healing?"

"Actually, he's not here anymore," Ginger said.

The Archivist pressed her lips together. "That's enough, Jalla."

The girl glanced at her mother with surprise and a hint of annoyance. Ginger wished the Archivist hadn't shushed her so fast. She was bursting to know how Darz fared. Taking a chance, she asked, "Have you had any news of Goodman Goldstone?"

The Archivist answered in a voice heavy with disapproval. "I assume he is doing whatever a pilgrim asking for forgiveness does during his penance."

Jalla looked from Ginger to her mother, her gaze alert. Ginger could almost feel her soaking in every word.

"He needs rest and tending," Ginger said. "He could die up there."

"Darz Goldstone is no longer your concern." The Archivist's voice could have chilled an ice dragon. "Perhaps you should look to your own penitence rather than inquiring after that which has no proper place in your life."

Ouch. Ginger wished she wasn't so sensitive to disapproval. If the elders had their way, which they probably would, she would never see Darz again. But it was for the best. Her interest in him could only hurt her.

As the Archivist and Jalla were leaving, walking with Ginger to one of the entrances, the Archivist spoke in an overly casual voice. "I've never seen that yellow light before."

Ginger improvised quickly. "It happens when sunlight reflects off openings in the roof." Which was true in the RayLight Chamber.

"How unusual," the Archivist said. "Especially since the sun had already gone down."

Ginger flushed, too disconcerted to think of an excuse. "I don't know, ma'am."

After her guests left, Ginger stood in the temple entrance and gazed beyond the rock gardens toward the village. Jalla and her mother were red-robed figures barely visible in a landscape lit only by the ruddy light of a fading sunset.

An anomaly registered on Ginger. South of the village, two mounted figures on a ridge were silhouetted against the red sky. They were too far to see clearly, but she thought they wore peaked cowls similar to those used by Jazid nomads. Unease rippled through her. From their vantage point, they could be gazing straight at the temple.

Kindle joined her. "So Jalla is going to be a baker."

"I guess so." Ginger indicated the cowled figures. "Do you know who they are?"

He squinted at the ridge. "Nomads? Or miners." A scowl creased his blocky features. "They won't find a welcome here."

"No, I imagine not," Ginger said dryly. Darz certainly hadn't. "Do you think they're dangerous?"

He pulled himself up straighter. "Not with my sentinels guarding the town."

She smiled at his pride in his men. Whatever she thought of

Kindle personally, he was a good Flame Sentinel. "We are fortunate to have them."

"Indeed." He regarded her curiously. "The Archivist didn't look happy."

"She's always in a bad mood around me," Ginger grumbled.

"She's jealous."

Ginger would have laughed if she hadn't been so disheartened. "Of what? I have nothing. She has a family and a high position in the village."

"Ginger, you truly can be dense sometimes."

She glared at him. "What does that mean?"

"She has a lot to envy." He wiped sweat off his forehead with his sleeve. "You're young, beautiful and voluptuous for starters."

"What does *voluptuous* mean?"

"For flaming sake!" His face turned the color of the sunset. "The Elder is right. You're too naïve for your own good."

"Come on, Kindle. What does it mean?"

He cleared his throat. "You have a, uh, womanly form."

"Oh." She doubted the Archivist could care less. "That sounds like something a man would think."

He looked exasperated. "In case you hadn't noticed, that's what I am." His voice took on an edge. "Maybe our Archivist found it offensive that a priestess doing penance would be so shameless as to ask after the man who had soiled her."

She felt as if he had slapped her. "That's horrible."

"Why *him?*" He sounded hurt as well as angry. "You never show such interest in—in anyone appropriate. Maybe if you didn't spend so much time alone out here, you wouldn't have so many inappropriate ideas."

"Inappropriate ideas? About *what?*"

"You should stop thinking about the interloper." He turned his head and spit in the rock garden. "Do what I tell you. Or else one of these days, the people who think you go too far will have enough fuel to make your life far hotter than you would ever like."

She stared at him. "Are you threatening me?"

"By the Dragon!" He looked as if he wanted to shake her, and he even started to reach for her. Then he swore and dropped his arms. "I'm *warning* you. Get yourself married to an acceptable man, Ginger-Sun, and soon, or the things people say about you could get a lot worse. If your behavior shames us before the dragon, it won't go easy on you."

With that, he turned and walked away, his back stiff. She stared after him, stunned. They condemned her when she had done nothing wrong. It was true she had hesitated when Darz kissed her. But she told him to stop. Even if the Dragon-Sun begrudged her companionship, she knew she couldn't have Darz. She couldn't hide from the dragon; surely he realized she accepted the realities of her life.

Perhaps she *had* done wrong by performing spells. Night magic. She felt worn down. If the Archivist suspected her of witchery, gods only knew what would happen. She dreaded to think how the people of Sky Flames would react if they decided she had so severely transgressed against the sun.

Dragon's Claw

Six days after the Archivist's visit, a crash reverberated through the temple. Alarmed, Ginger ran into the rock garden just as a thunder of falling rocks sounded.

Then it was quiet.

She stopped by an arch. The garden looked fine. Paths of blue gravel wound among cactus plants and beds of red pyramid-blossoms that opened at dawn. Vines with brilliant fire-lilies draped over graceful stone arches. Nowhere did she see anything that had crashed.

"Huh." She walked through the garden, listening. In the distance, someone swore vehemently. That sounded like Kindle. So she went in search of her truculent guest.

Ginger found the source of the noise beyond several ridges; a small bluff had collapsed into rubble. The air above it swirled with dust, and grit tickled her nose. She didn't know why the ridge would fall; it had looked perfectly stable the thousand or so times she had passed by this place.

"Kindle, where are you?" she shouted. Had he been under the bluff when it fell? "Are you all right? *Kindle!*"

A man walked out from behind the debris. When she realized it was Kindle, she gulped in a breath. How had he brought down the hill? Granted, it wasn't a big one, but even so. She couldn't fathom his purpose.

He grinned as she reached him. "You were worried about me."

"I heard the crash," she said, embarrassed now by her outburst. "I just came to see what happened."

He laughed good-naturedly. "You don't fool me. You were afraid I was hurt. Admit it."

Here she had thought he perished under a ton of rubble and out he comes, smirking. "Of course I came to check. I would be worried for anyone who brought a hill down on his head." Then she added, "Although some heads may be hard enough to survive."

He regarded her with innocence. "Why would I have anything to do with the hill?"

"Oh, I don't know," she said, hands on her hips. "Maybe because you are standing right here, looking guilty."

"Not guilty. Frustrated." He motioned at the rubble. "That wasn't supposed to happen."

Ginger had no idea what he had been doing. Although they had been together for nine days, she had avoided him since their argument about the Archivist. She left his meals in the room he had fixed up for himself, and she ate alone. Kindle, in turn, was gone for most of each day, ignoring the work Tajman had sent him here to do.

"Whatever are you doing out here?" she asked.

"What I promised you."

"I didn't ask you to crash rock."

"Not crash. Explode." He frowned at the collapsed hill. "I can't figure how to control the powder."

"You mean it *works?*" She gaped at him. "It really explodes?"

"Not very well." He squinted into the air, which smelled of acrid chemicals. "It makes more smoke than bang. Unless I use a lot." He turned back to her. "I followed the steps from the scroll. Even with that, it didn't work at first. Or second. Or third." Ruefully he said, "Or thirtieth. But I'm nothing if not persistent, eh, Ginger? I kept fiddling with ingredients, spark, trigger, confinement, everything. And finally it worked."

Her smile broke out. "Gracious, you did it! Kindle! You're brilliant. I never believed it would work."

He stood up straighter, as if he felt taller. "It wasn't that much." Then he scratched his head. "I can't make it do what I want, though. It'll take time to figure out the details. And I've no idea why this fellow Charles calls it gunpowder. I'd think dragon-powder would be more apt." He considered her. "Maybe all that reading you do has some use after all."

"I'm glad you think so." Ginger would take a qualified approval over scowls any day. She wasn't all that comfortable having the worth of her scholarship determined by her unearthing such a violent powder, but they might do a lot of good with it. The possibilities piled up in her mind. "It could help miners dig shafts. And we should send news to Quaaz! Tell the queen." When she realized what she had said, her face heated. "Not that I mean to imply we have such importance."

The entire time she spoke, Kindle was staring at the rubble. She wasn't even sure he was listening. But then he said, "You're right, we should write to Quaaz. No! Not a message." He swung around to her.

"I'll go myself, to the army. Just think of the weapons this could make."

"Weapons?" She didn't want her discovery to hurt people.

"Right now, I can't control it. It could just as easily blow up us as the enemy. But I can work on it. It will be a magnificent project." His face flushed with excitement. "Perhaps they will call it kindle-powder."

She smiled. "Or ginger-powder."

He blinked. "You can't call a weapon by a woman's name."

In truth, she didn't want her name attached to a means of death. It just bothered her that his plans didn't include her, after she had discovered the recipe for the powder. Knowing Kindle, by the time he reached Quaaz, his descriptions might leave her out altogether.

An idea came to her. She would have to present it with care, though, or he might blow up at her instead of blowing up hills. "Do you know how to see the queen? It must be difficult."

He wiped his perspiring face with his sleeve. "I'll have to go to an audience she holds for the public and present a petition to someone on her staff."

She beamed at him. "You'll write a great petition! I know it." Lest she get in trouble for bypassing proper protocols, she added, "You'll have to discuss it with the elders first, though."

He stiffened. "They can't stop me from going."

She wasn't so certain; in her experience, their decisions were often based on keeping things the same. But they all liked Kindle, so he would probably have a lot less trouble convincing them than if she suggested the trip.

"I'm sure you can win them over," she said. "Just show them your petition. If it can persuade a queen, it will certainly work on Tajman and the others."

"Queens don't know weapons, I'm sure. It's her generals I'll have to convince." After a long moment, he added, "Perhaps you could help me prepare the petition?"

His request didn't surprise her. She was almost certain he couldn't read or write. He had a good spoken vocabulary, though, and she had no doubt he could learn to read. She had thought she might offer to teach him, if she could find a way to suggest it without hurting his pride.

"I would be honored to help," she said. It would give her a chance to include details about the discovery of the powder. Wistfully, she added, "I wish I could go with you. To see Quaaz! It would be so exciting."

He was watching her oddly, with that intent focus so common in Sky Flames—and with something more. Hope?

"Do you mean that, Ginger-Sun?" he asked.

She suddenly realized what she had said. A woman couldn't travel alone with a man unless she was his wife. She thought frantically for a way out of her gaffe. "I know it would be improper," she said. "I didn't mean to offend, Sentinel Burr."

"No. You didn't." He seemed uncertain what to make of her. "Well, I should clean up. I'm starving."

Ginger nodded, relieved to escape the uncomfortable moment. "I'll have dinner ready when you get back to the temple."

"Thank you." As she started to leave, he said, "Ginger?"

She turned around. "Yes?"

"Would you—" he cleared his throat "—will you dine with me tonight?"

"Oh. Yes, of course." Caught off guard, she added the formal words. "It would be my honor."

He smiled, his teeth flashing white, and he scratched his stomach through his sweat-drenched shirt, where his once flat muscles were tending to fat. With no more preamble, he went back to his rubble, climbing up the mound.

As Ginger walked to the temple, she went over what had just happened. Could she marry Kindle? He did seem to want her, even if he was awkward in showing it, and the elders would probably approve the match. She just couldn't imagine living with his mercurial temper, always afraid to say the wrong thing lest he become violent. She would also lose her independence; he would expect her to serve him as she served the temple. It was the way of things with her people.

Ginger rubbed her eyes. Tomorrow was Kindle's last day here, and Darz's last on the Claw. No one would tell her how Darz was doing, and it enraged Kindle if she mentioned him. But if Darz had died, surely someone would have let her know. At the least, she would have noticed a change in the behavior of those who visited the temple.

She didn't know what would happen after tomorrow, but she could guess. Kindle would go to Quaaz, Darz would go to the army and she would be alone with the disapproval of Sky Flames.

Kindle and Ginger dined at a table in the gardens, under an arch heavy with yellow sun-snaps. She put her opal on the table as decoration, hoping Kindle would become so used to it that he stopped noticing it. She made curried lentils and rice and sweet-grain pancakes with honey, and she served it with cider from kegs in the cellar. She didn't realize until she took a swallow of the juice that it had fermented. Kindle had already consumed more than a glass. Fortunately, though, he didn't seem too affected. He wolfed down his meal with gratifying enthusiasm. Then he sat back in his chair, his face ruddy with the sunset, a glass of cider in his hand.

"That was really good," he told Ginger.

"I'm glad you liked it." She enjoyed cooking, especially when someone appreciated it.

He took a swallow of the cider, then gave a loud burp. When Ginger glared at him, he grinned. "It's a compliment." He drank more cider. "I could get used to living like this. At home, I have to eat my own cooking. Believe me, it's *not* a treat."

"I'm sure you do a fine job," she assured him, not because she had any idea, but because it was almost automatic for her to soothe with her words and deeds. She liked to help people feel better.

"Ginger." He was looking at her oddly. "You know…you could come to Quaaz."

She heard what he didn't say. *As my wife.* Awkwardly, she said, "Darz—I just don't think—"

"*What?*" He slammed his cider on the table. The glass shattered and gold liquid splattered everywhere.

She jumped up and grabbed her cloth napkin. As she sopped up the cider, she said, "Why the blazes did you do that?"

"Don't use that language with me," he shouted, his face red. He pushed back his chair and stood up, looming over the table.

Ginger backed up. This wasn't like when Darz got loud. She never feared he would strike out; he was just noisy. But she had no doubt Kindle would hit her if she angered him.

"I'm sorry," she said. "I don't understand what's wrong."

He spoke tightly. "My name is Kindle. Not *Darz*." He spit out the name as if it were an oath.

"Ai, I'm sorry!" She could have kicked herself. "That was stupid of me."

His fist clenched at his side. "You think too much about this intruder." He came around the table toward her. "I want to know why you keep bringing him up."

She took another step back. "He was almost dead. Now he's had to stay on the Claw. He still could die. I feel responsible."

He kept coming at her. "Why do you care, Ginger? Hoping he will take more liberties, is that it?"

"That's horrible to say."

"You *make* me say it! The way you act, tempting a man when he's forbidden to touch you. You're wicked."

"I'm not tempting anyone." Her anger flared. "If you like me, Kindle, that's something in you. Not me."

"Don't talk to me like that." He looked her up and down in a way he would never have done when he was sober. "You act like one of those Jazid pleasure girls."

"No I don't!" Not that she had the least idea how a Jazid pleasure girl acted. "I'm not interested in you that way." Too late, she realized how her words sounded, that it was probably the worst thing she could have said.

"Don't talk like that!" he shouted. His face blazed as he strode toward her. She tried to dart away, but her wrap caught her feet and she stumbled against the arch. Sun-snaps crushed around her, cloying in their sweet smell. Backed up against the stone, she stared up as Kindle loomed over her. He weighed twice as much as she did, and most of it was still muscle.

"You make me do this." He slapped her across the face, and her head snapped to the side, into the mashed flowers.

"No!" Frantic, her cheek burning, she shoved against his arms. It caught him by surprise, and he jerked back. She started to run for the temple, but the wrap tripped her. As she fell, he caught her around the waist and swung her back to the arch, lifting her off the ground. "Stay still," he shouted.

Her sense of time slowed down. She saw his hand descending and knew he wouldn't stop at a slap this time. She twisted hard and clawed her fingernails down his face. As he swore at her, his grip loosened. She lunged away and yanked on her wrap so hard that it ripped up her legs. Then she *ran*.

The thud of Kindle's boots pounded behind her. It took her only seconds to reach the temple, but it felt like forever. Her wrap ripped more with every step. She raced across the main room and threw herself into her suite. When she whirled around, he was only a few paces behind her. She heaved the door shut with a bang and slammed the bolt home.

"Open that up!" he shouted.

Gasping for breath, she sagged against the door and pressed her hands on its lacquered surface, as if that could push him away. She couldn't fathom his rages. No, she shouldn't have called him Darz. But no one, *no one,* had the right to beat her. If he didn't like the way she spoke, he could walk away, withdraw his marriage hints, refuse to eat with her, anything. She didn't *make* him hit her. He could have held back. She was so angry, she was tempted to yell that all through the door. She bit back the impulse, knowing it would only make matters worse.

"Ginger, open the door," he said. "I won't hurt you."

"That wasn't how it looked," she said.

"Why do you push me that way?" He hit the door. "Why can't you be as sweet to me as you are to other people?"

"I guess I'm not the right woman for you."

"Don't say that." He rattled the doorknob. "Let me in!"

"No! You can't come in my rooms. Go away."

"You don't give me orders. And you can't run around with your dress pulled up to your thighs, showing your legs." He pounded on the door. "You come out here. Don't make me break the door."

"No one makes you," she said. "*You* decide to break things. If you don't like the way I talk, fine. *Just go away*."

His pounding got louder. "Let me in! Or I'll—I'll—"

"You'll what?" she shouted. "Beat me until I can't walk?" The frustration, her loneliness, and her fear burst out of her. "That's brave, Flame Sentinel. Make war against someone who has half your strength and size."

"You'll regret treating me this way." His voice turned ugly. "I'll make sure you can never have what you want. *Never*."

"What does that mean?" When he didn't answer, her panic sparked. "Kindle! What does it mean?"

No answer.

"Kindle?" She was breathing hard, and it was loud in the sudden silence. Had he gone away? Or was he trying to trick her into coming out?

Ginger turned her back to the door and slid down until she was sitting on the floor. She pulled her knees to her chest and crossed her arms on them, then laid her forehead on her arms. She feared she could never leave her rooms, that he would always be out there waiting to punish her for saying things he didn't want to hear.

Tears filled her eyes. Her thoughts unrolled scenarios of what he meant by *I'll make sure you can never have what you want.* He could take so much: her independence, her life at the temple, the respect of people in Sky Flames, her freedom. The days when they burned women at the stake were long in the past, or she might have even feared for her life.

Ginger wiped her palm across her cheek, smearing the tears. How had such a quiet dinner gone awry? The cider, probably; the last time he had hit her, he had been drinking, too.

She couldn't hide forever. Nor could she live in fear of the people she had dedicated her life to serving. Right now she couldn't help but wonder why she had done such a thing. She had to remind herself the behavior of a few didn't negate the goodwill of the village. If she still had their goodwill. The dragon only knew what Kindle was doing.

Ginger climbed to her feet and leaned her ear against the door. The temple was quiet. Making as little noise as possible, she eased back the bolt. Then she edged the door open and peered out. She saw no one. She left her suite, alert to every sound: the scratching of birds on the terraces, the shoosh of the fountain, her own heartbeat. She held her breath, convinced Kindle would appear.

Silence.

After a moment, she breathed more easily. She crossed the temple, her bare feet silent on the stone. Outside, the sun had gone down and the horizon was a vivid wash of crimson and gold. In the rock garden, the remains of their dinner were untouched. She picked up her opal and squeezed until heat flared in the gem. It glowed in the same colors as the sunset.

"What are you trying to tell me?" she said softly.

Of course the stone had no answers. She tilted her face to the darkening sky. "Lord of the Sun and Lady of the Sunset, did you gift me with these spells? I will use them in honor of your greatness. If I presume in daring to hope you granted me this power, I entreat you to forgive my unconscionable presumption."

Ginger returned to the temple and set every candle she could find in a circle around and outside of the RayLight Chamber. Then she stood, holding the opal, and closed her eyes, envisioning flames. When she opened her eyes, a hundred candles were burning in the dusk-filled temple.

She entered the chamber. It symbolized the protection the Dragon-Sun gave his priestess, bathing her in fiery light as if she were immersed in his flames and yet unharmed by them. To meditate in the RayLight Chamber symbolized the trust a priestess gave the dragon, her faith that his fire wouldn't destroy her. This evening, no sunshine poured down from the skylights, but the candles shone through the glass and lit the lower portion of the room with tinted light. With the opal, Ginger added her own light until she flooded the chamber with radiance. So she sought to honor the Dragon-Sun and the Goddess. The colors filled her heart as if it were a stained-glass goblet, and she offered them her devotion in the hopes they would forgive her magic.

Ginger formed a spell of comfort greater than any she had tried before. It filled more than the chamber, more even than the temple. When it was ready, she sought Kindle with her thoughts, to allay his anger. She knew the moment she touched him. He blazed. His rage, his hurt, the pain of her rejection—it flared through her.

And in that instant, she knew what he intended.

"No!" Ginger broke off the spell. The light surged as if she had thrown oil on a fire, then sputtered and died. She threw open the door and ran out of the chamber. To the blazes with her seclusion. She had to stop Kindle.

If it wasn't too late.

Ginger had no time to change her wrap. She ran outside, not to town, where they would stop her, but north through a desert red with the lurid sunset. In the east, cactus fields stretched to the village; in the west, stone formations rose like teeth. She ran hard, and ignored the rocks stabbing her calloused feet. She had wasted so much time! She could only hope Kindle was too drunk to carry out his plans or that he had sobered up enough to regret what he intended.

Time flowed like molasses—it was taking forever—she would never arrive—and then the tip of her destination rose above the bluffs like a misshapen spire. The Dragon's Claw.

Her side burned with a stitch and the rocky path tore her feet. But she kept going, clutching the opal. She ran up the bluff, and the Claw rose before her until she reached the top of the hill. She was aware of two figures silhouetted against the red sky on a distant ridge, riders on horses. She kept running, though she was stumbling from exhaustion.

The Claw stood in the center of a rocky plain, jutting up like the crooked talon on a giant bird—or a dragon. It was a natural formation taller than any building in Sky Flames, taller even than the distant hills. The giant pillar ended in a huge claw of rock formations, eerie and desolate. She wouldn't be surprised to see the dragon himself rise out of the ground.

As she neared the tower, she looked for the sentinel who should be on duty. The barren plain left no place to hide, but no one was in sight, and the station at the base of the tower appeared empty. Foreboding rose within her. Either they had taken Darz down before his ten days were up or else the sentinel had deserted his post. She couldn't think of a good reason for either, but plenty of bad ones came to mind. Darz may have died. They may have locked him up in the cellar after all. Or Kindle had sent the sentinel home.

She slowed down as she reached the guard station, a small mesa at the base of the tower. Ten steps were carved into its side, and she took them two at a time. At the top, an overhang on one edge offered shade during the day. Only red shadows filled it now. No guard. She stopped and bent over, bracing her hands on her thighs while she gulped in huge breaths. Sweat had soaked her wrap, and it clung to her body. With the onset of night, a chill descended like the swoop of a black-wing hawk, and she shivered in her wet clothes.

Ginger descended from the mesa more slowly. She stood at the base of the Claw and stared bleakly at the trail that wound around it. If she was wrong in what she believed and she went up there, she would be in more trouble than she knew how to handle. Not only had she broken her seclusion, she was going to an isolated, unguarded place to see the man forbidden to her. But it didn't matter. She had to warn Darz, even if it meant she would lose her position as priestess. If he died because she had feared to act, she could never live with herself.

"Dragon-Sun, please understand," she said. Then she started up the trail.

Night settled over the land. It was dangerous to hurry in the dark, but she didn't dare take too long. So she made a spell. A dim sphere of red light formed, nothing like what she had done in the RayLight

Chamber with her energy high, but it was enough to show the steep path. The way up circled the Claw, with the tower to her right and a precarious drop off to her left.

As she went higher, the wind tossed her hair around her shoulders and arms. She had no protection except a ripped, damp wrap, and she shivered terribly. She tried to do two spells, heat and light, but she couldn't hold both, and the warmth faded. By the time she reached the top, she was so cold, she could barely walk. The apex was flat in the center and about thirty paces across. The outcroppings around its edges resembled twisted talons grasping at the sky. Although she saw no one, the eerily twisted rock formations offered plenty of places to hide. She wanted to call out, but the words seemed to freeze in her throat.

"What the hell?" a man said. "Who is that?"

"Darz!" She cried out her relief. "Where are you?"

He walked out from behind a crooked finger of stone. "Ginger? What are you doing here?" He came over to her with no trace of his limp from before. "Gods, you must be frozen!"

"I'm s-so glad you're all right." She barely got the words out. "We have to leave!"

He peered at her oddly. "How are you making that light?"

"It's not important. We must go. Kindle is going to make an explosion."

"I'm sure we're safe here."

"No! He brought down a bluff because he used too much. It d-doesn't always work, and he can't control it." Her teeth chattered. "He's furious. He thinks I won't marry him b-because of you. And he's drunk.".

"Ginger, slow down." He seemed bewildered. "If we leave, we're violating our agreement with your Elder. I've only this one night to go; then I can come down, and he's said he'll help me get supplies so I can be on my way. If we leave now, it will infuriate everyone." His voice softened. "I wish you could stay. You truly are a welcome sight. But if anyone finds you here, gods only know what they'll do."

"Please. I know it sounds mad. But if you stay here, you could die." Unless Kindle couldn't get the powder to work or he changed his mind. But she couldn't risk Darz's life on that hope.

He rubbed his face, which no longer had any bandage, just a stubbly beard. His bruises were almost gone. He would always have a scar, but it no longer looked as dire.

"I know this much," he said. "It's freezing here. I don't see how you can stand it, with that thin dress." He motioned to the boulders behind them. "I've a blanket back there. You can wrap it around you when we go down to the tower. I'll take you most of the way, but I don't think I should leave."

"You can't stay." She willed him to believe her. "Please."

"Ah, Ginger." He sounded torn. "Why are you so sure? And how the devil are you making that light?"

"I'm sure. I know Kindle." Self-conscious, she added, "The light is a gift from the Dragon-Sun and Sunset goddess."

"For flaming sake," he said. "You really believe all that pantheon nonsense, don't you?"

"Darz, don't." She couldn't bear the thought that he might offend the sun and sunset on what could be his last night of life. She knew how her people would react to any disaster here. If even someone as worldly as Darz didn't believe Kindle could cause trouble, no one would listen. They would find Darz tomorrow, burned and torn apart, and they would assume the dragon had meted out his punishment. If she accused Kindle, she would look either crazy or vindictive.

"Please," she entreated him. "No one was on guard below." She blanched as a thought hit her. Kindle could have come up earlier and was waiting for night so no one would see him. "We have to go!"

Darz's forehead furrowed. "You're sure about this?"

"Yes!"

After a long pause, while he stood frowning at her, he said, "Very well." He didn't sound happy. "I'll get my things."

She pulled on his arm. "We don't have time."

He took her hand. "If you'll forgive my touch, Ginger-Sun, I think we should hold each other, to ensure neither of us falls off the path in the dark."

"A-all right." Her skin tingled where he touched her. A nervous tickling started in her throat, and she had to swallow to make it go away. But as they walked toward the path, relief washed over her. They would be all right.

The night exploded below them.

10

Forbidden Sands

Light flared, followed by a great thunder—except that it was *below* them. Ginger and Darz stared at each other while the rumbling swelled.

"No!" she cried. *No.* Kindle wouldn't destroy the tower. She had expected him to come up here. She had no doubt he could kill if he thought it justified, but he would never attack the Dragon-Sun. He must have misjudged his efforts, or maybe he sobered up enough to change his mind, and the powder went off in the wrong place. Whatever had happened, rocks continued to fall beneath them in the aftermath of the explosion.

The Claw began to shake.

"Gods above!" Darz said. "It's going to come down."

"It can't come down!" she said. "It wasn't *that* big of an explosion."

"It wouldn't take much. This structure isn't stable." He drew her into the center where no pinnacles loomed over them. Then he crouched down, pulling her with him. "Sit with your head under your arms."

His voice was calm, but she heard his fear. She had gone beyond fear and turned numb, her only defense against terror. When she had done as he asked, he sat with his legs on either side of her body and pulled her into his arms. Then he bent his head over hers, making himself a shield. She could just barely see under his arm.

The rumbling grew louder, and the Claw shook. A spire of rock cracked at its base and crashed across the Claw only a few paces away. It shattered when it hit, and rock shards rained over them. As the shaking grew worse, Ginger squeezed her eyes shut and scrunched herself into as small a ball as possible.

"I'm sorry," Darz whispered. "I'm so sorry."

The world fell beneath them—they dropped through air—

Rocks crashed on top of them.

Her last thought was that she had died before she had barely even lived.

Cold.

Pain.

Ginger opened her eyes. The world was dark.

Time passed. Her body hurt. That didn't seem fair, if she was dead, that she felt pain.

"Darz?" she croaked.

No answer.

Her fingers twitched. She couldn't move them; they had spasmed around the opal. Rocks jabbed her legs and a weight pressed on her body. When she tried to move, boulders shifted and pebbles clattered somewhere. She went still, afraid to start a rockfall.

A man groaned.

"Darz!"

"Gods be damned," he muttered, along with several other choice oaths that normally would have left her ears burning. Right now she was just glad to hear him speak.

"The Claw must not have fallen all the way," she said.

"It feels like the whole cursed mountain is on my back."

Her grip on her opal had relaxed enough for her to set it down. She stretched out her arm, past rocks and under Darz's leg. Her fingers scraped dirt, then passed through open space. "I don't think we're totally buried."

"Must be a cavity."

Her pulse was racing. "Does that mean if we move, the rocks could fall the rest of the way?"

"I'm afraid so." He sounded as if he had to push out the words. "But if I don't move whatever is on top of me, it'll crush me anyway."

She knew she couldn't lie this way long, either, under the weight of his body and whatever pressed on him. Claustrophobia lurked at the edges of her mind.

"Can you move?" she asked.

"Maybe—"

She held her breath as he eased off her. Each time he shifted, dislodged rocks pelted their bodies. Grinding noises came from above them, and a miniature avalanche started. She bit her lip so hard, she tasted blood.

After the rain of pebbles stopped, Darz muttered an oath. "I'm stuck. Something is jabbing my back."

"Can you push it off?"

"I'm afraid I'll bring down the ceiling. But—ah! It *hurts.* I have to—" With a grunt, he gave a jerk. The rocks above them grated against one another as if gnashing their teeth. Ginger clawed the dirt and held her breath.

Then the rumbling stopped. After it was silent for a few moments, Darz squeezed down behind her with his front against her back. The air around them smelled dusty and hurt her throat, but she could breathe again.

"No more moving," he said raggedly. "Whatever is holding these boulders off us isn't fixed in place."

"Are you hurt?" she asked.

"Bumps and bruises. I don't think anything broke."

"It's the same for me."

He leaned what felt like his forehead against the back of her head. "Now what?"

"Maybe someone will dig us out."

"Maybe." He didn't sound optimistic. "I wish I had my blanket. It's so blasted cold."

Ginger slid her hand to where she had put the opal—and it was gone. "No!"

Darz tensed behind her. "What happened?"

"I lost it!" The talisman was a rock, not their salvation, but right now it was her touchstone. She *couldn't* lose it.

"Please," she said, entreating whatever god would listen.

"It'll be all right," Darz said softly.

Her fingers nudged a pyramid of stone.

"Thank you," she murmured to the dragon and sunset, and to Darz as well, for being alive. She closed her fingers around the opal. "It wasn't lost."

"What is 'it?'"

"A good luck charm." What she said now could affect the rest of her life, even destroy it. If she antagonized Darz, he could cause great trouble. But he hardly seemed the type, besides which, she might have no life left. So she spoke.

"Which would you like more?" she asked. "Light or heat?"

His laugh sounded frayed. "How about light, to see where we are."

He thought she was joking. She smiled wanly and focused on the opal. Slowly, a red glow spread around them. It wasn't much, but she could see.

"Gods almighty," Darz said. "How did you do that?"

"I don't know. It's a spell."

"A spell? That's impossible."

She smiled slightly. "Well, perhaps we have just imagined this light."

"You brought a candle with you." Awkwardly, he added, "A, uh, red candle."

"I have no candle of any color," Ginger assured him. She peered into the dim light but saw nothing promising, just a lot of rock.

"I don't believe in spells." He sounded more stubborn than certain. "Not yours and not those in Aronsdale."

"Why Aronsdale?" She had little to lose now by telling him about herself, and as long as they kept talking, it held her panic at bay. "My grandfather came from there."

"So that's where you get that hair." He leaned over to see what lay in front of her. "Surely you have a lamp there."

"No." She could hardly move with the two of them crammed together, but she opened her hand to show him the stone. "Just my opal." She was enormously aware of his muscled self pressed against her body.

He leaned farther to see the stone. "How does it do that?"

"Darz, you're going to flatten me."

"Oh!" He pulled back. "Sorry."

"I can't hold this light much longer. It tires me."

"You don't have to hold your, uh…spell." He grunted at the word. "I mostly wanted to see where we were. Look up if you can. I think those slabs are the reason we're alive."

She had enough room to maneuver onto her back, with Darz lying on his side next to her, propped up on his elbow. Above them, two slabs of rock had hit each other at an angle and leaned together in a sort of peaked roof. A projection on one jutted into the cavity and was probably what had jabbed Darz. Another portion had buried itself behind him, forming a wall at his back. On Ginger's other side, a fall of rock blocked their way. They were trapped, but with space to breathe.

For now.

"It doesn't look as if it will fall," she said with more confidence than she felt.

"Not right away." The dusty air blurred the contours of his face. "If we try to dig out, the rest will go. Our safest bet is to stay still and hope someone can get to us."

Her voice caught. "I don't want to die."

"Ach, Ginger," he murmured. "We'll be all right."

"I should never have told Kindle about the powder."

"You really think he caused this?"

"The explosion, yes." She thought back to what Kindle had told her. "I doubt he meant to destroy the tower. I think he just wanted a small explosion that would affect you. Maybe he sobered up and changed his mind. But something must have gone wrong. He says he hardly knows what to do with the powder, how much to use, how to control the results."

"Well, it sure as hell works."

Claustrophobia was closing in on her. She needed to think about something else besides the collapse. *Anything*.

"We must be a mess," she said. It was a ludicrous comment, but it was the best she could do.

His face gentled. "You look beautiful, even after a tower fell on you."

Ginger's eyes filled with tears. She heard tender words so rarely. Never, in fact. She wanted to tell him, but she didn't know how to say it, and the spell was tiring her. With a sigh, she let it fade into darkness.

"I meant no offense," Darz said.

"You didn't give any." Softly she added, "And I doubt the dragon will hear." He seemed to have turned away from them, leaving her bereft.

Darz brushed his lips across her forehead. "You take this dragon business so seriously."

"Don't you?" She should have just said, *Don't,* but if she was going to die, she wanted to know at least a few moments of affection in her parched life.

"The tales are pretty," he said. "But hard to credit. The sun is just a ball of fire and the sunset a lot of colors." He sounded frustrated. "People can't even be consistent. In some places, they call the goddess Sky-Rose. In Aronsdale, they worship Verdant, who gives life to meadows and forests, and Azure, who supposedly glazes the sky. In the Misted Cliffs it's Aquamarine, for the ocean. There's Lapis Lazuli, the wind; Granite, for thunder; and Alabaster, who strummed stars into the night. It's too many. It makes my head hurt."

She didn't want him to die without the good graces of those deities. "Even with an aching head, you must pay proper homage."

Catherine Asaro

"Always homage, to some myth," he grumbled. "The Aronsdale man who married our queen does tricks with light. But I certainly don't believe he's a warlock."

She wondered if the prince consort would know a way to free them from this nightmare. "Have you ever seen him?"

"They sometimes stand on a balcony of the palace above a plaza. They wave. People cheer."

"But not you."

"I am honored to serve Her Majesty. I would lay down my life for her." His hair brushed her cheek as if he were shaking his head. "It's this alliance with Aronsdale that bothers me. But we need it, even if it is unpalatable. The king of the Misted Cliffs, the man they call Cobalt the Dark—*he* frightens me. Before last year, Jazid had never been conquered. Now Cobalt rules there instead of the rightful heir to the Onyx throne."

"Poor little boy," she murmured.

Darz snorted. "That 'poor little boy' would probably have grown up to be a despot, just like his papa." Then he added, "But at least he would have been our ally."

"Darz—" She couldn't keep up this distracting talk.

"We'll be fine," he said.

"Do you think anyone will find us?"

He was silent for too long. Then he said, "They will."

"I can't *breathe*."

He pressed his lips against her temple. "It will be all right, Ginger-Sun."

She fought back her panic. "Tell me a story. Tell me about Quaaz and all the fine happenings there."

He stroked her hair and switched into a storyteller's voice. "It is a fine city, full of people and excitement and life. The queen is beautiful, and the people love her." After a moment, he spoke in his normal voice. "Well, most of them. Some wanted a man on the throne. No longer, though, given who she married. No one wants her husband to rule."

"You mean the man from Aronsdale?"

"That's right," he growled.

"He must be very handsome."

Darz gave an exasperated snort. "Why do women always say things like that? *Why* must he be very handsome?"

"It makes a better story." Her voice caught. "Just as it does in the tale of the priestess caught in a rockfall with the handsome soldier from Quaaz."

"Don't cry." Darz put one arm over her waist and the other behind her head, as close as he could come to an embrace in their confined space. "Everything will work out."

She turned her head toward him, seeking a comfort older than any taboos. Her cheek brushed his chin, and his beard scratched her skin. Bending his head, he searched until he found her lips with his. His kiss stirred her like the colors of sunset or the sensual nighttime landscape of dunes under the stars.

But when he slid his hand over her breast, she stopped him. Even now, she couldn't break her oath to the sun. Tears ran down her face for what she had given up in her life. The topaz desert under the glazed sky sheltered her people, yet it also scoured their spirit. She would never know tenderness, for here beneath the claw of the dragon, the pitiless desert would claim their lives.

The Claw

They slept in the dark. Ginger lay curled into Darz, and he kept his arm across her body. How much time passed, she had no idea. When the cold became unbearable, she formed spells of warmth to keep them alive.

She knew when day arrived. Its heat came gently, relief from the icy night. It seeped into the rocks, and they were finally able to rest with a respite from cold.

Then it turned hotter.

Trapped under the stones, their cavity became an oven. Just as the rocks had held the cold during the night, now the heat became smothering. Hours passed, and the temperature rose, relentless and unforgiving.

"Darz." Sweat drenched Ginger's body. "I can't bear it."

"I thought we would die from suffocation." His words were a croak. "Or thirst, or crushed. Never this."

"I would do anything for ice."

"If you can create heat, can you take it?"

Her brain felt dull. "Take it?"

"Make it cold. If you can make heat, can you make cold?"

"I never have." His idea soaked into her charred mind. "I can't do spells during the day. Only in the dark."

"We haven't any light. It can't get any darker."

Ginger didn't know if it was the lack of light or the position of the sun that affected her spells. "I'll try." She closed her eyes, though she could see nothing anyway. This time, as she focused, she imagined cold. It felt strange, as if she were plowing through sand. Spells had never been this difficult. So hot…so very hot…

Cold, she thought. *Cold as a desert night…*

She lost track of time and floated in a haze. Only gradually did she realize the heat had receded. It wasn't cold, but it was bearable.

"Did the sun go down?" she mumbled. Her lips were swollen.

"It hasn't been long enough." His breath stirred the hairs at her temples. "Thank you, Ginger-Sun."

"I wish we had water. Food, too."

"You know what I would like?" His voice cracked. "A haunch of boar roasted over a pit. And a jug of wine. No, a lake."

"Wine comes in lakes?"

"In my fantasy, it does."

A smile creased her dusty face. "In mine…I am riding through Quaaz, past houses with gilded roofs. The streets are ankle deep in gold hexa-coins."

"That many, eh? Riding would be hard."

"I could just go with the gilded roofs."

"Would you go with me?" he said softly.

Tears gathered in her eyes for what she could never have. "It would be an honor. We could call on the queen."

Catherine Asaro

"Bah," he muttered. "She would throw me out of her palace for tracking in mud." He caressed her hair. "But I do wish I could take you to Quaaz."

"I couldn't go. A priestess may travel with no man except her kin. Or her husband."

He didn't answer, and she felt stupid, fearing he would think her comment a clumsy ploy to gain a vow from him.

But then he said, "I do think you would be so very good for me. In Quaaz."

Ginger flushed, knowing he spoke that way only because he would never have to follow through with the suggestion implicit in his words. She could just imagine how people would respond to his comment. Her ears burned, thinking about it. "The elders would never let me leave Sky Flames like that and still be priestess when I came back."

"The Elder Sentinel doesn't seem so bad."

She kept her thoughts about Tajman to herself. He led the village well, but he dealt better with men. Sometimes he stared at her when he didn't realize she knew. Later he would bring his wife to the temple for a blessing or his children or even his grandchildren. It was as if he were reminding himself of what he valued. His decision to put her with Kindle felt that way, too, as if he were pushing them together to protect himself. She knew Tajman meant well, but he had been suffocating her as surely as this oven of a prison.

After a while, Darz spoke in a rasp. "Are you sure you can't make water?"

"I don't think so. With light and heat, I'm not creating anything, just changing it. I don't know why, but light seems like little invisible particles to me. I gather them into a small place. With heat, I speed up the air. To cool it, I slow it down. With water, I would have to *add* something."

"Ah, well." He sounded disappointed but unsurprised.

Ginger sighed. "I might as well try. We've nothing else to do." She concentrated on the air, feeling its excited motes, hundreds, thousands, millions, an uncountable number, like stars at night. She soothed them as she would soothe a person. They calmed and the air cooled, as it had done before. Perhaps she could gather them into water, not creating something new, just rearranging it. She imagined recombining motes, but it was difficult. In fact, only when she let them speed up again did the spell even feel as if it might work. But the air was mostly the wrong motes. It was absurd, anyway, invisible particles in the air and the sky and the clouds—

Clouds! She needed *clouds.* She had only a tiny bit of what she needed, but it *was* here…

"Gods above," Darz whispered. "It's *raining.*"

A drop landed on Ginger's nose; another splattered her cheek. She opened her mouth, and water drizzled over her cracked lips. She gulped convulsively. Liquid ran down her shoulders, and she tried to catch it in her cupped hands.

The rain lasted only a few minutes, but it was enough to drink, and it dampened their clothes, cooling them. After it stopped, Ginger gave thanks to the dragon. She actually had no idea if he was punishing or helping them; she knew only that she was glad to be alive. She hadn't expected to survive this long.

"I thought you couldn't do that," Darz said.

"It was hard. And I think I used up whatever I needed to make the water." Fatigue settled over her like a cloak. "The big spells tire me out…"

"Sleep, Ginger-Sun," he murmured.

She closed her eyes and slept.

Night came, even colder than before. Darz held her while they shivered in the dark. Exhausted from creating the rain, she could manage no more than a weak spell of warmth. They clung together, wracked by hunger, thirst and cold, until she wondered if she had done no more than prolong the misery of their dying.

"Darz?" she said.

He rubbed his forehead against the top of her head. "Yes?"

"If—if someone does try to dig us out—won't the rocks fall and crush us under them?"

"I have to believe that won't happen. I can't lie here with no hope."

She had no answer for that, for she had begun to lose hope. Instead she said, "Thank you."

"For what? Getting you killed?"

"For holding me. No one else ever has. No man, I mean."

He pressed his lips on her forehead. "Not a single kiss?"

"Not even a touch." Her voice caught. "At least I won't die wondering what it was like."

She thought he would insist they were going to live. Instead, he said, "If I could have given you the sunset itself, the fire in the sky and the fire in my heart, I would have done it." His voice cracked. "Goodbye, Ginger-Sun."

"Goodbye," she whispered.

* * *

Thunder crashed. Ginger started awake, lifting her head in the dark. The night's chill had eased but the killing heat hadn't yet descended. Above them, the world rumbled. It was only when it kept going that she realized it wasn't thunder. Rocks were falling.

"Do you hear?" Darz asked when she tensed against him.

Ginger had gone beyond panic. "The Claw is collapsing."

He put his arm around her. "I think it's stopping."

The rumble was indeed petering away. She lay still, afraid to breathe.

Someone called out.

In the same instant, Ginger said, "Did you hear?" and Darz said, "Someone is out there!"

"Help us!" Ginger shouted.

"Down here!" Darz bellowed with his wonderfully *loud* voice.

More rumbles came from above, then scrabbling, and the clatter of stones falling over stones.

"*Careful!*" Darz shouted. "The rocks aren't stable."

"Can you hear us?" someone called.

"We're here!" Ginger shouted.

"Down below you!" Darz yelled. "Careful with those rocks!"

The scrabbling continued. Ginger wanted to laugh and then cry, her relief all mixed in with her fear of what would happen when their rescuers disturbed their precarious roof.

The thunder started again, this time almost on top of them. Darz pulled Ginger's head against his chest and curled over her, protecting his own head with his arms. With a groan of rock, the slabs above them shifted, resettled—

And fell.

Ginger gasped as the ceiling collapsed. Rocks piled up on top of them until she was suffocating. Even with her face pressed against Darz's chest, dust clogged her nose and mouth. She couldn't believe they had been buried this close to help. Rocks entombed them.

"Here!" someone shouted.

A terrible weight suddenly lifted off her body—and light flared around her. Someone or something hauled her up into the open air. The light blinded her. She could barely see the men crowded around the hole. Someone was holding her up, and dirt and pebbles rained away from her body. Voices blended around her, a cacophony of noise.

"Thank you," she whispered. "Thank you."

"I can't believe they're alive!" someone said.

"It's a miracle!" another voice exulted.

"Or something else," someone said, more darkly.

"They're a mess," someone else said.

She managed a smile at that last. She wanted to shout, cry, laugh and exult all at once. Her eyes were adjusting to the light better now, enough so she could see them helping Darz out of the hole. Dirt covered him, and his clothes were soiled and rumpled. She had never seen such a beautiful sight.

Someone handed her a bag of cured hide. She fumbled at it with one hand, too dazed to do more, until the same someone took it away. Belatedly, she realized it was Harjan. He opened the bag and helped her tilt it to her lips. Water, beautiful water, ran smooth and cool down her throat. She gulped convulsively until he tugged it away with gentle hands.

"Not so fast," he said. "It will make you sick."

Ginger sagged, and Harjan put his arm around her shoulders to keep her from collapsing.

"Don't touch her," someone snapped. It was Dirk Bauxite, the builder who had challenged her at the town meeting.

Harjan frowned at him, but he let Ginger go. Unable to stand on her wobbly legs, she sat down on a crag of rock. She was uncomfortably aware of Dirk staring at her, but she kept her gaze away from his and her opal hidden in her hand.

Harjan offered her the bag again, and this time she drank more slowly, closing her eyes with relief. When she opened them, she realized the day was nowhere near as bright as she had thought. Dawn tinged the sky, but the sun had yet to rise.

"How did you survive?" Dirk was asking Darz. "It seems impossible."

"I don't think we could have much longer," Darz said.

"It's incredible," another man said. It was Spark, the Second Sentinel.

"Here, Priestess." Harjan spoke in a low voice. "Cover yourself before they complain." He offered her a linen shawl dyed in rose and yellow hues.

"Thank you," she said softly. The falling rocks had shredded her already torn wrap, and the rips revealed stretches of skin on her torso and legs. She pulled the shawl around herself and shot Harjan a grateful look.

"Where is Kindle?" she asked.

"We finally got him to rest," Harjan said. "He insisted on working every shift, looking for you. We had to force him to go home or he would have collapsed." He motioned toward the edge of the Claw. "The Elder Sentinel has another team over there."

She followed his gaze and finally took in the surroundings. It was a sobering sight. They were still up high; the Claw had about two thirds of its former height. Rubble from its partial collapse had scattered so far, she could see mounds of it on the plain below even from up here. Great portions of the tower probably lay heaped around its base. The Claw itself had vanished, the magnificent spires buckled into a twisted landscape of debris.

"It's such a great loss," she said.

"It's only rock," Harjan said. "You lived. That's what matters." His eyes were glossy, as if filled with tears.

"It's not normal," Spark said. "No ordinary human being could survive being buried that way."

His stare unsettled Ginger. Emotions played across his face: relief, but also anger and an ugly quality that frightened her. She had a sudden feeling he hadn't *wanted* her to live.

"Their survival is a blessing." Harjan indicated the dust-laden sky, which was turning red-orange, the color that gave their village its name. "From the dragon and the sunrise."

"Is it a blessing?" Dirk asked, his gaze hard. "Or an omen?"

"Hasn't Kindle talked to anyone about the dragon-powder?" Ginger asked. They all just looked at her blankly.

"Why were you on the Claw?" Spark demanded. "Tajman clearly specified you were to remain in the temple until after the intru—" He glanced at Darz. "Until after Goldstone left the village."

"Stop interrogating them," Harjan said. "We need to get them back to the village before they collapse."

Ginger shivered, though the dawn wasn't cold. She rose slowly to her feet, stronger now, but still exhausted. As they walked forward, she fell in with Darz and discreetly pushed her opal into his hand. When he started to speak, she just barely shook her head.

She wasn't certain why she gave it into his safekeeping; she knew only that she didn't feel much safer now than she had before their rescue.

Led by Dirk Bauxite and Second Sentinel Spark, the rescue party brought Ginger to her brother's home. However, Harjan went with Darz, taking him to some other place. Tanner, one of the miners who worked with Harjan, was waiting at Ginger's house. His face lit up when he saw her, and he greeted her with joy. Dirk Bauxite was another story. His censure saturated the air like an acrid dust.

Second Sentinel Spark assigned Dirk and Tanner to watch Ginger and told her not to leave the house. She had no intention of going anywhere; she could barely stay on her feet. After declining Tanner's kind offer to bring the healer, she went to the bathing room and washed away the grit of her ordeal. She had scrapes and bruises, but nothing serious. When she finished, she retired to her old bedroom and slept like a stone.

Ginger awoke into shadows. She dragged herself out of bed and slipped on her robe. The colors of the room seemed muted in the dim light, which fit the way she felt.

She wondered what had happened to Darz. She wished she could go to him, but she knew it was impossible. It would only hurt to see him anyway. Sky Flames wasn't his home. He had spoken of a future with her only when he thought they had no future.

She walked into the front parlor, yawning, and found Dirk relaxed in what had been her father's favorite chair before he died. Dirk was whittling. Ginger stared dully at the wood shavings all over the tapestry rug.

He rose to his feet. "Light of the evening." His knife glinted in the glow from a candle on the mantle. The window behind him showed the purpling sky that followed sunset and the glitter of the first few stars.

Ginger returned the traditional greeting. "Light." She was too tired to say more.

"Elder Tajman was here earlier," Dirk said. "He and the Archivist want to talk to you tomorrow. I imagine they will ask how you survived being buried."

"Well, we weren't that deep," she said, rubbing her bleary eyes. "I'm surprised it took two days to find us."

He stepped forward, clenching his knife, his face red. "Take care with your accusations!"

Dismayed, she backed away. What had brought that on? She knew he and Spark believed she had broken her oath to the dragon, and they wanted her to suffer consequences. But it was more than that. They were *afraid* of her, and it made them like fuel ready to ignite.

Dirk's voice hardened. "You better have a good explanation for why you were on the Claw, why it fell and how you lived."

She stared at him, and the rest of his words finally soaked into her sleep-slowed mind. The Archivist wanted to talk to her. The Archivist. The person who had seen her make yellow light.

Ginger spoke with a formality she hoped hid her fear of him. "I regret if I misspoke, Goodman Bauxite. I will be ready tomorrow to meet with the Elder and the Archivist."

"See that you are." He opened and closed his fist as if he were preparing for something. She didn't intend to find out what. With a nod, she retreated from the room.

Inside her bedroom, Ginger slumped against the wall. She could see what was happening, but she didn't know how to stop it. They believed she had done evil, experimented with forbidden arts and that the Dragon-Sun had brought down his claw in retribution. They might strip her of her title, even exile her.

Surely Kindle wouldn't stand by while they accused her of evil. Or would he? She had felt his anger when she rejected him. They all seemed bent on seeing her pay for what they considered her misdeeds.

Dirk was the only guard at the house when Ginger awoke in the morning. Someone had sent Tanner home. It disquieted her, for Tanner was the only one of them who seemed sympathetic to her. When the Elder and Archivist arrived, the Elder looked exhausted, with dark bags under his eyes, and the Archivist watched Ginger with her lips pressed together. Second Sentinel Spark came with them, stout and frowning. Ginger sensed no support from anyone, only suspicion and hostility.

She offered them chairs in the parlor, but no one wanted to sit. So she also stood, though she was still tired. She didn't dare ask after Darz; she could think of little else that would inflame the situation more. Gods only knew what would happen if they found out he had kissed her again. She wanted to believe they would understand how two people who thought they were going to die would comfort each other, but seeing their faces, she knew that would never happen.

"We must decide what to do about your crimes," the Elder said. Anger edged his voice. "I told you to stay in the temple. The last place I expected you to go was the Claw, to see *him*. Now we have to deal with the aftermath of your behavior."

"Elder Limestone, I greatly respect your judgment." She spoke quietly. "That is why I ask you to hear me out. What appears as a transgression on my part was an attempt to save his life. I went to warn him about the explosion. I was too late. But I had to try, even if it meant going against your just and fair ruling that I stay in the temple." The words felt like dust in her mouth, saying "just and fair" for a sentence he had given *her* because Darz had broken the temple taboos and Kindle had hit her. But she had to protect herself.

"How did you know the Dragon-Sun intended to lower his claw?" the Archivist demanded. "What did you do to bring his wrath upon us all?" Her voice rose as she spoke.

"I did nothing wrong." Ginger hoped it was true. She had never sought harm with her spells; she sought only to heal and give comfort. But they were still night spells. "Hasn't Kindle explained about the powder?"

"What is this prattle you keep on about a powder?" Spark snapped.

Tajman held up his hand. "Enough. As long as she remains our priestess, you must speak with respect."

Ginger didn't miss his phrasing, and she doubted anyone else did, either. *As long as.*

"Ask Kindle," she said. "He's done something great, worthy of the queen's notice. But it's hard to control."

"What are you talking about?" the Archivist asked. "It makes no sense."

"The dragon-powder," Ginger said. "I found a description in one of the old scrolls. The powder explodes. Kindle was going to present a proposal to you for his taking it to Quaaz." She left out his request that she help write it; that would go over right now about as well as another collapse of the tower.

The Elder was shaking his head. "He has said nothing."

"Nothing? But—but surely he told you."

The Archivist spoke. "You blame Kindle for the debacle at the Claw? I would have hoped you had more integrity. But we've seen the truth of that these past days."

Ginger met her stare, and the Archivist's gaze slid away from hers. And then Ginger knew. Kindle *had* told someone. The Archivist. And she had no intention of revealing it to anyone. Like Spark and Dirk, she wanted Ginger punished. They would say it was because Ginger had done evil, but other currents were swirling here, dark and cold.

"Elder Tajman, please," she said. "I ask that you speak with Kindle again."

He looked as if he were in pain. "I wouldn't have thought you would deny responsibility for your actions. To manipulate the affections of a man who loves you in an attempt to make him shoulder the blame for your offenses is appalling."

"I'm not doing that! I'm telling the truth."

The Elder glanced at the Archivist, and she shook her head.

Tajman spoke wearily to Ginger, as if he were under a weight greater than he knew how to bear. "I had hoped to avoid this." He straightened up, seeming to gird himself. "There are those who demand you stand trial. We will commence immediately."

"Trial?" This was the worst she had feared. "For what?"

The lines on his face were deeply etched. "For breaking your vows to the temple and the Dragon-Sun, for your suggestive behavior—" Quietly he said, "And for witchcraft."

"You can't mean that," Ginger said. Had her attempts to hide her spells failed that badly? She had thought that except for that moment with the Archivist, she had protected herself.

No one answered. Their stares chilled her. Ginger looked at them and felt as if she couldn't breathe. "No one has been tried as a witch for ages."

"This will be the first such trial in one hundred and ninety-two years," the Archivist said.

"Witch," Dirk said, low and ugly. His gaze raked her body.

"No! I'm not!" Ginger's heart was pounding. "Has—has the sentence ever been changed?"

"No." The Archivist met her gaze. "It is still execution."

Fire Trial

The Tender's Hall had been crammed the last time Ginger was here. Now no one was present except the elders: Tajman, the Archivist and Second Sentinel Spark. Dirk Bauxite also came at their request, to ensure Ginger didn't try to run. With alarm, she realized they intended to hold her trial in secret.

The elders sat at the table on the platform at the front of the room. Ginger stood in the open space below them with her wrists bound behind her back and Dirk directly behind her, on guard. The high neck of her wrap felt as if it was cutting off her air; she couldn't *breathe*.

"Ginger Clovia," the Elder said, using her full name instead of the honorific "Ginger-Sun." "You are sworn to tell the truth. Do you understand?"

"Yes," she said.

"Then we shall begin." Tajman looked at Spark to his left and the Archivist to his right. "Are we agreed on the charges?"

"I believe so." The Archivist rose to her feet and picked up one of two scrolls on the table. She untied the black ribbon and unrolled the parchment. "Ginger Clovia, you are accused of sacrilege, of violating your oath and of lascivious behavior." Her voice hardened. "Moreover, you stand accused of witchery and dark arts."

"I'm not evil." Frustration bubbled into Ginger's voice despite her intention to stay composed. Even with her own doubts about spells, she would never believe she deserved to *die*. "You all know I'm not!"

"Ginger." Elder Tajman looked as if he were dying inside. "You must not interrupt. You will have a chance to speak."

The Archivist stared down from their high platform as if Ginger were a bug rather than the priestess who had served them for years and blessed the Archivist's own daughter. Then she took her seat and set the parchment in front of the Elder.

Tajman turned to Spark, whose beefy face had turned red. "Please present your evidence."

Ginger blinked. Evidence? What could Spark possibly have?

The Second Sentinel stood and regarded her with a pitiless stare. "Three days ago, while the accused was supposedly serving her sentence, she left the temple. She ran with abandon through the desert. Her wrap was slit to her hip, showing her legs. It became soaked with sweat, and she made no attempt to cover herself." His eyes glinted. "The cloth clung to her body. You could even see her nipples through it."

Heat flushed Ginger's face. What the blazes had Spark been doing, spying on her? Protection was one thing, but this felt invasive.

"She went to the Claw," Spark said. "Despite your order forbidding her to see the stranger. She ran to him. Almost as soon as their illicit tryst began, the Dragon-Sun smote the Claw and buried them. They were under the earth for over a day and a half, yet when we found them, they were hardly affected." He stretched out his arm to point at Ginger. "That woman was dressed in even less when we pulled her out. Much of her body showed through tears in her clothes."

The Elder was staring hard at Ginger as if he were seeing her in a new and unwelcome light. She couldn't believe what Spark was saying. It wasn't that any of it was untrue, but he twisted everything around.

"Of course my clothes were torn," she said. "A tower fell on me."

"You were in remarkably good shape for someone who had been buried under a mountain!" Spark shouted. "Amazing that your clothes suffered, but you were fine. What were you doing under there, witch?"

"Spark, enough," the Elder said. He sounded exhausted. To Ginger, he said, "Do not disrupt these proceedings."

The Second Sentinel said, "My apology, Elder Tajman." He nodded to Tajman and the Archivist. "That is my testimony." Then he sat down.

Ginger barely controlled the protests roiling within her. Her clenched fists caused the thongs binding her wrists to bite into her skin, but she was so tense, she couldn't relax her hands.

Tajman turned to the Archivist. "Present your evidence."

She rose to her feet. "I saw the accused create light out of a rock. She had no candle, no flint, no flame. And she did it to my *daughter*. We came for a blessing, and instead she cursed Jalla." She took a deep breath. "I have other times suspected her of working with such witchery. She always does it at night, in hiding. She fools people into thinking she is sweet. Men lose their good sense, lie for her, even destroy their lives for her. It is bad enough she dabbles in forbidden arts. But to do such spells of darkness within the sun temple is a desecration so great, it is no wonder the dragon smote her down."

"That's not true!" Ginger said. "I would never harm—"

"Enough!" the Elder warned. "Ginger, if you cannot respect the rules of this trial, I'll have to have Dirk gag you. Do you understand? This is your last warning."

She stared in disbelief. Never had he spoken to her this way. He knew she wasn't evil. Was it such a terrible crime to want tenderness and love?

"I asked a question," he said quietly. "You may answer."

"Yes, I understand." She hated the way her voice trembled. "May I ask a question?"

"Now, no," he said. "But in a few moments, you will have the opportunity." He glanced at Spark. "Did you have anything else to present?"

"I could detail more of her behavior," Spark said. "But it's all similar. She's grown brazen and wicked." His face paled. "She will bring evil here if we don't protect ourselves."

His fear dismayed Ginger. He genuinely believed she had enraged the Dragon-Sun. All of them did.

The Elder turned to the Archivist. "And you?"

"If you need more testimony, I can provide that for the record," she said. "It is all of a similar nature."

"Very well." Tajman turned to Ginger and spoke with pain. "I have known you all your life, since when you were a charming if unruly child, throughout your years as an acolyte and then as priestess. You've been well-liked, Ginger, and you've served well. But some folk have raised concerns. In the past, I have let my fondness for you overrule my judgment. I must not let that happen now. The severity of your behavior demands we respond." He took a breath as if to steady himself. "If you have anything to say you may speak."

She struggled to restrain the explosion of words within her. "I deeply regret if anything I have done has appeared inappropriate in thought, word or deed. Please know, all of you, I would *never* seek harm against anyone." She turned to the Archivist. "Jalla is dear to me. I would never hurt her."

"You speak your lies so convincingly," the Archivist said.

"I sought to *save* a life. Kindle can tell you." Ginger looked at the hall behind her with its empty benches. Dirk was watching her, his gaze implacable. Rattled, she turned back to the Elder. "Why is no one here to speak for me?"

"You mean Kindle?" He looked disappointed, as if he had hoped she wouldn't bring up the Flame Sentinel. "We cannot allow you to sway a good man into falsely taking blame on himself so you can avoid justice."

"If you won't hear those who would speak in my defense," she said angrily, "the Dragon-Sun will know. He'll punish you."

The Archivist jumped to her feet. "How dare you invoke the name of the dragon you have dishonored. You're an abomination!"

"I have done nothing wrong!" Ginger cried.

Spark was on his feet now, too. "You're lewd and wicked!"

"Stop it!" The Elder stood between them, his face red. "Silence, both of you!" He raked his hand through his hair, his gaze fixed on Ginger. "Do you repent your actions?"

"Yes," she said, desperate. "I swear, I do."

"She lies!" Spark said.

The Archivist spoke. "We cannot endanger the village by keeping among us someone who has so angered the sun, he brought down a mountain in retribution."

Watching Tajman, Ginger realized even he believed what the Archivist said. Her voice trembled. "What must I do to convince you I mean no harm?"

The Archivist spoke severely. "If you are genuinely true to the Dragon-Sun, it will be impossible for you to burn, for he protects his priestesses from the inferno of his power."

Ginger felt as if the room were whirling around her. "From the fire of the *sun*. Not the fire of man."

The Elder narrowed his gaze at her. "You would reinterpret the ancient scrolls for your own benefit?"

Ginger felt as if she couldn't say anything right. She had spent her life avoiding speeches, and now she had no compelling phrases to roll off her tongue. She struggled for the words. "The fire referred to in those scrolls is symbolic."

"The scrolls say fire," the Archivist said flatly. "Not 'fire as a symbol' for the convenience of blasphemous priestesses."

"I would never speak blasphemy against the dragon!"

The Elder pushed his hand through his hair, moving as if he carried a great weight. "I have heard the evidence, Ginger. I do not want to believe. But it is damning. We cannot ignore it, not after the dragon himself has smote the land." He pulled himself up straighter. "But the Dragon-Sun has also heard your claim of repentance. If you speak truly, he will grant you mercy. We must leave it in his hands." Still looking at Ginger, he said, "Archivist, do you have the sentence?"

The Archivist picked up the other scroll in front of her. She unrolled the aged parchment, taking care with its frayed edges. "In the last trial with such charges, the sentence was thus." Holding the ancient document with both hands, she read, "For lewd and licentious behavior, the accused is sentenced to twenty lashes. For the charge of witchery, she will be bound to a stake at sunset, the time where both the Dragon and Goddess reign. Peat, brush and desic-cated fire-lily vines shall be piled around the stake. They shall be put to flame with three torches. If the Dragon-Sun so wishes to punish the witch for her misdeeds, she will burn."

"You can't do this!" Ginger cried. She stepped toward the table. "Tajman, surely you can't mean this!"

Dirk pulled her back. "Stay away from them, witch."

"No, let me go!" She tried to wrench out of his grip. As he caught her around the waist, she twisted in his hold to face the others. "If you go through with this, you're *murderers*."

"Silence her!" the Archivist shouted. She looked panicked. "Before the Dragon-Sun brings this hall down on all of us!"

As Ginger struggled, Dirk shoved a cloth in her mouth and tied another around her head in a gag. Spark came down from the platform and strode over to her. He took one of her upper arms while Dirk held the other, and they swung her around to face the table where the Elder and the Archivist stood.

"Take her to the cellar with the riding gear," Tajman said. He looked as if he were ill. "We must be quick. It's almost sunset."

Ginger struggled as they pulled her to a door behind the platform and onto a landing with one candle burning in a niche there. Tajman lifted a torch off the wall and lit it with the candle. Holding the torch high, he descended the cracked stone steps. Ginger planted her feet on the ground and resisted when Spark and Dirk tried to pull her forward. Even if she hadn't balked, her wrap would have kept her from descending the stairs as fast as they were trying to go. They finally lifted her by her arms and carried her down the stairs, her toes just barely hitting the stone.

At the bottom, despite her struggles, they dragged her down a tunnel with crumbling walls. The smell of wine permeated the air. They stopped at a stone door braced by strips of black iron, and the Archivist heaved it open. In the cellar beyond, kegs of ale stood in front of racks that held wine bottles. Big copper serving plates hung on the far wall. Closer by, bridles, saddles, ropes and riding quirts dangled on pegs.

When Ginger saw the Elder take a quirt off the wall, panic swept over her. Instead of fighting, she suddenly let herself go limp. It caught Spark and Dirk off guard, and their grip loosened. Wrenching free, she lunged for the door. She could have raced upstairs ahead of them if only she had been wearing her leggings. But she tripped in the wrap, and Dirk easily caught her.

Spark and Dirk dragged her to a table and bent her over it, face down. When Spark unbound her wrists, for one heady moment she thought she could wrest free. Then he pulled her arms over her head, ripping her sleeves, and he and the Elder held her down. In the copper plate on the wall to one side, she glimpsed Dirk's face. The hunger in his expression terrified her. He grabbed her wrap where it stretched across her back and yanked. It ripped to her waist, leaving only scraps of cloth and the wires that held it in place over her breasts. The Archivist stayed in the corner, watching. Ginger saw her fear, but also her satisfaction that they were dealing with the threat she thought Ginger posed to Sky Flames.

Ginger cried when Dirk lashed her. The leather shredded her back, and the pain was unbearable. By the time he finished, she was sobbing. They pulled her to her feet, and the Elder wrapped a shawl around the tatters of her wrap. Tears poured down her cheeks as she stared up at him. He looked as if he had aged twenty years. She hoped this gave him screaming nightmares for the rest of his godforsaken life.

She could barely walk. Her ears rang as if thunder had crashed too close, and her back was on fire. No, not fire! Anything but fire. She hurt too much to struggle, and she knew then the purpose of the lashes. Whipping someone they were about to execute made little sense in terms of justice, but it served them well by decreasing her ability to resist. If only she had her opal! She would blast them with fire the moment the sun went down. She was becoming exactly what they feared, and she dreaded that knowledge, but if she could have attacked them, she would have done so in an instant.

They exited the Tender's Hall into an alley. Brackish water ran down the center of the lane. The strip of sky above them was darkening; they had timed her trial so they could carry out the sentence immediately. Did they fear she would have more chance to fight back if they didn't finish this as fast as possible? They were right. Except she had never formed a spell without the opal. Had she not given it to Darz, they would have taken it away. Gods, she hoped they hadn't also sentenced him to die.

The alley ended at a pavilion that shaded the village water-well. The central square lay beyond the well, but she was hidden from the view of anyone there by columns that held up the pavilion roof. She heard a buzz of voices. The people might not know they were about to see their priestess burned, but they surely realized something was about to happen.

Dirk and Spark leaned her over the retaining wall so she was staring down into the well. Moist air wafted up, and she caught a faint splash of water. The Elder and Archivist were standing in front of the well, blocking Ginger's view of the plaza. She knew why they were hiding her: to minimize the chance anyone could interfere in their plans.

With a strength driven by desperation, Ginger twisted with a great heave and jerked free. The gag muffled her cries, but she made enough noise to rise above the hum of voices beyond the well. Spark and Dirk caught her, and she cried out when Dirk's hand scraped the lacerations on her back.

Tajman groaned. "By the dragon, let's get this terrible business over with."

Dirk dragged her from behind the well—and she inhaled sharply. People filled the plaza. Sunset wasn't normally a busy time; by now the buildings of commerce here were empty and most everyone had headed home. But it took very little to start rumors. Word must have spread that something was happening, for the square was as crowded as midday, though twilight was descending. Some people held torches. The smoky glow barely chased away the encroaching night, and it lit their faces with inconstant flares of light.

It was too much. She couldn't handle it all. When she sagged, Dark and Spark lifted her up until her feet barely touched the ground, so they were practically carrying her. At the edge of the crowd, two cowled figures stood watching, tall in their charcoal-gray robes. Peaked hoods covered their heads and gray scarves wrapped around their faces. Nothing showed except their dark gazes, which followed Ginger as Dirk and Spark dragged her past them.

Then she saw what had drawn the onlookers. A platform stood in front of one of the buildings that bordered the plaza. Constructed from uneven boards, the stage had the unfinished look of a structure thrown together too fast.

In its center, stood a stake.

The pole was taller than Ginger and as thick as a tree. A base and supports held it in place, and coils of rope lay beside it. Two women were climbing the stairs of the platform, their arms loaded with stripped branches and dried fire-lily vines.

The sight jolted Ginger out of her shock. She renewed her struggles with such vehemence, Dirk and Spark had to stop. Spark swore vividly under his breath. "Why won't she *give up?*"

Ginger had no intention of making it easier for them. She would never give up as long as she could breathe. They believed that because she was tender, she must also be weak, but if they thought she would go to her death without protest, they were mad.

She kept fighting as they took her to the platform. Dusk was spreading, and ruddy torchlight lit the plaza. Her shawl caught on the top step and dragged off her shoulders, flapping in the rising night wind. A multitude of faces were turned up to watch her, and rumbles of shock stirred among the crowd. It may have been the harsh, wavering light, but the people seemed avid to Ginger, hungry for the gruesome spectacle.

The stake loomed before her. Several villagers now were piling firewood around the base, and a man came to help Dirk and Spark pull her forward. No one would meet her frantic gaze. They forced her to stand with her back to the stake so she faced the crowd. She moaned as the wood scraped her wounds. They tied her wrists behind the thick pole and bound her ankles to the bottom.

Please, Ginger thought. *Stop, please.* Did Harjan know what was happening? Tanner? Her brother was gone. This had happened so fast, most townsfolk wouldn't learn until tomorrow that the elders had executed their priestess. Heath would come home to find his sister dead.

The crowd fell quiet. For one heart-stopping instant she thought someone had come to light the firewood at her feet. The acrid smell of torches, with their oils and cinders, saturated her senses, making her ill. But no, too many people were on the platform. They couldn't light the flames yet, because when they did, this entire structure would burn.

Elder Tajman walked into view, to the front of the platform, and she understood then why everyone had fallen silent. They were waiting to hear what explanation he could possibly offer for this atrocity.

He spoke in the resonant voice that had earned him such renown as an orator. His words rolled across the plaza. "Good people, listen well!" Wind blew his silvered hair back from his face, accenting his sculpted profile. "You all know the Dragon-Sun brought down his Claw. He toppled a tower that has stood sentinel over our people for thousands of years!" He turned and stretched his arm out to point at Ginger. "He has smote this witch for her sacrilege! His wrath came down, and so will it come down on us all if we cannot appease him."

Cries rose from the crowd, and Ginger knew then she had no hope. Until this moment, she hadn't really believed Tajman would go through with it. Deep inside, she had trusted him. She was a fool. She had trusted them *all,* assuming the gratitude they expressed for her work meant she had their goodwill. She had been so achingly naïve, and learning that truth hurt at a level so deep, she felt as if she broke inside.

They were afraid. In a village this small, the tale would have circled a hundred times, embellished and twisted until she no longer recognized herself. The malevolent sorceress, the temptress who committed unspeakable evils and lured men to their deaths. They believed the Dragon-Sun would strike Sky Flames as he had struck his Claw, and that only her death would satisfy the angry god.

Flames
of Glass

A chill wind buffeted Ginger, and the torchlight wavered. With dread, she realized Tajman and everyone else was leaving the platform—except two men and a woman who held torches. The Archivist's words came back to her: *The wood shall be put to flame with three torches.* Nothing was going to stop them, no protests, no sudden rain, no clemency from the dragon.

If only she had the opal. If only she could bring water out of the air. But that drizzle she made would never put out the inferno they were preparing. She had neither the means to create a spell nor the calm to focus on even a small one, let alone downpour the size of what she needed.

Tears streamed down her face. *Dragon-Sun, don't let me die this way. If I have offended you, give me a chance to make it right.* But if he heard her plea, he gave no sign. The fiery colors of his setting were gone from the sky.

As the torch bearers came forward, Ginger stared over the crowd, trying to distance her mind from her body. The Arch-Tower stood across the square, the tallest building in Sky Flames. It had the only stained glass window in the village proper, a large circle depicting a black-wing hawk soaring through the sky. Set under the bulb of the tower, the glass caught torchlight and glowed red, as if it were on fire. Gazing at its round shape, she willed her mind to recede from the flaring torches.

A spell stirred within Ginger.

The torch bearers stopped in front of her. They blocked her view of the tower, dousing her spell, and she was suddenly more aware of the pain in the gashes and welts on her back, especially where her skin pressed into the pole. Had she imagined the spell in her desperation? The trio with the torches watched her with fear. She tried to speak, to entreat them to stop, but her cries were lost to the gag and the rumble of voices below. The smell of burning hemp and the oil that soaked the torches nauseated her. Ashes twirled in the air, and an ember singed her bared shoulder.

Together, in a single motion, they dropped their torches into the firewood around the stake.

"NO!" Ginger screamed.

The torches crackled at her feet, and the trio backed away as if she had cursed them. They strode from the platform, out of her view, and their feet thudded on the stairs.

Ginger could see the clock window again, and she stared at it, struggling for a spell, *any* spell, while the torches burned at her feet. With a whoosh, dried branches caught fire, and flames jumped in the wood piled around her. Heat licked her legs. It would only be moments before the fire caught her clothes.

As the flames rose, so did the cries of the crowd. Yells came from somewhere, but the lurid torchlight left too many shadows for her to see who was shouting, and the crackle of the flames drowned out whatever they were yelling at her. She focused on the window—

And a heat spell rose within her.

The window was glass, not opal, but it was so much larger. It stoked her spell. In a strike of insight that came far too late, she realized it wasn't the opal that catalyzed her spells, but its *shape*. The circle couldn't do it as well, but it worked.

For one incredible moment Ginger thought she could bring rain. But that spell was beyond her reach. She inhaled smoke instead of air and choked for breath. She had no time to focus, none of the calm she needed; she was *heat*, terrible, terrible heat. In the past, she had created spells of comfort and light to honor the dragon, but now he had deserted her. Flame seared her legs, and she screamed. In this terrible moment, as she burned alive, she grasped the roiling power within her and let a spell surge out, huge and wild, driven by fear, with no control.

If I am to burn, then so shall you all.

The buildings surrounding the plaza erupted into flame. Fire leapt into the sky, red against the night. People shouted and ran from blazes that suddenly were everywhere. Through the veil of flame around her, Ginger saw them pointing toward her, their faces contorted with fear.

The hem of her wrap caught fire. She cried out as heat engulfed her calves. Everything was burning, her clothes, the platform, the buildings, the sky, the entire world. The crowd had turned into a panicked mob. Through the flames, she saw a running mass of people on foot and horseback—

Horses?

Someone on a horse was slashing with a sword! No, it was a

mirage; no one in Sky Flames had a horse but a few sentinels and the elders. The flames were leaping too high for her to see anything but a red blur. Something gouged her ankles, and the ropes binding her feet to the stake scraped her legs. She sobbed from the heat as her hair caught fire.

A sharp edge scraped her wrists—and her arms fell free! She lurched forward, her ankles tearing away from the stake. Even as heat blasted her face, something jerked her back, out of the flames. She couldn't move—she had been tied too long—but someone kept pulling her, and she stumbled into the area behind the stake. The fire hadn't yet caught the platform here. Wild with the fear pumping through her body, she stared up into the face of the person who had freed her from the stake.

Heath!

Her brother's hair whipped around his head in the wind. He ripped the gag off her mouth and yelled, "We have to get down." He half carried, half supported her as they ran for the stairs. Ginger coughed raggedly, heaving in breath after glorious breath. Right now she would have run on broken legs if necessary. Fire roared behind them, but cool air blew across her face like a gift.

Two men were at the bottom of the stairs, fighting against four of the village sentinels. She recognized one of the men immediately: Harjan had come to help. And the other—was Kindle! Incredibly, the Flame Sentinel was battling his own men.

Ginger swallowed; she and Heath could go no farther with the sentinels blocking them. Heath took her halfway down the steps, then set her against the rail and jumped down into the midst of the fighting. The four sentinels had Harjan and Kindle backed up against the platform. Her giant of a brother took on two of them while Harjan and Kindle grappled with the others.

Ginger had no intention of staying here while they fought for her life. She grabbed the hem of her cursed wrap and ripped it so she could move. Agony stabbed her burned and scraped feet as she stepped down the stairs. When she moved, two of the sentinels stopped fighting Kindle and looked up.

Ginger went utterly still. They stared at her, their faces streaked with sweat and lit in orange by the fires. One of them looked at Kindle, who was breathing hard, poised to take them on again. Then incredibly, the two sentinels stepped back. The others had noticed and stopped fighting Heath. They looked at Ginger, at Kindle, back at Ginger. Then they all moved away.

Ginger couldn't believe it. She limped down the last step, painfully aware of the sentinels. They were, miraculously, letting her go, but they could change their minds at any moment.

With all the noise of the flames roaring behind them, Heath had to shout to make Kindle and Harjan hear him. "I don't know how much longer he can hold them off! Get his attention while I take Ginger. We have to go *now*."

He? Ginger looked to where he pointed—and gasped.

A man on horseback was fighting in the center of the plaza, surrounded by armed sentinels on horseback and more on foot. None of his assailants had backed off; their faces were drawn in snarls. The man reared his horse, raising his curved sword high over his head, and the garish light of the fires glittered on its edges like molten lava. His horse pawed the air, and his war cry tore through the air as if it were the scream of dragons. Then he came down, slashing with his sword, and the sentinels scattered like chaff before a blazing wind.

Darz.

He was one man, alone, fighting three others on horseback and six on foot, yet he held them off. He struck harder and parried faster. He advanced, blocked their moves, backed away when they surged against him, then came at them again.

"He'll catch up with us," Heath said, urging Ginger forward. She stumbled with him toward a lane between two burning buildings. When hooves pounded behind them, she summoned up an extra spurt of speed. But still the horse gained. It pulled alongside of them and a sentinel leaned down to grab her.

"No!" She strove to run faster on her burned, aching feet.

"Ginger!" he shouted. It wasn't a sentinel, it was Darz. Leaning down, he reached for her. She had no time to think; she grabbed his hands with hers as she had often done with Heath when they were children practicing mounts on the horse owned by their father, who had been a sentinel. Darz heaved her up in a practiced motion, and she scrambled astride the bare back while Darz held her in front of him.

"Go!" Heath shouted. "Get her safe!"

With one arm clamped around Ginger, Darz kicked the horse and leaned forward. It raced into the alley and thundered past the blazing walls on either side.

They rapidly left the flames behind. Darkness closed around them, but not the full night, for the burning plaza cast a glow that reddened the shadows. The fire bell in the plaza began to clang, calling fire-tenders to battle the inferno. Ginger was clenching her fists so hard, her nails tore her palms.

It wasn't until they had left the plaza far behind and were riding through the outskirts of the village that her grip eased. She drew in a deep, shuddering breath. Her head swam and she swayed until Darz tightened his hold, keeping her from falling off the horse. As her head cleared, she recognized the animal as Grayrider, Kindle's fine stallion.

They were riding too hard for normal conversation, but Darz bent his head so his lips touched her ear. "Are you all right?"

She managed a nod. She wasn't all right; welts, gashes, lacerations and minor burns covered her body. Nothing was left of her clothes but scorched, bloodied rags. She hurt everywhere so very much, but it was far better than burning alive.

They soon reached the desert. When she looked back, the village was no more than a glow in the sky. Out here, only the moon lit their way, and Darz let Grayrider slow down.

"The Flame Sentinel told me he left supplies for us in the Flint Maze," Darz said. "Do you know where that is?"

"West of the temple." Her voice caught. "I can't think of enough ways to thank you."

"I owe you, Ginger-Sun," he said gruffly. "I almost got you burned alive because I couldn't keep my hands where they belonged."

"You didn't make this town brutal." She had always known the harsh life of the desert could harden people, but she would never have believed they could turn on her this way. She spoke with a pain that bandages and salves could never heal. "They're responsible for what they did, Darz. Not you."

"How could they do it?" His voice crackled with disbelief. "It's so illegal to burn someone alive, I can't count the number of laws they've broken."

"They're scared."

"They ought to be. When I report this—"

"Darz, don't."

"Why the hell not?"

"It hurts too much," she whispered.

"Ginger—"

She just shook her head. "Not yet." She was too upset to think through what had happened, not only what the elders had done, but her final act of fury. She needed time. Right now, she just wanted to fold up and nurse her wounds.

"Is that the temple?" Darz asked.

It took her a moment to recognize its terraced roof against the starred sky. "Yes, that's it." Moonlight glinted on the skylights at the tip of the RayLight Chamber where she had spent so many hours in meditation. Or making spells.

"Maybe they're right," she said dully. "Maybe I am evil."

"What? That's absurd. You're one of the kindest people I've ever met." He punctuated his assertion with colorful oaths expressing his opinion of Sky Flames. He caught himself midway through one. "Sorry," he said. "I'm too used to traveling with the army."

"It's all right." She motioned up ahead. "The Maze is a five-minute ride past the temple."

"I mean it, Ginger. You aren't evil."

It would have been easy to let him reassure her. But she couldn't lie. "I do the things they claimed."

"Like hell."

"I make spells, Darz."

"I don't believe in spells," he said. "But if I did, I would have to point out that the kings of Aronsdale choose their brides for their ability as mages. Whatever that means."

She smiled wanly. "But you don't believe it." After what had happened to them in the cave, he might accept far more than he was willing to admit.

"I know this much," Darz said. "You had nothing to do with the Dragon's Claw falling. Your Flame Sentinel says he did exactly what you thought. Apparently he sobered up enough to change his mind, but this powder of his blew anyway. He lost control of it."

"Then he admitted everything?"

"To me. To your Archivist. To your brother." In a wry voice, he added, "To the guards confining him in his house. That was before he beat them up and left."

That sounded like Kindle, but for once she was grateful. "Then he found you and Heath?"

"Me, yes. One of the miners, a man named Tanner, went yesterday to get your brother. Tanner says he was at your house when they brought you back from the Claw."

"I remember." She tried to collect her thoughts. "When I awoke today, only Dirk Bauxite was guarding me. Tanner was gone."

"Yes, well, he got suspicious when the elders sent him away and left you with Bauxite."

"But how did he find my brother? Heath was in J'Hiza. It's half a day's ride from here, and Tanner has no horse."

Darz cleared his throat. "He, uh, borrowed one from a sentinel."

From his tone, she suspected the sentinel hadn't known about the loan. Softly she said, "I am in their debt. And yours. I thought you were gone for good."

His voice quieted. "Your elders turned me loose yesterday with nothing. They told me never to come back." He sounded annoyed. "Did they really think I would just walk away after what had happened? I snuck back last night. I was looking for you when the Flame Sentinel caught up with me."

That surprised Ginger. She had thought Kindle hated Darz. "After he tried to kill you, he asked for your help?"

"He feels guilty as hell. He ought to." Awkwardly, he added, "He also seems to believe you prefer me over him."

"I hardly know you."

He gave a snort. "Your hulking monster of a brother thinks otherwise. He gave me quite a speaking to. He's furious."

She could well imagine. "We've always been close."

"So I gathered." He shifted behind her. "You can't return to that town."

"I know." She couldn't bring herself to think farther ahead than that. "Do you see those shadows up there? The tall ones?"

"I think so."

"That's the Maze. It's a lot of rock slabs sticking up out of the desert." To Ginger, it had always looked like it could be an ancient palace of the gods blasted into ruins.

"It's hard to see anything in this dark."

She paused, thinking of the stake. But Darz already knew about her spells. "I could help with the light." A disheartening thought came to her. "Unless you didn't keep my opal."

"I kept it. It was all I had to remember you by."

She was glad he had cared enough to want a keepsake. "I hope you don't mind my asking for it back."

He let go of her, and a rustling came from behind her, the scrape of the ties on a suede riding pouch. Then he pressed the opal into her hands. "It's yours. But I don't think we should use a light. It would make us easy to spot."

"Oh. Yes. Of course." The opal warmed her palm, so very welcome, as if in some subtle way it increased her well-being. She formed a spell of succor. It couldn't heal her, but her pain receded to a more bearable level.

She wondered if Darz might prefer the opal to remember her by rather than have the responsibility of her person. He was right: she couldn't go home. That thought came with such pain. If she could reach J'Hiza before anyone heard about what happened here, she might arrange passage to someplace safe. Where, she didn't know, but she couldn't give up. She couldn't ask Heath to leave with her, though; he needed to stay and protect their family's mining interests, lest the elders challenge his claims after what he had done tonight.

"Could you take me to J'Hiza?" she asked. "I won't trouble you after that. But it's too far to walk." She didn't know how they had expected Darz to make it without supplies, a horse, or a guide, especially after all he had been through. Maybe they had hoped the desert would finish the job his attackers started.

He spoke awkwardly. "I don't think you understand."

"Understand?" she asked, distracted. They were almost to the Maze, and the tall, uneven slabs of rock were easier to see. So was the yellow glow leaking around them. "Darz, you may not have wanted a light, but someone else out here does."

"I see." He guided Grayrider in the other direction around the Maze, away from the light.

Ginger squinted at the yellow glow. "I see a man walking. He has a lamp."

"You can see that from so far away?" Darz asked.

"Definitely. Two people. No…three. And two horses." She was

suddenly aware she had no weapons. Darz had his sword, but she had nothing more than her fingernails.

Darz walked the horse behind an outcropping of slabs on the edge of the Maze. The night was silent, without even the call of a black-wing. Voices drifted to them.

Relief washed over Ginger. "That's Heath."

"Your brother?"

"Yes. The other two are probably Harjan and Kindle."

"Either that, or the sentinels caught your brother and tortured him until he told them where they could find you."

"They would never—" Then she stopped. Today people she had known all her life had condemned her, whipped her and tried to kill her. She had blessed Dirk just last year when he wanted luck for the houses he built. Yet he hadn't hesitated to lash her in the cellar. She blanched, remembering the hunger in his face as he tore off her wrap. He had *wanted* to hurt her.

"You're sure you saw two horses?" Darz asked. "I thought only your village sentinels had them."

"Heath has one," she said. "Not Harjan. You have Kindle's."

"Where would they get a second?"

"I don't know."

"We shouldn't just go over there. I'll check first."

Grayrider stood quietly as Darz dismounted. Alone on the horse, Ginger shivered as the wind chilled her bare arms and shoulders. She hadn't realized until Darz moved away that his clothes had a familiar smell of the red dye used in Sky Flames. Would she ever smell it again? For all she knew, they didn't even have the same dye in J'Hiza.

In just a few days, she had lost everything. She was still a priestess; they hadn't stripped away her title. Why bother, when she would soon be dead? But she no longer had a temple to serve. She didn't want to blame Darz; she had meant it when she told him it wasn't his fault. Yet she couldn't help but think that if he had never come to Sky Flames, none of this would have happened. She might have married Kindle or spent her life alone, but she wouldn't be exiled from everything she loved.

"Ginger?" Darz said.

She realized he had reached up to her. With a sigh, she eased off the horse. Darz caught her, holding her in his arms, and she groaned when his sleeve scraped her back.

He turned her around. "Gods! What did they do to you?"

"Twenty lashes."

"Bastards." His touch was unexpectedly gentle. "You need a healer. If these wounds aren't tended, they'll fester."

"I'll be all right."

"No, damn it, you won't." He turned her to face him. "My men say the same thing when they're injured. 'I'm all right.' Stop being so stoic. If we don't tend your wounds, you could die. I don't let my men get away with that knuckleheaded bravery, and I won't let you, either."

The hint of a smile softened her face. "Are you comparing me to a soldier in Her Majesty's army?" He had called her brave. Knuckleheaded, too, but she could live with that.

"Ach!" he muttered, sounding loud even when his voice was barely audible. "I didn't mean to insult you."

"You didn't." She touched his cheek. "Go see who came to meet us." Her eyes filled with moisture. "If it's safe, I would like to say goodbye to my brother and the others."

He folded his fingers around hers. "I'll leave you with a dagger. If anyone comes, scream." Bluntly he added, "And stab the hell out of them."

Even a few days ago, she wouldn't have believed she could stab anyone. Tonight she had seen a violence within herself she had never known existed. She could have burned every person and building in that plaza. Part of her believed the elders were right, she was a dark witch. Another part of her raged. *They* were responsible for their cruelty and their lust, not her. And they were the ones who had decreed: *If the Dragon-Sun so wishes to punish the witch for her misdeeds, she will burn.* Well, she hadn't burned, so the Dragon-Sun hadn't wanted her punished, and the hell with all of them.

She recognized the dagger Darz withdrew from his belt; it belonged to the Elder, who had lent it to Darz for his stay on the tower. She closed her hand around the roughly cast hilt and didn't miss the irony, that Tajman's weapon would help her escape the execution Tajman had ordered.

Darz slipped into the Maze. Just like that, he vanished. She couldn't even hear him. Whether or not he would return, she didn't know; this was his chance to escape the burden of her dependence on him. She didn't think he would turn from someone in need, but her confidence in her ability to judge the good in people was gone.

Grayrider stood motionless, drawing no attention. Kindle had bought the horse after he became a sergeant and trained Grayrider as a cavalry mount. Silence pressed on Ginger. The night shouldn't be so quiet. No sand-chirpers. They were similar to crickets but even noisier, and usually they clacked until dawn. They must have gone silent because of her and her brother's group. No one else was here.

Catherine Asaro

She had to believe that. Folding her arms against the chill, she scanned the hills beyond her hiding place.

On top of a ridge, two figures on horseback were silhouetted against the sky.

14

Desert
Oath

Ginger gulped in a breath. The silhouettes had vanished—if indeed
they had been there at all.

Voices drifted to her. "…have to stop them from taking our
family's holdings, or we would ride to J'Hiza with you."

She closed her eyes with gratitude. That was Heath.

"Many people in town will stand against them," Harjan said.
"Ginger is well-liked."

"People fear her, too." That was Kindle. "The Archivist didn't
believe me about the powder. She thinks I'm bewitched."

"Well, we should reach J'Hiza tomorrow," Darz said. "If we ride
most of tonight."

Light leaked around the slabs, and a large man appeared between
the two great stones. The light from his lamp nearly blinded her.
Shielding her eyes, she clenched the hilt of the dagger and raised her
arm to strike.

"Ah, Ginger." Heath came forward, lowering the lamp so she

could see him. He carried two travel bags over his shoulder. "They truly have done malice, if you fear even your own kin."

"Never you." Her voice caught. "I wasn't sure who you were."

Darz and Kindle stepped through the opening, then Harjan. Kindle had a sword strapped across his back, which was odd, because Darz had been using Kindle's when he fought the sentinels, and as far as she knew, Kindle only owned one such weapon. It wasn't until Heath pried her fingers off the dagger that she realized she was still threatening him with the blade. She sagged against the slab next to her.

"Ginger, honey, are you all right?" Heath asked.

She tried futilely to smile at him. "I will be." Her voice felt as unsteady as her legs.

"She needs the salve," Darz said.

"I have it here." Heath set his lamp on a shelf of rock and dropped one of the travel bags on the ground. Opening the other, he rummaged through its contents.

"I saw someone on the ridge," Ginger said. "Two riders."

Kindle scanned the area, or at least as much as he could see between the slabs of rock. "Are you sure?"

"Actually, no." She shivered and crossed her arms.

"Would you like the riding blanket?" Darz asked.

"I'm all right," she said. Heath was watching Darz with a narrowed gaze, and she didn't want to aggravate their tension. Besides, the blanket would scratch her back.

Kindle climbed up on one of the slabs and crouched on a ledge behind its jagged top. "It's hard to see with that lamp. Can you douse it?"

"I'll do it," Harjan said quickly. He stepped around, putting himself between Heath and Darz.

Ginger glanced from Darz to her brother. Darz's fist was clenched and his face dark; her brother had that look he wore when he defended someone he cared for. Harjan was pretending to be engrossed in the lamp, but she wasn't fooled. He had positioned himself so he could intervene if Darz and Heath came to blows.

Harjan doused the lamp, and darkness surrounded them. Heath finally found what he was looking for in the bag, a vial she recognized, one of the salves from her supplies.

"We should treat your wounds," he said.

"We don't have time. What if someone comes after us?" She blanched. "Those riders could have been from the village."

"I don't see anyone," Kindle said from his post above them.

"I'm afraid of their fire," she whispered.

Heath reached out to touch her cheek as he had so often in her childhood, when he offered comfort. Then he stopped, caught by the strictures of her title. "We'll take care of you."

She rubbed her palm across her cheek, wiping away tears.

"Don't cry," Darz said. He also reached for her, and also stopped, though in his case it was because Heath put out an arm to block him, his gaze hard.

Darz frowned at him. "If you give me the salve, I'll tend her injuries."

Ginger had absolutely no doubt Heath would refuse—so she almost fell over when he handed the vial to Darz. Her brother spoke stiffly. "See that you take care with her."

"You have my word," Darz said.

Ginger squinted at the two of them. They were talking about more than salve. Currents of meaning and intent were flowing here that she didn't understand.

Heath took a bundle out of the bag and gave it to her. "We brought your tunic and leggings."

She nodded her thanks, too full of love and grief to speak. He looked as if his heart were breaking. "You'll be well again," he murmured. "Harjan, Kindle and I will set things right in the village before anyone can spread false tales about you."

"Can you go back?" They were only three against a town. "It isn't safe."

"We have support." His eyes were dark in the moonlight. "They went too far, Ginger. And *still* you survived. It is a sign from the Dragon-Sun. They cannot deny it."

"It's flaming blasted illegal," Darz said, along with several other choice oaths.

Heath scowled at him. "My sister is a priestess, Goldstone. Show some respect."

She expected Darz to growl, but instead he reddened. Then he said, "My apology, Ginger-Sun."

"It's all right...." She was just barely keeping to her feet. "I think I should sit down."

"Ach," Darz muttered. "I'm an insensitive clod." He reached for her tunic. "I'll spread that out, so you don't have to sit in dirt." Then he stopped. "No, I can't do that. You're going to wear it."

Even now, Ginger couldn't help but smile at his confusion. He could fight off nine men in Sky Flames and face ten days on the Dragon's Claw without a flinch, but when it came to the details of women's lives, he seemed completely lost.

"Here." Heath withdrew a bulky roll from the travel bag and gave it to Darz. "Use this."

Darz opened the roll into a riding blanket. "Yes, that will do." He knelt and spread out the cloth. Then he awkwardly held out his hand to Ginger. "You can sit here."

With his help, she let herself down. Heath stood watching, his posture so stiff, she wondered his muscles didn't crack. She could tell he wanted to punch Darz. Harjan's worried look was plain even in the moonlight. Kindle watched from his post as if he were ready to jump down at any moment. Yet they let Darz help her sit. Maybe after everything that had happened, the proscription against touching her seemed as ludicrous to everyone else as it did to her.

She knelt on the blanket, exhausted. Darz fumbled with the vial, and the honey-scent of the salve wafted around her.

"Do you have water?" he asked someone. "Soap?"

"Soap?" Heath asked. "Why soap?"

"She'll heal faster if I clean and debride the wounds."

Heath didn't look convinced, but he seemed willing to take Darz's word. He dug out a soap and water sac and several cloths, and gave them to Darz. Then he and Harjan moved away, leaving Ginger and Darz in privacy. Their behavior bewildered her, that they would let Darz do this, but she was too worn out to worry about it. Closing her eyes, she bent her head.

Darz knelt behind her and laid a wet cloth on her back. It caught on a shred of her wrap, and she flinched when the cloth pulled a gash in her skin. Darz fumbled with the material, then slipped his hand under the ribbing that held the wrap over her breasts and clumsily snapped the wire. Even knowing he had to remove the cloth to clean her wounds, it was all she could do to stop herself from knocking away his hand as he peeled off what little remained of her wrap. Excruciatingly self-conscious, she folded her arms across her breasts.

"Ginger-Sun, I'm sorry." He sounded as dismayed as she felt. "I don't know how else to clean it properly."

"It's all right." It wasn't, and she didn't know if anything ever would be again. For the second time in her life, the elders had torn apart her family. She knew Heath didn't want her to go away, and she kept expecting him to challenge Darz. She needed help to clean her wounds, but it baffled her that they allowed Darz to give her that aid.

Then, suddenly, she understood. Of course. It was obvious. Darz had tried to tell her earlier: *Your brother has spoken to me.* Darz had compromised her. Then they had lain together under the Claw for over a day. And she would have to travel with him. Heath and Harjan had probably told Darz that if he didn't marry her and restore her honor, they would kill him.

A flush of shame went through Ginger. She turned her head. "You don't have to do this. If my brother is forcing you—"

"Ginger-Sun." He spoke in a low voice. "It's my honor as well as yours. I did this to you, even if I wasn't the one who raised the whip or lit the fire." Awkwardly, he added, "I can't promise to be the husband a woman like you deserves. I'm a firebrand who knows curses far better than words appropriate for a highborn woman. But I'll do my best."

"I'm sorry," she whispered.

"For having to marry me, I can see why. But I'll endeavor to be tolerable." When she gave a small laugh, he kissed her cheek, the barest touch of his lips to her skin. He was such a study in contrasts, rough yet gentle; full of rude oaths one moment, articulate and well-spoken the next; hot-tempered, yes, but he had never directed it against her. So far.

"We don't have any marriage documents," she said.

"Your brother and Harjan wrote the scrolls while they waited for us. They'll keep a copy and give us the others." He parted her hair and put it in front of her shoulders, then went to work cleaning her back. "They certainly got here fast. Apparently someone named Jalla lent them her horse. They say it's the fastest in the village."

"Jalla? You mean the *Archivist's* daughter?"

"That's what they said." He paused in treating her wounds when she flinched. "She thinks you're a treasure. She told your brother the blessing you gave her was a gift."

"I've always liked her." Bitterly she said, "Her mother hates me." At least Kindle hadn't said *I told you so*.

"They see you as a threat." He spread salve over a burn on her shoulder. "And they can't control you because of your status as a priestess. It frightens them."

"But it doesn't bother you?"

"Why should it?" he asked. "Hell, people claim our queen married a warlock or some such nonsense. And look at Aronsdale. The royal house of Dawnfield is supposedly full of mage women. If their kings can choose their brides that way, so can I."

She started to smile, then jerked as he dressed the cuts on her lower back. It was hard to make spells of soothing when she hurt so much, but she managed a small one, and the pain receded.

When Darz finished her back, she turned around. She kept her eyes downcast and her arms folded over her breasts, too self-conscious to look at him. He cleaned the cuts on her face and the outer side of her arms, and smoothed salve over the burns. She couldn't bring herself to unfold her arms or legs. He didn't push; he left it up to her what she would allow.

Finally he set down his cloth and vial. "I can wait out there while you change, if you would like."

"Yes," she said softly. "That would be good."

He went to join the others, leaving her alone in the pocket of rock. With relief, she peeled off the remains of her wrap and did her best to treat her other wounds. Then she put on the tunic and leggings, wincing as they scratched her skin.

When Ginger rejoined the others, Darz was readying Grayrider for travel. She hugged Heath hard, uncaring about the taboos, and squeezed Harjan's hand. It was the first time she had touched either of them in years. None of them could hide their tears. She promised to send news after she and Darz were settled.

When Kindle climbed down from his post, she laid her hand on Grayrider's flank and said, "We'll send him back with a caravan. Your sword, too."

Kindle sounded subdued. "I never meant for this to happen. If I could have taken your place at that stake, I would have done it in a second."

Ginger shuddered. "I'm glad you didn't have to."

He reached over his shoulder, and for a moment she thought he was drawing a weapon. But instead of the sword she had thought he was wearing, he pulled out two scrolls. "I got these from the archive at the temple."

Puzzled, she took the scrolls. "What are they?" It couldn't have been easy for him to fetch them; from what she knew of his reading, he could barely recognize enough symbols to piece out their titles.

Kindle indicated Darz, who was watching from the other side of the horse as he fastened the bags across Grayrider's flanks. "He serves in the army. He thinks he can get a hearing with the queen, or at least her officers."

Ginger knew then what one of the scrolls contained. She hadn't expected him to give up the powder. "I don't know what to say. Thank you."

"If they have an interest in developing it—" He was stuttering. "I know I have no right—after what I did…"

"I'll tell them you can develop it," she promised. She lifted the other scroll. "And this?"

"I don't know what it is—I mean, I do." He spread his hands. "It's your history. I always meant to ask you about it. But I didn't want you to know I—well, I couldn't read it."

Never in an eon would she have thought Kindle, of all people, would realize how she felt about her meager attempts at scholarship. She had assumed she would lose the history. Her voice caught. "I can hardly tell you how much this means to me."

He pushed his hand through his thinning hair. "It all turned out so differently from what I had hoped."

"Be well, Kindle. Promise you won't drink so much ale, yes? And don't be embarrassed about the reading. Talk to Tanner. He can help you." Then she added, "Don't let the elders take away your title over this. You're a good Flame Sentinel."

"I'll miss you, Ginger-Sun." His flush was visible even in the moonlight. He stepped back as Darz came around the horse.

"We should go," Darz said.

Ginger bit her lip, uncertain with her new husband.

Darz wasn't quite ready, though. He pulled out the marriage scrolls to check the wording and added two statements. After his name, he penned *Ar'Quaaz*. It meant "Of Quaaz." It seemed unnecessary to Ginger, until she realized other cities might have other Darz Goldstones. He started to rewrite his entire name, but after he smudged *Darz*, he gave up and left it alone. He also wrote that she and their children would be heirs to his name and all he owned. The marriage already made that true, and from what he had told her, he didn't own a great deal, but it touched her that he wanted to be certain.

Ginger wasn't sure how to be the wife of a soldier. So far he had been rough but kind. It could bode well for the future. She didn't want to think about the other possibility, given what she had seen of his temper, that he would be prone to rages. Although he had never been violent toward her, she had never seen him after he had been drinking.

Darz packed the scrolls, then mounted Grayrider and helped Ginger up in front of him. They rode out into the desert and the night, headed into the unknown.

15

Topaz Passage

Ginger hadn't expected to sleep, but exhaustion weighed on her, and she dozed as they rode. Several times she jerked awake when her head nodded forward. Another time she didn't stir until Darz shifted her upright after she started to slide off the horse. Although the moon gave some light, they couldn't ride fast. She thought Darz would stop, but either he didn't need sleep or he managed to do it sitting up, too. Maybe he had learned in the army how to sleep on a horse without falling off. Grayrider plodded onward.

The next time she awoke, dawn was lighting the sky. A simmering arousal pulled her out of slumber, and gradually she realized Darz was stroking her breast. With each caress, he pulled the scooped neckline of her tunic down a little farther. Much more, and her nipples would be exposed.

Ginger made a noise of protest. With a sigh, he slid his hand to her waist and gave up his campaign on her beleaguered neckline.

"Light of the morning," he said.

"And you," she mumbled, too groggy to think of anything more intelligent.

"You're my light," he said, bending his head to kiss her cheek. Flustered, she pulled away.

"Ah, Ginger," he sighed. "You torture me."

Torture, indeed. He didn't sound the least bit agonized; his voice had a drowsy, sensual quality that suggested pleasure more than anything else.

"I'm sure I don't," she said.

He laughed good-naturedly. "Ah, well, I suppose horseback isn't the most pleasant way to spend your wedding night."

Ginger wasn't certain what to think about it all. It was strange to feel his touch after years of solitude, but not unpleasant. Now, however, she hurt all over. It would be days before she could imagine lying with a man. No, not "a man." Her husband. He wasn't part of the violence she had suffered in the village, but those events darkened everything in her life, including her response to Darz. Her sentence supposedly had nothing to do with sex, but an ugly current of lust had run through the way Dirk Bauxite treated her, Spark, even the Elder, though he tried to hide it, even from himself.

She couldn't tell Darz all that, though. So she said only, "I need some time."

He didn't answer. Nervous, she focused on her opal to make a spell of soothing—and realized it was gone.

"No!" she cried. "My charm. We have to go back—"

"Ginger-Sun." He stopped her by laying his fingers on her lips. "Don't you remember?"

The moment he touched her mouth, she thought of when Dirk

had gagged her. With a frantic reflex, she shoved away his hand. "Remember what?"

"You dropped your rock while you were asleep," he said sharply. "I stopped to retrieve it and let the horse rest. It's in the bags." Then he added, "And damn it, don't push my hand. I don't like it."

Ginger froze. "My apology." With tense formality, she added, "Thank you for picking up the opal." Would he be like Kindle after all? Her mood dimmed.

The desert stretched endlessly around them, shimmering. Heat hadn't yet parched the day, and the golden rolls of land were just touched by the lightening sky. It was beautiful, but unfamiliar. She had no idea where they were and recognized no landmarks.

"Do you know where this is?" she asked. Immediately she regretted the words. If he didn't like her pushing his hand, he would probably resent even more any implication that she doubted his judgment. Spark always reacted that way, and the Archivist.

Darz just said, "Yes, I'm pretty certain. We're traveling southeast, which is the right direction."

"Ah." She heard how stiff that sounded.

He swore under his breath. "Listen, I'm not the most tactful man alive, all right?"

Bewildered, she said, "All right."

"Someone once shoved my hand like that," he said. "Several times, actually. I was eleven. It was my father's cousin. He told me I was stupid, and he knocked away my hand because I was trying to wear armor and I couldn't get on the helmet. It's a silly memory that shouldn't bother me, but it did. So I yelled at you. I shouldn't have." He sounded relieved, as if he hadn't been sure he could get it all out.

Ginger had no idea how to react. No man in Sky Flames would

ever offer an explanation. It just wasn't done. It took her a while to find her voice. Finally she said, "I thought you were angry at me for saying I needed more time before we, well…" She couldn't so easily forget the taboos, even of speaking about such subjects. "You know."

"For saints sake! Do you think I'm a monster?"

Ginger winced. "No. Just loud." Too late, her common sense caught up with her mouth and she realized how much tact *that* reply lacked. This morning her mind was full of cotton. It wasn't surprising given the way she had spent the night, but she didn't want to alienate Darz before she even had a chance to know him.

To her surprise, he let out a hearty laugh. "So everyone tells me." He leaned forward so he could see her face. "Take as much time as you need. You are so delectable, though, I can't promise I won't misbehave. If I do, just slap me, eh?"

It took her a moment to comprehend he was teasing her. Men in Sky Flames *never* teased. They also rarely gave compliments. She knew her father had loved her mother, but she had never heard him tell her so or say she was beautiful.

Her shoulders came down from their hunched posture. She was beginning to suspect that behind Darz's bluster was a man with more kindness than he felt it appropriate for a warrior to show.

"If you misbehave," she said, her lips curving upward, "I shall send you to your room without dinner."

"Is that a smile I see?" He sat up straighter behind her. "You should do it more often. It's lovely."

"Thank you," she said softly.

They continued in silence, but it was less strained. Darz let Gray-rider walk, to rest the horse. Sunrise, another aspect of the Sunset, spread her rosy glow across the desert. Every now and then Darz brought Grayrider around to face the way they had come. For several moments he would scan the desert. Then they would continue on their way.

Eventually he said, "No one seems to have followed us."

"Good." If they were lucky, the elders wouldn't send anyone after her.

"Those riders last night," Darz said. "Have you seen them before?"

"I think so." His question felt off, she couldn't say why. "I don't know where. I don't think they're from Sky Flames."

"How can you tell?"

She realized what was odd: he listened to her. The Elder and Archivist often dismissed her observations. Spark never paid attention. Darz just talked to her, naturally, without strain. It was a good question, too. She wasn't sure *how* she knew the riders.

After a moment, she said, "Their manner of dress."

"You could tell from so far away, in the dark?"

"It's their hoods, with those peaked cowls. No one in Sky Flames wears those." Suddenly it hit her. "They were in the plaza! Two men from Jazid, I think. Nomads. They had those charcoal scarves knitted from a thick yarn."

"Saints almighty," Darz said. "You could get all that while you were being dragged to your death?"

"Well, they were right in front of me."

"I wish my trail scouts were that observant," he muttered. "Why would two nomads from Jazid be in Sky Flames?"

"I've no idea. But we aren't that far from the border."

Darz was quiet for a while. Then he said, "Your brother's group was carrying lights. We weren't. If the nomads followed anyone, it was probably them. They might not have seen us leave."

She shifted uneasily. "Why would they follow us?"

"Did they see you in the square?"

"Dirk and Spark dragged me right past them."

"So they saw you bound to that pole up on the platform?"

Her face heated. "Yes. They and half the village." It hadn't actually been that many, but it felt that way. "Why?"

"I should think it is obvious."

"It's not to me."

He cleared his throat. "You are very pretty and very, shall we say, womanly in your shape, Ginger-Sun. You also obviously didn't have anyone's protection. They probably wanted to see if I was going to strand you in the desert. They would have picked you up."

"You really think they would have helped me?"

He gave a harsh laugh. "Hell, no. The T'Ambera nomad tribe in Jazid sells pleasure slaves."

"Oh." The more she learned about the world she had thought would be so exciting, the less she liked it.

"Do you remember that scream in the temple?" Darz asked.

"It was awful."

"You've reminded me where I've heard it before." His hand tightened on her waist. "In battle. It's a Jazid war cry."

It made no sense to Ginger. "Why would a Jazid warrior come into the temple and scream? Were they chasing you?"

"It's possible. But it doesn't make sense. Why attack me? We and Jazid fought on the same side. Besides, if they were after me and knew I was there, they would have killed me."

"Then why scream in my temple?"

"To frighten you. Same with the blood in your room. They hound their targets. You were guarded, so they wanted to panic you, drive you into the open or into doing something unwise." He spoke grimly. "You're lucky Harjan posted guards that night. You're even lucky Spark followed you to the Dragon's Claw. If you were the one the nomads wanted, those guards are probably the only reason you're here with me instead of in chains."

She didn't want to believe her freedom could be that ephemeral. "They wouldn't kidnap a priestess."

He snorted. "They would damn well take any woman they wanted. Besides, Jazid doesn't have priestesses. Their temples serve the Shadow Dragon."

"The Shadow Dragon is evil."

"Oh, Ginger."

"He's *not* a myth."

He wrapped his arms around her. "I certainly have no doubt the nomads exist. They won't get near you. I swear it."

"But I don't understand why they were in Sky Flames." It was ludicrous to think they would travel to some isolated village in Taka Mal on the off chance they might find a nubile priestess to carry off.

"They might be the ones who attacked me," Darz said uneasily. "I was actually glad your Elder sentenced me to stay up on that promontory. It was the most inaccessible place in this region, and he posted guards to ensure I didn't sneak off. I was safer there than in town."

"But it gets so cold! And how did you bring supplies?"

His voice lightened. "You should have more confidence in your husband. I've dealt with worse conditions in training exercises." After a pause, he admitted, "Carrying my gear up wasn't easy. But once I was there, I just wrapped up in the blankets and slept for most of four days."

"So even if the nomads knew, they couldn't get to you."

"Apparently." He shifted his arms protectively around her. "Or they might have nothing to do with me. They may just be travelers looking for Taka Mal women."

"Whatever for?"

He answered obliquely. "Jazid is an incredibly wealthy country. They have even richer mineral deposits than we do. But the population is sparse, given the rough land and climate. They've long offered incentives to miners to immigrate—free land in the most lucrative areas. In return, the miner gives a portion of his profits to the government."

"It sounds sensible," Ginger said. "But I don't see what that has to do with Taka Mal women."

"Only men come. Few women want to go to a country with such harsh laws, where legally they're property." He shifted her in his hold. "And girl infants don't always receive the same care as boys. So their mortality rate is higher. Add it all together, century after century, and you get an imbalance. Estimates of their population range from sixty to eighty percent male."

"Gods," she murmured. "That's even worse than Sky Flames."

He guided Grayrider more to the north. "Taka Mal had similar problems in the past. We've changed a lot, though, and the balance is much better here. But in Jazid the customs are too entrenched. The rarer women become, the more restricted their lives."

It sounded unpleasant. "I can't imagine Sky Flames would be a place to look for more. There's so few of us."

"It would be an odd choice," he acknowledged.

She shivered in his arms, though the day was warming as the sun rose. "Maybe those riders were spirit executioners sent by the Shadow Dragon to find you."

"Shadows, eh? I better watch out."

"Don't laugh. You were the one who told me about them."

"I did?"

"Yes. Or perhaps you said assassins."

"Oh. You mean the political sect." The humor faded from his voice. "They're very much men, not spirits. Supposedly the former King of Jazid, the Atajazid D'az Ozar, formed their sect. It could just be a story, though."

Her alarm surged. "Darz! They must be looking for you. They might try to assassinate you again."

"Slow down," he said, laughing. "We don't even know if the assassins exist, much less that two Jazid nomads who happen by your village are secret killers out to get me, of all people."

"Have you ever antagonized anyone in the Jazid army?"

He didn't answer, and that made her wonder.

Eventually he did say, "No, I don't think so."

She spoke uneasily. "Why did you wait so long to answer?"

"I know nothing about you. Yet you want me to trust you."

She blinked at that. "You mean you don't?"

"How do I know you have nothing to do with those nomads?"

"How can you even *ask* such a thing?"

His breath stirred her hair. "What happened to me was no robbery that escalated into violence. They wanted me dead, and the harder I fought, the more viciously they ripped me apart. Now you're bothered because I don't trust the lovely, vulnerable maiden who tended me back to health and I somehow ended up married to her under threat of death from her brother. A girl I really don't know at all. Would *you* trust you, if you were me?"

"Probably not," she admitted. Softly she said, "We live in such a violent world. It's a wonder any of us survive."

"I know. And something else." Tension crackled in his voice.

"Yes?"

"We had trouble getting to you in the plaza last night. It wasn't just the sentinels trying to stop us. The place was crowded with people who wouldn't let us by."

"But you got through." She would be forever grateful.

"Well, that's just the thing, Ginger. Everyone suddenly started to run away. Not from us. From the plaza."

"Oh." She knew what he was getting at now. Sweat broke out on her brow.

"I might believe that sparks from the stake started fires in one or two of the buildings around the plaza," he told her. "But *all* of them? At *exactly* the same moment?"

"The Dragon-Sun was making his displeasure known."

"Like hell."

Ah, well. She hadn't really expected that to work. She gazed at the topaz desert with its rolling landscape. "What do you think caused it, Darz?"

"What I think," he said, "is that you don't need that rock to do spells."

She decided that was better left unanswered, lest she provoke him into abandoning her out here.

"Ginger, answer me," he said.

"I don't know what you expect me to say."

"This dragon-powder Kindle created—I think it may have a great deal of military potential."

She wasn't sure why he switched topics, but it relieved her. "You saw what it could do."

"He says you told him how to make it."

"Not me. A scroll in the archive. The one he gave me last night just before we left."

"Did you make that up so he wouldn't suspect you caused the explosions?"

"What!" She saw what he was getting at. "I absolutely did not cause any explosions, Darz Goldstone."

"No explosions."

"None!"

"Just fires."

"Yes." Too late, she realized what she had admitted. "Damn," she muttered.

He chuckled. "I thought priestesses didn't know such language."

He was devilishly clever. Would he condemn her now that he realized the extent of her transgressions?

"How do you do it?" Darz said.

Ginger blinked. In Sky Flames, they had only one response for unwelcome behavior: censure the guilty person. A simple, "How do you do it?" was outside of her experience.

"I don't know," was all she could say.

"I had thought it was linked to your opal," he mused. "But I had the rock when the fires in the plaza started."

"I thought it was the opal, too." She felt defenseless, exposing her vulnerability. "But it may be the shape. A round window in the Arch-Tower worked. It wasn't as strong, but it was larger, so it gave—gave me—" She stopped. After years of hiding, she couldn't reveal so much, especially not here, where she had nowhere to go if he cast her off.

"What's wrong?" he said.

"Are you going to turn me out?"

"Gods above, why would I do that?"

"They did in the village." To put it mildly.

"That was their stupidity." His hair rustled as he shook his head. "Look at what they had. A priestess who genuinely wanted to improve their lives, someone who enjoyed dedicating her life to them. A girl who shouldered far more responsibility for their temple than they had any right to expect, and who has done it since she was a child. Without complaining. Someone who found time to educate herself, and who knew how to unearth valuable knowledge in their archives. Someone who might have abilities that could benefit their entire village, gifts of warmth, light, comfort. An incredibly beautiful girl that the men in that town should have been down on their knees courting. And what did the idiots do with this gift from the gods? Try to burn her at the stake. Right. They didn't deserve you, Ginger-Sun."

His viewpoint was so different, it took a while to turn it around in her thoughts. Finally she said, "You have an unusual way of seeing things."

"That was tactful." He gave his vigorous laugh. "Better than, 'You're a strange man, Darz Goldstone.'"

Ginger began to relax. Apparently he didn't plan to turn her out. In fact, he didn't seem angry at all.

"Tell me something," he said. "If I had asked you to go away with me before all this happened, would you have?"

Leave the familiar? He had the allure of the unknown, of exciting places and events, but she couldn't have imagined her life away from Sky Flames.

"The elders would never have allowed it," she said.

"What about what you wanted?"

16

Sun King

J'Hiza was the first town Ginger had ever seen besides Sky Flames. It was gigantic, teeming with life, over a thousand citizens. Grayrider's hooves clopped on the yellow cobblestones as Darz rode down a street, guiding Grayrider through people, sheep, geese, and squawking rock-hens. Signs creaked on poles, and merchants stood in front of their shops, gossiping with their neighbors. Scents filled the air: spices, perfumes, and the stink of animals crammed together.

"What do you think?" Darz asked. "Too noisy?"

"It's different." She hesitated. "But interesting."

He laughed in that easy way of his. "I'm not sure that's an accolade to J'Hiza."

She wasn't certain, either. "Where are we going?"

"To the guilds, to find merchants who are about to travel. They might let us go with them if we pay."

"We have no coins." They had nothing to trade, either, except the horse and sword, neither of which belonged to them.

"They choose a husband for the priestess."

"For flaming sake. That practice stopped ages ago."

"Not in Sky Flames."

He gave a snort. "You know why? Because they all wanted you in their bed. They didn't want to admit it, though, because they aren't supposed to think of you that way."

"Darz!" Her face was hot. "You think about sex too much."

His laugh softened. "What do you expect, when I have my sexy bride sitting in front of me with her body rubbing mine every time the horse takes a damn step? It's driving me mad."

She couldn't help but smile. "Is this where I get to slap you?" She would have never dared tease a man in Sky Flames that way. She didn't know what possessed her to do it now.

"I shouldn't have said that," Darz grumbled. "You'll never let me forget." Although he kissed the back of her neck. "I saw you smile, Ginger. Someday yet I may get you to laugh."

She flushed, and this time it wasn't from embarrassment. He stirred reactions she wasn't ready for, she enjoyed them.

But then she said, "I think not yet."

"Why the blazes not?"

"We have more to worry about." She pointed west where, shimmering in the pure light of early morning, the bulb towers of a city glistened.

"Your brother gave me your dowry," Darz said.

She hadn't expected *that*. "What dowry?"

"One hundred silver hexa-coins."

"Really?" It was a decent amount, more than she had ever seen. "I didn't know. I hope you aren't disappointed." She had no idea if he came from a well enough placed family to expect a larger dowry.

He brushed his hand over her hair. "It's fine."

"Darz?"

"Hmm?"

"Will it disappoint your family when you show up with me?"

He was quiet for so long, she wished she hadn't asked. Then he said, "I don't think so."

That wasn't exactly a ringing assertion. "You aren't sure?"

"It's complicated. My family is small. But intense."

"Oh. I see." She didn't really, but she was too tired to pursue it, even if he had been willing to tell her about them. It hurt too much to think about facing more censure. Nor was that her only concern. Now that the sun had risen, she couldn't create spells of succor, and her injuries hurt terribly.

"Can we stop first, before we go to the guild?" she asked.

He sighed, and she thought he would tell her no. Instead he said, "Aye, Ginger-Sun. I meant to." He bent his head over her. "You are different from other women I've known."

She wasn't certain how to take that. "Why?"

"They expect coddling. You keep going, always stoic, and hesitate to make even the simplest, most reasonable request."

"Oh." That didn't sound like he was disappointed. "Thank you."

So they went, looking for an inn.

* * *

Darz dumped the bags on the floor of their room, which was on the second story of the inn. Logs were stacked by the fireplace, but Ginger couldn't imagine needing a fire. The morning had barely started, yet already the heat sweltered, making it hard to remember how cold the desert became at night. The room had a table with two rickety chairs, and a bed against one wall with a chamber pot beneath it. A washstand in one corner held an earthenware bowl, a ewer, and a metal tray with soap. High in the wall, a window glowed with early morning light, though the sun was too low to slant through the glass.

"You rest," Darz said. "I'll find the guilds. I've seen signs for glass-makers, weavers and crop houses."

"You need to rest, too." She stood in the center of the room, acutely aware she was alone in a strange town with a man she had known for less time than anyone else in her life.

Now that she could see Darz in the light, she realized how awful he looked. A ragged black beard covered his face, bristly and thick, and sand crusted his clothes. The scar snaked from the corner of his eye to his ear. His hair hadn't been washed or brushed since the last time she had done it, fourteen days ago. He was a mess. She didn't even know what he actually looked like. He had been injured at first, covered with bandages, and then the two of them had been buried.

Perhaps that was why neither Kindle nor Heath recognized him. She had hoped one of them might know Darz from their time in the army, to corroborate what he had said about himself. She told herself he looked different with his beard. Besides, thousands of men served in the army. Their chances of meeting him were slim. She could almost believe that explanation. Almost.

"Why are you staring as if I am a misbehaved boy?" he asked.

She felt her face redden. "My apology."

"Accepted," he growled. "Now please answer my question."

"It's just that—are you going out like that to see if anyone will let us travel with them?"

"Like what?"

She cleared her throat and shifted her feet. Watching her, Darz squinted. Then he went to the wash table and dumped the soap off the tray. Holding up the metal, he peered at his reflection. With a wince, he said, "Ah, Ginger-Sun, you are ever the soul of diplomacy. I look like an ogre someone dug out of a mine." He glanced at her. "Don't worry. I'll make myself presentable."

She hesitated. "Perhaps a bath, too, if they have one."

"Ach! All right." Laughing, he said, "I am not usually this scruffy, wife. You haven't married a scalawag."

A tentative smile curved her lips. "I'm glad."

He stretched his arms. "Do you need more salve on your back?"

"Later." Shyly, she said, "I would like to clean up now."

"Ah." He stood and smiled at her. After a moment, though, he said, "Oh! Do you want me to leave?"

"If you don't mind."

"Ah, well," he said. "I wouldn't want to be around my smelly self, either, if I were you."

This time she did smile. "It is good for everything about a man to be strong."

He burst out laughing. "All right! I'll find a bathhouse."

"I'll wait here." She heard how soft her voice was next to his robust style. She hoped he didn't think she sounded as if she were in need of coddling.

"I'll try not to be long." He hefted up one of the bags and went to the door. Pausing, he looked back at her. "Don't open this for anyone. I'm going to lock it, and I have a key, so you won't need to let anyone in. Don't go out, not even down to the common room. It looked a little rough."

"I'm just going to sleep," she said.

"Good." He grinned at her. "I'll see you, then."

"That sounds fine." It felt unreal to be with him in this strange place. She had to remind herself the taboos no longer applied. Yet as strange as this felt, it wasn't unwelcome. For the first time in years, she looked forward to her life. She felt apprehension, too, for the unknown and her uncertainties about Darz. She had no idea what to expect, whether they would suit each other or struggle to eke out a living. But her new life held promise, if she and Darz could find their way together. Right now, on the doorstep of a future she had never imagined, she could hope, for reality hadn't yet given her a reason otherwise.

After Darz left, Ginger undressed and washed with the soap and the water in the ewer. She treated her injuries as best she could, steeling herself against the pain. To dry off, she used a clean shirt she found in the travel bag, and silently promised Darz she would wash it later. It was odd to think she would be doing such tasks for him now, too, as well as herself.

It was too hot to wear anything. Nor did she want garments to abrade her wounds while she slept. So she slipped under the sheets in her bare skin. Although worn and patched, the linens smelled of soap. It wasn't such a bad place, nothing as pleasant as the temple, but she could adapt.

Ginger didn't know what wages an army officer earned. At least she and Darz had her dowry to help them get established. She might be able to join a temple in Quaaz, not as a priestess, since they would have their own, but as an assistant. She and Darz couldn't live in the temple if she wasn't the priestess. Perhaps he lived in a barracks. Or maybe he had a house. She didn't need anywhere grand, just a home where they could raise their children.

The thought of making those children made her body tingle the way it had this morning when she awoke to his caresses. Her thoughts drifted....

Light awoke Ginger. She sensed it even with her eyes closed. Heat surrounded her, and she should have been afraid after what happened in Sky Flames. But this inviting warmth didn't hurt. She could burn in this fire unharmed and survive as if it were a crucible.

Disoriented, she opened her eyes to find that golden light filled the room. Holding the sheet in front of her body, she sat up with her back to the wall. Through the glare, she could just make out the door; it was still closed and bolted. Sweat beaded her forehead and palms and dripped down her body. No candle glowed in the room. No lamp burned. Nothing showed anywhere to cause this incredible radiance.

A shape took form within—and of—the light.

At first it was no more than a swirl of color: gold, red, yellow, topaz. Gradually a figure of fire emerged. Its long neck arched to the high ceiling. The great reptilian wings spanned the room and went *through* the walls, unconfined by barriers. Its gigantic tail curled around on the floor and ended in a deadly ball of spikes. Flaming scales covered its body.

"Dragon-Sun," she whispered. "Have you come for me?"

The colors coalesced into a new shape, no longer a dragon, but a form she had never seen in any statue or picture. He had become a man. He wore clothes of flame and his skin glowed with the luminance of the sun. He was twice the height of a mortal man, and his head reached the ceiling. His hair of flames wavered in the air. When he stepped forward, fire rippled along his body. She shrank against the wall and clenched the sheet to her chest.

The man blazed, yet nothing burned. He sat on the bed, and the sheets didn't burst into fire. Flames from his body enveloped her with warmth but caused no harm. Even sitting, he was taller than any man, his head larger, his shoulders broader, his legs longer. He reached out his arm, and she pressed back against the wall.

Ginger-Sun. His voice filled her mind.

She didn't try to speak, knowing her voice would tremble. *I am your priestess*, she thought.

He touched her shoulder. I am pleased.

I'm sorry I transgressed against you.

You have not. His thought darkened as he lowered his arm. The others have transgressed.

Would you have let them burn me?

I am a ball of fire, not the conscience of man. I cannot control the minds of you who call yourselves humanity. You are responsible for your choices and the deeds you commit, whether they be great or heinous. The flames around his body flared until they blinded her. She lifted the sheet and covered her eyes.

Look at me, Ginger-Sun.

Shaking, she lowered her hands. She could see, but his light filled the room, radiant and terrifying. *Will you burn me?*

No. His voice rumbled within her. Seeing you in agony did not please me. Had no one taken you from those flames, then when I rose the next morning I would have burned the land until it set the village afire.

Then you aren't angry with me?

No. You are my bride, Ginger-Sun.

Ah, no. It was true, she had taken the vow. But she had assumed it was symbolic. *All priestesses are your brides.*

This is true. But you please me more than the others.

Dragon-Sun—I am sworn to another.

Anger saturated his thought. He calls me a myth. A tale. A lie.

He doesn't understand! Please, don't kill him.

I shall not. The light brightened, so brilliant she could barely make out his shape. I have another punishment for him. He reached forward and pulled off the sheet she was holding. Terrified, she grabbed for it, but it burned away in front of her, leaving the bed untouched, no ashes, no sign it had ever existed. She crossed her arms over her breasts.

You are not his wife yet.

We have documents—

But you have not yet been wife to him. So you shall be to me. His punishment will be to lose his bride to the sun.

No! Ginger thought she must be mad to refuse the sun-god. *He is my husband. I must be true to him.*

His radiance vanished. Nor did any light come from the window outside. The room went dark. Nothing showed in that blackness but the burning gold orbs of his eyes.

You dare to defy the sun?

She was shaking too much to speak. But she could form words in her mind. *I cannot betray my vow to him.*

And what of yours to me?

But…I thought it was a symbol. Not literal.

For other priestesses.

I am not worthy to be your consort.

If I choose you, then you are worthy.

She wanted to entreat him to change his mind. But she had given her oath to him before she ever met Darz. She couldn't deny that promise. Never in a thousand years would she have presumed to think of herself as the sun's true consort. She had no right to want Darz instead. Knowing that didn't change how she felt about Darz, but she couldn't break her vow.

A tear ran down her face. *Dragon-Sun, I am honored beyond words.*

Do not cry, Ginger-Sun. His light returned, softer than before. With reluctance, he added, He is a fortunate man.

Her breath caught. Did he mean what she thought?

If you want him, you may have him.

An intense relief washed over her. *I thank you.*

He leaned across the bed, his torso so large that the space between them was nothing. I can be generous. But not quite yet—He put his blazing hand behind her neck and drew her forward. She tried to turn away, but he caught her chin, and flames flared around her face. Heat surged in her. When he kissed her, and touched her, she blazed in an erotic fire.

Don't! she thought. He tempted her with a passion that could consume her if she let it. *Stop.*

I will not force you. His thoughts faded as he let her go. You are true to him. It is good. The light was almost gone. But, ah, Ginger-Sun, I have wanted to do that since the day you pledged yourself to me….

Then the room was empty, and outside, the sky was light again. Trembling, she lay down and pulled the other sheet over her body.

She closed her eyes, not because she thought she could ever sleep again, but to hide from the sunlight slanting through the window.

Sleep, his thought whispered.

Ginger awoke knowing she wasn't alone. The sunlight was gone from the room, and the sky outside had darkened into purple twilight. The air had cooled with the onset of night, and the one remaining sheet on the bed wasn't enough. But someone was lying behind her, his body warm against hers, the contours of his chest ridged against her back. She lay still, afraid the dragon had changed his mind and decided against generosity.

The man behind her snored.

Her lips curved upward. She knew that noisy sound from when she had sat vigil over her patient in the temple. She turned over—and almost screamed.

A stranger lay with her. She started to push him away, then stopped with her palms on his shoulders. The "stranger" had a scar running from the outer corner of his eye to his ear. It was Darz, but unlike she had ever seen him. No trace of his beard remained. His clean-shaven face revealed his high cheekbones and regular features. He had washed, brushed and trimmed his hair. He smelled good, too, like soap.

He grunted in his sleep and snorted, sounding like scalawag Darz instead of this finely apportioned stranger. She smiled, grateful to find him alive and well, instead of burned to death by an angry dragon.

She sank back into sleep.

"Ginger?" Darz's voice curled into her sensual dreams.

Opening her eyes, she looked up at him in the moonlight that flowed through the window. She was lying on her back, and he was stretched out alongside her, his head propped up on one arm as he looked down at her.

"Light of the moon," she said.

"How do you feel?"

"Better." She wouldn't have expected to recover so fast, but her wounds hardly hurt at all. She was aware she was bare under Darz, but in the moonlight, it didn't embarrass her.

"You look very fine," she said.

His expression softened, and he kissed her, though just lightly. Perhaps he was waiting to see if she really would slap him. She put her arms around his neck and returned the kiss. Having almost lost him had made her realize just how much she wanted him.

With an exhale, Darz lowered himself on top of her. When he caressed her, she felt as if she were an instrument tuned by the dragon and then left unplayed. She pulled him closer, and his kiss deepened.

He moved his lips to her ear. "Your skin is hot. Like you have a fever."

"For you," she said. She had refused a sun-god for him, and in return, or perhaps retaliation, the dragon had left her with this unquenched fever.

Darz explored her in ways she had thought no one would ever know. Then he slid down and took her breast into his mouth. She was so startled, she almost pushed him away. But his lips closed around her nipple where the Dragon-Sun had touched her, and heat burst over her, exquisite. Her fingers tangled in his hair while she sighed.

"Ah, Ginger, I can't—" He pulled himself up along her body and kissed her some more. When he touched her below, at first she thought it was his hand. Then he groaned and thrust hard, tearing into her. She cried out, not only from pain, but from the blaze that flared through her. She pressed against him and he responded with a powerful rhythm, until the heat broke in a surge of pleasure. He covered her mouth with a kiss and muffled her cries.

Ginger slowly came back to herself, enough to realize Darz was still on top of her, his body flattening hers. She shifted under him and he grunted as he rolled onto the mattress. He lay alongside her with one leg thrown across both of hers. She turned her head toward him, and her forehead scraped the hint of stubble on his chin.

"I liked that," she whispered.

He gave a low, uneven laugh. "I could tell." He kissed her forehead. "So did I." He lay for a while, his breath calming. Then he said, "Did I hurt you?"

"No...a little. It's fine." With a yawn, she added, "I would have thought it would bother my back more."

"We should make sure it's all right."

"Tomorrow..."

Sleepily, he said, "I know. But we should check now. You may not feel pain, but if anything tore open, we should treat it. Or it might get worse."

Too drowsy to protest, she rolled onto her stomach. She felt his hand on her back, exploring. His palm moved over her behind, where she had no cuts at all, and between her legs, where she still tingled. She lay enjoying it for a while, until finally she murmured, "Behave yourself."

He laughed softly and slid his hand up her spine, over her shoulders, and along her arms. "That's odd."

"Hmmm…?"

"The cuts, the welts, the burns—they're almost gone."

"They can't be already."

"I know. But they are." He paused. "Maybe you just needed sleep."

"I've tended people with similar injuries. Sleep helps, but never this much, this fast." She hesitated, not wanting him to become angry or ridicule her. "Darz?"

"Yes?" He lay down and turned her over so he could pull her into his arms.

"You mustn't get upset."

His arm muscles tensed. "About what?"

"I had a visitor today."

"*What?*" He pushed up on his elbow. "I told you not to open the door!"

"I didn't."

"Then how did someone get in?"

"He didn't need the door."

"*He?*" He grasped her arm. "What happened?"

"It was the Dragon-Sun."

His grip eased. "Oh, Ginger."

"It's true. He came here at noon. He said he would punish you for not believing in him. I told him I was promised to you. He was angry. At first. Then he wasn't anymore."

She expected him to say she had dreamt it all. She wasn't even certain she hadn't. When instead Darz just kept looking at her, she blinked.

"What is it?" she asked.

"You said this happened at noon?"

"Yes. The sun was shining through the window."

"How long did it last?"

"Maybe fifteen minutes."

"And then what?" His voice had an odd quality. Fear?

"He let me go and went back into the sky."

"Gods above," he said. "It can't be."

This certainly wasn't the response she had expected. "What do you mean?"

"Something impossible happened today. At noon, for about fifteen minutes, we had an eclipse."

"A what?"

"When the moon passes in front of the sun."

"I don't understand."

He spoke uneasily. "I'm not sure I do, either. The palace astronomers in Quaaz claim the earth goes around the sun, not the reverse. And the moon goes around the earth. Sometimes it gets between the earth and the sun. When that happens, we cannot see the sun. So it gets dark."

"And that happened today?"

"Yes. It scared a lot of people." He shook his head. "We had a full moon last night. If it was on that side of the earth, how could it get between the earth and the sun today?"

She just looked up at him.

"I'm not saying it's true," he added. "But if it were…"

"Yes?"

"You would really defy the Dragon-Sun for me?"

"Yes."

His grin flashed. "Brave woman." He lay down and tickled her belly button. "You were as fiery as the sun tonight."

Her lips curved upward. "I thought you were sleepy."

"That was before."

He drew her closer, and she responded with an intensity she wouldn't have expected even a few days ago. For so long she had thought she would never know a man's embrace. Darz was a gift. She didn't know if this passion had always been within her, waiting for its time, or if the sun had released it, but she soon stopped caring, or thinking at all, as she and Darz celebrated their own fire.

The potter's caravan was small, only six merchants and a handful of helpers. They were headed to Quaaz instead of Taza Qu, but Darz seemed reconciled to the change in his plans. They agreed to take the newlyweds if Darz would guard the caravan. Although Ginger could see it was an equitable arrangement, it meant he spent all day riding up and down the procession. She hardly saw him, and she missed his company.

The merchants wore cowled robes over leggings and tunics, similar to Jazid nomads, but they dyed the cloth yellow and topaz rather than charcoal. They all looked the same; she recognized Darz only because he was taller and huskier than the other men. No one seemed bothered when she adopted their style of dress. Even if they had known she was a priestess, which they didn't, she doubted they would expect her to wear the wrap. If she did, they would have to carry her in a litter, which would be annoying for everyone. She gladly quit the ceremonial garments; she loved this freedom.

The days stretched out as they traveled west, and the sun blazed. At night, temperatures plummeted, but she and Darz didn't mind, ensconced in their tent. She learned the ways of his touch and his scarred body, yet not of his heart. She wanted to believe he had begun to trust her, but he remained silent about himself.

He also bought her a horse. In Sky Flames, no one had wanted her to ride. She had learned by coaxing Heath, who could never tell her "no" on anything. These merchants took it for granted that anyone who traveled with a caravan could ride and do it in sensible clothes. For now, the lifestyle of the caravan suited her.

Ginger missed the temple and her work, though, tending to people and the village. She missed the cool stone spaces and burbling fountain. She longed for the serenity of those days, before reality had shredded her illusions.

Today Darz patrolled the heavily laden wagons on horseback. He intended to return Grayrider to Kindle as soon as he and Ginger were settled and he found an army company or caravan traveling east. As Ginger rode up alongside him, he maneuvered Grayrider to give her room. Only his dark eyes were visible; he kept a scarf over his face as protection from the sun and wind-driven sand. Far up ahead in the topaz desert, the green line of an oasis bordered the horizon.

"The caravan master tells me we will reach Quaaz the day after tomorrow," Ginger said. "Maybe tomorrow night."

He nodded, surveying the land around them. "It will be good to be home."

"Do you have a house there?" She had tried asking more obliquely, with no success.

He continued to scan the desert. "I live with my cousin and her husband."

She hadn't expected that. "Do you mean the cousin you were pledged to marry?"

"That's right."

No wonder he avoided talking about his living arrangements. "Isn't that awkward?"

He glanced at her, his eyes enigmatic. "No. Should it be?"

"Her husband trusts you?"

He gave a snort. "Her husband doesn't like me in the least. But that would be true regardless. He knows if Lima and I had wanted to marry, we would have done so long ago."

It still sounded thorny to Ginger. But maybe they couldn't afford separate households. "Will there be room for me?"

"Enough." He went back to studying the desert. He always seemed on guard these days, alert for an attack. It might be his normal state. Or maybe he was tense because of what had happened to him. She wished he would talk to her more.

"Is there a temple near where you live?" she asked.

"I think so."

"And?"

He peered at a ridge to their south, shading his eyes with his hand. "And what?"

"Will you tell me about it?"

"Nothing to tell, really."

Dryly she said, "Perhaps I should try to extract one of your teeth. You might be more willing to let me do that."

He shot her a startled look. "I should hope not."

"Why won't you talk to me? Don't you want to?"

"Well, yes." He sounded bewildered.

"But?"

"But I think I should pay attention to my duties instead of chatting with my distracting wife."

"Oh. Of course." She flushed with embarrassment. "I'm sorry. I will leave you to your work."

"Ginger—"

She nodded formally, then wheeled her horse around and rode toward the end of the caravan. She felt like a fool. If she kept making such mistakes, he would rue the day he ended up saddled with her. But saints, she dreaded the thought of living in the same house with his former betrothed, especially if Darz was often like this, so distant and preoccupied. She kicked her horse into a gallop and sped past the end of the caravan, her robe billowing out behind her.

After a few minutes, she took a deep breath and slowed her horse to a walk. It wasn't Darz's fault. He had never asked for a wife; Heath and Harjan had forced her on him. She knew other men who didn't talk to their wives. Perhaps, because he held her so close at night, she read more into his interest than existed.

In the ten days they had been traveling, thoughts of Sky Flames had haunted her. She couldn't believe they had sentenced her to die. Darz expected her to demand vengeance, but that felt hollow. She wanted justice. She wanted the elders to *know* what they had done was wrong and abhorrent. She wanted them to have no choice but to face the truth, now and for as long as they lived. That would mean more to her than any act of revenge.

The power to exact vengeance simmered within her, ready to erupt. She had never before comprehended her ability to do violence. Calling forth the killing spells of fire had left her feeling ill, but if she ever was that desperate again, she might again evoke that dark power. It was *within* her, and she didn't know how to deal with it. She turned away from revenge because she feared herself more than those who had wronged her.

Ginger brought her horse around and headed for the caravan. It had moved ahead, and it would take a while to catch up, but as long as she had them in sight, she wasn't worried. She valued her freedom out here in the vast desert.

After a few minutes, a man came galloping back to her. She wasn't sure who; without a comparison to others, she couldn't tell if he was large enough to be Darz. As he drew nearer, though, she thought it was him. It wasn't his size so much as the way he held himself, as if he could command the world from horseback. She thought he was probably a cavalry man. He wouldn't talk about his military service, though. If he hadn't been willing to go back to Quaaz, she would have wondered if he were a deserter after all.

As he reached her, the man reined in his horse, and it stamped its hooves, impatient. "Never come out here alone!" he bellowed. "Gods only know what could happen! Stay with the caravan!"

That was definitely Darz. "Don't yell," she said, rubbing her ear. "I hear you fine."

"Someone could pick you off the desert," he thundered. "Just like sand-cats prey on stragglers from the goat herds. Ba-zing! You're gone."

Ba-zing? She tried not to smile, because he was obviously upset. "I'm sorry."

He spoke more quietly. "You worried me. You shouldn't let yourself be separated from the others."

She hadn't meant to trouble him. "I'll be more careful."

"Good." He rode with her toward the caravan. "Why were you angry with me before?"

"I wasn't angry." She felt at such a loss. "My whole life has been turned around and spilled out until I have only the unknown. And you. But the only time we do anything together is at night."

"It's good," he said, his voice warming.

"I need more."

"More?" He grinned. "You'll wear me out." He didn't sound at all displeased with the prospect of his imminent exhaustion.

Her face heated. "That's not what I meant."

"You are my wife. It is what a man does with his wife."

"You can talk to me, too."

"I do!"

"But you say so little."

Frustration leaked into his voice. "Women talk a great deal to one another. All this gossip and such. I am not a woman."

"What do you do when you have to command your men?" she inquired, exasperated. "Grunt?"

"That's different." His voice lightened. "They at least do what I tell them."

She couldn't see his face, but she recognized his tone. He was teasing her. "They have my sympathy."

He brought Grayrider in as close as he could to her horse and leaned over to her. "If you bedevil me," he said in a low voice, "tonight I will find a suitable way to return the favor."

She couldn't help but laugh. He would undoubtedly tickle her mercilessly, which he had discovered made her laugh and struggle. "Darz, it is you who bedevil me."

"Hah! I will see you tonight." He took off then. They had reached the caravan, and she rode in back while he ranged ahead. She wondered who he thought could threaten them out here. She could see for leagues in every direction. Spears of rock jutted up in places, but it was mostly flat ground. It wasn't as dry as the area around Sky Flames; they had passed a river this morning, and tonight they would camp at a real lake.

Water mirages rippled across the sands, obscuring details. The robes everyone wore out here were the same color as the desert. It made a person hard to see from far away. That was true for the colors worn by the Jazid nomads, too, among the rocks. Unsettled by the thought, she spurred her horse closer in to the caravan.

They reached the oasis in midafternoon, as the sun slanted long rays across the sand. Cook, the man who prepared their meals, had told her to expect only a small lake, but it was more water in one place than she had ever seen. Cliffs overhung it on one side, and a waterfall cascaded down them. She sent thanks for this haven to the dragon as he descended in the sky.

They weren't the only ones at the lake. It was exciting to see groups from all over Taka Mal, from solitary travelers to another caravan as large as theirs. Riding past them, Ginger felt like a wide-eyed child on festival night. All too soon, she had to dismount and help set up their camp. She unloaded supplies with Cook. On her first night with the caravan, she had prepared supper for her hosts, and afterward Cook had asked if she would do the meals with him. She was glad to have a skill she could offer in exchange for their letting her and Darz accompany them.

Before they started cooking, she wanted to clean up. Darz was busy checking the other groups at the lake, so she asked Cook if he would mind doing guard duty. He came along good-naturedly, telling her rowdy jokes and terrible puns, and helped her find a spring in a pocket of rocks above the lake. He waited outside the enclosed area, positioned so he could see her as he blocked the view of the pocket to anyone else. Kneeling down, she washed her face and hands. The water was bliss. The air had a different smell than in Sky Flames, with a sweet scent of jasmine. Standing up, she stretched her arms—

Someone yanked her backward. It happened so fast, she had no time to shout. He clamped his hand over her mouth and pinned her arms to her sides with his other arm. She rammed her elbow into whoever was behind her, and he grunted.

"Hurry up," someone said.

As she fought, someone came around in front of her, his features shadowed by the cowl of his charcoal robe and masked by a dark scarf. He was a wraith without a face, inhuman in robes that blended with the rocks.

He pressed a wet cloth over her face. Caught off guard, she gasped in a breath. A cloying smell saturated her senses, sickly sweet. He kept pressing the cloth… She couldn't breathe…

17

The General

A continuous bumping shook Ginger awake. She opened her eyes into the dim interior of a wagon. It resembled those used by the gypsies who wandered the borders between Jazid and Taka Mal. She lifted her head, then groaned as vertigo hit her.

She was lying near the front on a pile of carpets woven in blue and gold, with red accents that in her dazed state looked far too much like blood. Blue canvas walls enclosed the wagon. Its roof was patterned in gray-and-charcoal triangles, with red tassels at the edges that bounced as the wagon jolted. She couldn't have been out long; daylight sifted through the canvas walls, and she didn't think she had been unconscious long enough for night to have come and gone. The light had the aged feel of late afternoon rather than the freshness of dawn.

One of the nomads was sitting on a bench several feet away, deftly sewing a hole in a shirt despite the unsteady ride. His hood was pushed off his head, and the scarf hung down around his neck. He had sharp features, with small pox scars marking his skin. Black stubble covered his jaw. Another nomad was sitting across from him, a giant man with tangled black hair. He held a whetstone in one hand and a dagger in the other. He was staring, however, straight at Ginger. The hairs on her neck prickled.

"She's awake," the giant said. His voice was so deep, it seemed to boom even though he spoke at a normal volume.

The man stitching his shirt glanced at her. "So she is."

"Where are you taking me?" Ginger asked. She sounded like she felt, thick and dazed.

The stitcher narrowed his gaze at her. "You've given us a lot of trouble."

"I don't even know who you are," she said. "How could I give you trouble?"

He didn't answer; he just went back to sewing. She pulled herself up to sit cross-legged on the rugs. Bile rose in her throat, and she willed her stomach to settle. When she felt steadier, she said, "What did you do to Cook?"

The stitcher shrugged. "Nothing."

She clenched her fists in the carpet. "You didn't kill him, did you?" She had grown to like the plump cook and his bad puns.

He smiled slightly, the barest lifting of his mouth, his attention still on his repairs. "I told you. We did nothing."

She didn't believe it. "How did you get past him to me?"

"It was easy." He finally looked up at her. "You shouldn't travel with such greedy people."

"You *bribed* him?" She couldn't believe Cook would sell her.

This time he smiled fully, and she wished he hadn't. It was an ugly expression, derisive and covetous at the same time. "He sold your freedom for what he thought was a lot of gold. It's nothing compared to what we've been promised for you."

A sense of betrayal swept over her, followed by anger at herself. When would she learn to stop trusting people?

"You can't sell me," she said.

"Of course we can." He went back to sewing. "We've had a buyer ready since we told him we had seen you in that temple."

"You're a hard one to catch, priestess," the giant man rumbled. "Too many people around."

Ginger felt as if she were spinning. "No. You can't. My husband will look for me." She wasn't certain that was true. Sometimes he seemed to care for her, and he had braved a frenzied mob to free her from the stake. But she didn't know how much of that had been his idea and how much Heath had forced him. For all she knew, this provided him with a convenient way to rid himself of an unwanted bride. She didn't want to believe that about Darz, especially not after their nights together, but he had told her so little about himself, she was constantly on edge with him.

"Your husband, eh?" The giant laughed. "Is that the story?"

She stiffened. "It's true."

"What wedding?" the stitcher asked. "Those people were going to burn you alive. Some fellows rode off with you. We found the inn where you stayed, and they didn't say horse-shit about a wedding. You sure as hell didn't marry him on the caravan. You're a concubine, girl. Don't pretend otherwise."

"That's not true," she said.

"She could have married him while we were looking for her," the giant said. "It's not impossible."

The stitcher glanced at him, then at Ginger. "Whatever your man is, he would be a fool to chase us. He's just some rube from a little town. And he's only one against many of us."

She wanted to tell him what she thought of the "many of us," but she bit back the retort. The giant was sharpening his dagger, and the scrape of metal against stone grated. She didn't doubt he found opportunities to use his weapon. She felt cold. Was that the knife that had left so many wounds in Darz? She stared at it, then lifted her gaze to the giant. He regarded her with no hint of sympathy.

Ginger had felt constrained in Sky Flames, but she realized now she had taken for granted a level of safety that didn't exist in most places. She questioned whether it had ever existed at home, either. Naïve and idealistic in her airy temple, she had seen the world as if the sunset gilded it with rosy colors.

The giant was watching her. Holding up the dagger, he touched its edge and blood welled out of a cut on his thumb. Then he went back to sharpening the blade. With a shudder, she looked away.

If only she had brought her opal to the water hole. In daylight, for such a short stop, it hadn't occurred to her. She couldn't make spells with the sun up, but it couldn't be more than few hours until sunset. In the plaza she had used a large circle to focus her spell. She didn't know if she could use the ragged shapes here in the wagon, but she was ready to try anything.

And then what? She had spent her life using her talents to nurture people, to create light, real and symbolic. She truly enjoyed her calling in the temple. Before that night in the plaza, she could no more have imagined committing violence than she could have envisioned the sky breaking apart. But if she didn't disable or kill her guards, they would catch her again.

She rubbed her eyes. Her head ached from whatever they had used to knock her out. Regardless, she had to escape soon, before they traveled too far for her to get back. She couldn't set out without a map, horse, or supplies; if she did, the nomads would recapture her or the desert would kill her.

"You think he will pay the price he agreed to?" the giant asked the other man. "She's a mess."

Ginger squinted at herself. She wasn't a mess. She had just bathed. Her leggings and tunic were clean and well kept. Sand covered her boots, but what did they expect in a desert?

"You dress like a man," the stitcher told her. "You looked better in the temple."

"Well, since I'm so unattractive," she said sourly, "you might as well take me back to my unfortunate husband."

"Oh, I didn't say that," he answered. "Just that it isn't showing properly for us to get the best price."

She regarded him uneasily. "My clothes are fine."

He studied her. "We need to leave some mystery. We don't want to be too obvious." He got up and walked over, his gait uneven with the swaying of the wagon.

"What are you doing?" She slid back on the carpets.

The giant lifted his dagger. "Priestess, do you see this?"

She froze, her gaze on the blade. It glinted in light that leaked between two panels of the canvas walls. "Yes," she said.

He leaned forward. "A little blood on the purchase isn't going to dissuade our buyer. In fact, given what I know of him, he might pay more."

"Don't," she said.

"Don't what?" he asked, turning his dagger.

Somehow she kept her voice steady. "Don't use that on me."

"Then cooperate."

She swallowed. "I won't fight."

"Good." He sat back and continued sharpening the blade.

I lied, she thought. She would fight—when she had her weapon, the spells of fire. He was making it easier for her to face what she would have to do. *If* she could find a good shape. *If* the spells worked. Too many ifs.

The stitcher sat next to her and put his arm around her waist, pulling her against his side. Then he reached under her tunic and pulled her leggings off her hips.

"Don't!" Her face heated as she pushed him away.

"Hey!" The giant's voice snapped like breaking stone. He towered when he stood up, and he reached the carpets in one step. Kneeling behind Ginger, he touched the tip of his dagger to the nape of her neck, through her hair. "I thought we had an agreement."

She went still. "Don't cut me."

"Don't balk, then."

She forced herself to remain still while the stitcher took off her boots and leggings. The giant lifted her arms, the flat of his blade scraping her skin, and the stitcher pulled off her tunic. They left her in the undertunic, a translucent shift that came over her hips and thighs.

"That's better," the stitcher said. "Give him something to think about while we're settling terms."

Ginger crossed her arms in front of herself, her palms on her shoulders. She wanted to fold up and hide.

A shout came from outside. At first she didn't understand the caller's thick Jazid accent. Then she realized he had said, "Which pavilion do you want?"

The stitcher leaned past her to the front of the wagon and rapped on the wood that separated them from the driver. "The large gray one on the south end."

"Aya," the call came back. The wagon lurched as it changed direction, throwing Ginger against the stitcher, away from the man with the knife.

"Heh." He pushed her into the giant, lifting and resettling her so she was kneeling with her back against the huge nomad. She grasped the carpet at her sides while she stared at the stitcher. The giant put his hands on her shoulders, holding her in place, the hilt of his knife pressing her skin. His breath rustled her hair, with a strong smell of onions.

Only moments ago, it seemed, she had been with Darz. The future had been uncertain, but also exciting, filled with promise. That *couldn't* all be gone. It couldn't be. Life couldn't be that cruel.

The stitcher traced his finger along her lip. "Priestess, you should learn to hide your outrage. It will only get you hurt. Accept the way of the desert. It has always been like this. Men die and women suffer. Those of us who are strong survive. The rest of you serve our bidding."

She wanted to tell him he could rot in a slime lair. The way he was leaning over her, with his hands braced on her thighs and the giant holding her in place from behind, she feared they would hurt her before they reached their destination. So instead of an oath, she reminded him why they should do nothing to her.

"You kept saying 'he' before," she said. "You're taking me to 'him.' To *who?*"

The stitcher sat back on his haunches and rested his palms on his knees. "You wouldn't know him, I don't think. Not unless you're familiar with the generals from Jazid who fought in the war against the Misted Cliffs."

"I don't know much about Jazid," she admitted. "Why is he in Taka Mal?"

"Why are any of us anywhere?" the giant said behind her, holding her shoulders. "We have no army to fight for anymore. Only conquerors who occupy our country."

"And take our lives." The stitcher's voice crackled with anger. "The king of the Misted Cliffs has demanded our soldiers swear allegiance to him or face execution."

"You're soldiers?" she asked. "I thought you were nomads."

"We are." He motioned to the man behind her. "He comes from the Kublaqui tribe. So does our driver. I'm of the T'Ambera. Our tribes have always supported the Jazid army."

She tried to remember what Darz had told her about the war. "But your king, your atajazid—he is dead now, yes? His seven-year-old son would sit on the throne but he has been imprisoned by the king of the Misted Cliffs."

"So you've paid attention, eh?" He spoke grimly. "Yes, Cobalt the Dark murdered our king and put himself on the Onyx Throne. But he does not have the boy."

She didn't know whether or not to believe him; the boy's freedom could be a rumor the displaced army had started to lift the morale of their people. If the claim were true, it didn't bode well for the Misted Cliffs. Either way, as long as the nomads were talking about armies, they were leaving her alone. "Where is the prince, then?"

"In a place you'll never see," the stitcher said.

"And the general?" Sweat gathered on her palms, and she rubbed them on the carpet. "Who is he?"

"Dusk Yargazon," he said. "Do you know of him? His family takes their name in honor of the Shadow Dragon."

She shook her head, disquieted by the fierce quality of his gaze when he spoke of the general. She knew people in Jazid took names such as Dusk and Shade to honor their shadow god, just as they favored the gray-and-charcoal patterns, but it had always seemed a dark choice to her.

He leaned forward, trapping her between himself and the giant. "You *should* know of him. Everyone in your ungrateful country should honor his name. He is a general greater than any who fought in Taka Mal. It is *he* who sat in the war council after the Battle of the Rocklands and faced down the atajazid's murderer, Cobalt the Dark. It was he who won the prince's life." His eyes blazed with the too-bright gaze of fanaticism. "And it is he who will put the boy back on a throne."

She shrank away from him. "Then why are you in Taka Mal? We cannot put him on his throne."

The stitcher put his hands on either side of her hips, on top of her hands, pinning them to the carpet. "Maybe we're here to find a reprieve from the hardships of our exiled lives." He was so close, his lips were almost touching hers.

She turned her head away. "The desert is as harsh here as in Jazid."

"Oh, I don't know." He put his palm against her cheek and turned her head so she had to look at him. "They say you Taka Mal priest-esses are forbidden. No man may touch you." He slid his other hand up her thigh. "What happens to a man who does, eh? Shall your Dragon-Sun smite me down?" He glanced up at the sky, pretending to crane his neck. Then he looked back at her. "It seems not. Perhaps it excites him to see the taboos violated."

She spoke through gritted teeth. "Leave me alone."

Outside, the driver called out. The wagon jolted to a stop,

knocking the stitcher back from Ginger, and she fell forward, catching herself on her hands. As the stitcher stood up, someone pushed aside the blue canvas at the back of the wagon. A third nomad looked in, this one with a hood shadowing his face.

"General Yargazon is in a meeting with his men," he said. "He'll see us when he's done." He nodded toward Ginger. "Best make sure she doesn't cause a ruckus."

Ginger recognized the man's voice. He was the driver.

"We'll take care of it," the stitcher said. "Let us know when he's ready."

The driver nodded and withdrew, leaving the flap swinging in his wake. The stitcher went back to his sewing and took several lengths of cord from his pile of yarns and cloth. He came back to Ginger with the leather cords looped around his hands and gave them to the giant behind her.

She tried to turn around. "What are you doing?"

"Stay still." The giant turned her forward, then handed his dagger to the stitcher. Standing in front of her, the stitcher held the dagger by his side, level with her eyes. She stared at the glinting blade and shuddered.

The giant pulled her arms behind her back and crossed her forearms, one on top the other. He bound them together with two of the cords, then tugged the third tight around her upper arms, drawing her shoulder blades together until it forced her to arch her back slightly. She felt ill. She wanted this to be over, to be away from the nightmare. The nomads seemed balanced on the edge of violence, ready to erupt, and she feared by the time the sun set, she would be too injured to do anything at all, let alone call up the capricious spells that were her only defense.

The driver opened the back flaps and looked into the wagon again. "They're ready for you."

"Good." The stitcher grasped Ginger's arm and heaved her to her feet. The effects of the drug they had used to knock her out hadn't worn off as much as she thought, and her head reeled. He returned the dagger to the giant. Then, holding her upper arms, the two nomads walked her to the back of the wagon.

They came out into an evening even hotter than in Sky Flames. Although she didn't recognize the land, she thought they had gone south. The desert was no longer flat; it stepped up in stark ridges, higher and higher until they became the razor-thin foothills of the Jagged Teeth Mountains that dominated northern Jazid. Beyond them, in the purpling distance, the Jagged Teeth towered against the sky. It was a cruel landscape, like the people who lived in it, their souls parched and starved.

The area below the foothills formed a basin that might have once held a shallow sea. If water had ever softened this land, it had long since dried away. The sun was low in the west, and shadows stretched across the desert. Tents filled the basin. Soldiers moved down there, hundreds, even thousands, and the many tenders who served an encamped army. A good portion of the Jazid military must be there, in exile, hiding in the badlands of Taka Mal while they plotted against the usurpers in their land.

Only a few tents stood here, one large pavilion and several smaller ones. To the north, away from the camp, horses were drinking from a trough in a corral. Closer by, a group of soldiers had gathered around a fire to cook a meal. They watched the three nomads bringing Ginger to the pavilion. Her face heated as the wind molded the under-tunic to her body and rippled it around her legs.

A man in leather and bronze armor with a heavy sword on his belt stood at the entrance of the pavilion. He wore a dragon helmet with a point on the top shaped like a tetrahedron. Power shifted within Ginger. She couldn't call it forth yet, for the sun still shone, but if she could see one of the helmets after sunset, she might use the tetrahedron to drive her spells.

The guard either expected them or recognized the nomads, for he didn't call challenge, he simply stepped aside. Inside, the pavilion was larger than the garden in the house where Ginger had lived as a child. Plush cushions were strewn across the carpeted floor and around low tables tiled in charcoal and black. Torches on poles added light and smoke. Across the tent, a wall map of Taka Mal was tacked to a beam support, and a large group of men were gathered before it. They all wore the black-and-silver uniforms of Jazid military officers. A painful thought hit Ginger; she had never seen Darz in his Taka Mal uniform. She didn't even know if he was a full officer, and unless she managed a miracle with her spells, she would probably never find out.

The warrior motioned them over to a corner of the tent. The nomads drew her with them, and they waited by a brazier that curled smoke in the air. The giant stood behind her, tall and silent, with the tip of his dagger against her spine. Across the tent, the officers were deep in a debate.

Sweat gathered on Ginger's forehead and ran down her neck. The heat from the brazier bothered her, but after the sun set and cold rushed in, she would welcome its warmth. She looked around the tent for shapes. Although she saw no pyramids or circles, triangle patterns were everywhere. But they stirred no response within her, not even a sense of potential. Usually in daylight she could feel the banked power of her spells waiting for release. It worried her; the triangles seemed too weak to drive her spells.

As the officers argued, she caught the words "Quaaz palace" and "Topaz throne." She picked up only fragments, but it was enough to dismay her. They intended to invade Quaaz, the capital of Taka Mal. She didn't understand; Jazid and Taka Mal weren't enemies and had often allied in their violent histories. They had fought together in the last war to drive back the Misted Cliffs. She couldn't fathom why Jazid would plot against the country most likely to support them against their conquerors.

She had to warn Darz! It sounded like Jazid agents were targeting commanders in the Taka Mal army, kidnapping the highest-ranked officers for interrogation and killing the rest. If they found out Darz had survived—and was headed to Quaaz with tales of murder—they would go after him, and this time they would make sure they finished the job.

One of the men rubbed the small of his back and glanced around the tent. His gaze scraped over Ginger. He turned to another man, a tall officer, probably in his fifties, with a great deal of silver on the shoulders and sleeves of his uniform. The first man said something, and the tall one glanced at Ginger. Then they returned to their discussions.

After a few moments, though, they brought their war council to an end. The officers left in groups of three and four, still deep in discussion. The tall man remained and conferred with two younger soldiers who had far less silver on their uniforms. After they departed, the older man walked to where Ginger stood with the nomads. The giant nomad moved the point of his dagger against her back, and the stitcher and the driver flanked her, each holding one of her upper arms. She was trapped and vulnerable, unable to retreat.

When the officer reached then, the stitcher bowed deeply. "You honor us with your presence, General Yargazon."

Yargazon inclined his head in acceptance of the formal words. He was staring at Ginger, however, and she flushed under his scrutiny. Her shoulder blades ached from being pulled back by the cord. She wanted to fold her arms over her torso, as if that meager effort could protect her against Yargazon's formidable presence.

The general spoke in a voice like rust. "It appears, Ji, that I owe you an apology. I had assumed you exaggerated when you described her. I was wrong."

The stitcher, who was apparently Ji, said, "Makes it worth the chase, eh?"

"Indeed." Yargazon stepped forward and slid his hand into Ginger's hair. "Is this color real?"

She looked up at him, unable to speak. With the giant behind her, Ji on one side, the driver on the other, and Yargazon towering over her, she felt suffocated.

The general yanked back her head by her hair. "I asked you a question."

"Y-yes," she said. "It's real."

"I've never seen such a color."

Staring at him, she knew he was more dangerous than any sentinel. The sun had weathered his face and prominent nose, turning his skin leathery. Wrinkles creased the corners of his eyes and bracketed his mouth, but he otherwise had the robust appearance of a man half his age. His uniform accented his height and powerful physique. Its stark black lines and silver ribbing gave him a shadowed aspect.

The heavily corded tendons in his neck slanted into the muscles of his shoulders and under his stiff tunic. His expression had a steel quality, as if he had seen too many wars and killed too many men. Ginger shrank back and felt the nick of the dagger against her spine.

The general took her face in his hands. She froze as he bent his head. When he kissed her, she tried to pull away, but the nomads held her in place.

Yargazon took his time kissing her, stroking his thumbs on her cheeks and then her nipples. Then he pulled the undertunic up to her shoulders and touched her more. She tried to disassociate herself from it, as if she were someone else, but it was hard when her arms ached.

After a while he lifted his head. "Such sweetness," he murmured. Stepping back, he pulled down her tunic. "You were a priestess in one of those temples, yes?"

"Yes." She lifted her chin. "I serve the Dragon-Sun."

"Do you now?" He seemed amused. "It is a quaint idea, to have sun priestesses bless and nurture people. Rather charming. Take a lovely, innocent girl, put her all alone in a temple, and then say no man may touch her. One wonders if the people of Taka Mal are deliberately provoking us or just plain stupid."

Gritting her teeth, she held back the urge to tell him their temples didn't exist to serve the whims of Jazid warlords.

He glanced at Ji. "She is the one who tended the body?"

"That's right," Ji said. "They brought it into the temple."

Yargazon rubbed his chin while he considered Ginger. "What did you do with it?"

"It?" She endeavored to look blank. "What do you mean?"

"The corpse the miners took to you."

She shuddered at the memory of when they had brought Darz into the temple, believing him dead. She didn't miss the irony, that the nomads had spied on her, even invaded the temple, yet didn't seem to realize Darz had been asleep in one of the cells, recovering from his stab wounds.

"I gave him the Sunset Rites," she lied. "We cremated him."

He spoke to Ji. "Can you verify that?"

"We didn't see any smoke," Ji said. "But they never carried him out for a burial, and his body wasn't in the Sunset Room."

"Perhaps next time," the general said tightly, "you will take care of the burial yourself instead of hiding when you hear a few harmless miners."

Ji's gaze never wavered. "We completed our mission."

"Your orders included burying the body," Yargazon said.

"We've brought you the girl."

"At an exorbitantly high price."

"You've seen her," Ji said. "She's worth it, for the information as well as the pleasure."

Information? What did that mean? Ginger had a sense of undercurrents here she only partially understood. The general and Ji were parrying. They continued their veiled battle of words, and she listened intently, though she hid her attention by acting dazed. The lives of women in Jazid were even more limited than in Taka Mal, but it offered an unexpected advantage; they didn't seem to consider her presence a deterrent to their discussions the way they would have if she had been a man. She suspected it didn't even occur to them she could pose a danger to their plans.

It was difficult to sort out the hierarchy between them. Yargazon was obviously in command, but the nomads weren't soldiers. It sounded as if they were part of a covert sect he had hired to kill certain Taka Mal officers. At Sky Flames, the miners had appeared unexpectedly, forcing the nomads to hide while Harjan and the others carried the body into the temple.

They had no idea Darz was alive. Incredibly, they had stood in the plaza less than two tendays later and watched him fight off the sentinels, never realizing they were seeing a man they had left for dead. With his beard, on a horse, Darz had looked too different for them to recognize.

Although the general censured Ji for his failure to bury the body, she had a feeling he agreed with the way they had dealt with the situation. But he was using it to claim that bringing "the priestess" was part of their mission, so he could question her. The nomads didn't consider it a military matter. They served Yargazon by choice but had other livelihoods, including this transaction. Ji saw it purely as a matter of selling a commodity—Ginger—the general had arranged for him to acquire.

It was chilling how well they knew how to bargain. Both clearly understood the purpose of their supposed disagreement. Within moments they settled on a price, less than what Ji wanted, but an amount of gold coin and gems so large, it bewildered Ginger. She had never seen even a tenth that much wealth.

When they finished, Yargazon turned to her. "Were you the only witness to the cremation?"

She hesitated. If they had been watching the temple, they would know the miners guarding it had stayed outside that night.

"Yes," she said. The shorter her answers, the better. She tried to keep her face blank, so they wouldn't suspect how closely she was following all they said.

"What did you find on his person?" the general asked.

His person? "Nothing."

He spoke sharply. "Answer my question. I want to know what you saw when you gave 'sunset rights' to this man."

She was growing confused. "Nothing."

His voice turned cold. "We've heard rumors of actions by the Taka Mal army in the area of your village. Are you people sheltering anyone? Do they have a base of operations?"

She shook her head. "I know nothing of such things."

"You priestesses hold a high position among your people. Don't expect me to believe you've heard nothing."

"I've nothing to tell you." She doubted the army had been in the area doing something hidden. "I don't know anything about the military."

The entrance flap of the pavilion rustled, and an officer pushed aside the canvas. "Permission to speak with you, sir."

Yargazon walked over to him. "Go ahead, Lieutenant."

"I think we have all we're going to get," the lieutenant said. "We have scrolls for you."

"Very well." The general glanced at Ji. "I must attend to another matter." Motioning at Ginger, he said, "Bring her. I'll have my men get your payment."

Ji drew her forward. She wanted to resist, but the driver took her other arm and the giant followed them, a looming presence at her back.

Outside, the sun was almost to the horizon. Ginger thought the dragon was truly a harsh deity to serve, that he would burn in the sky knowing such cruelty took place below him. She could hear his voice: *I am a ball of fire, not the conscience of man. I cannot control the*

Catherine Asaro

minds of you who call yourselves human. You are responsible for the deeds you commit, whether they be great or heinous.

Yes, she thought, they were responsible for their deeds. But it was the people like her and Darz who paid the brutal price of those who chose what was heinous.

The Tent

Yargazon and his aide walked ahead, conferring in low voices. Neither wore a helmet, nor did Ginger see other shapes she could use. They went to a small tent under an overhang of rock. As they reached the entrance, a ragged scream from inside shattered the evening.

Ginger stopped, terrified. This wasn't the bloodcurdling war cry she had heard in the temple. It was a scream of agony.

The general and his aide went inside, and the nomads dragged Ginger after them. The interior was dim, lit only by one torch, and the overhang outside blocked what little of the aged sunlight might have filtered through the canvas. It took a moment for her eyes to adjust enough so she could make out the scene on the far side of the tent. A man was lying on a slanted surface, and several Jazid warriors were gathered around him. None of them wore helmets.

As her group approached, she inhaled sharply. The man wasn't lying down, he was manacled to a rack that stretched him out, his arms and legs spread-eagled. What remained of his clothing was ripped and bloody, and welts crisscrossed his torso and legs. But she could make out enough to know he had worn a uniform with gold and red colors. He was an officer in the Taka Mal army.

One of the Jazid warriors came over to Yargazon and showed him a scroll. "We got troop and cavalry deployments, postings for twenty officers, and the names of two covert operatives, one in Aronsdale and the other in our army."

Yargazon raised an eyebrow. "A Taka Mal spy is here?"

"Not here. He's with a regiment in Jazid." The man tapped one of the scrolls. "His location, cover identity and assignment are all here."

"You've done well." Yargazon glanced at the man on the rack. "You can take him down and finish matters. Make it quick, so he doesn't suffer anymore. And cremate the body."

Bile rose in Ginger's throat. She had read accounts of military campaigns, but they always described battles, which invariably were either glorious or dire, depending on whether the historian was from the winning or losing side. They never revealed this side of war, the bitter stories of soldiers who lost their lives far from the field of battle.

The warriors released the Taka Mal man and two of them took him out of the tent. They had to carry him; he was incapable of walking. Tears gathered in Ginger's eyes as she turned to Yargazon. "Can't you let him live?"

The general answered with a softness that jarred with the orders he had just given. "Such a sweet, gentle priestess." He put his hand under her chin and wiped the tear on her cheek with his thumb. "Are you really so innocent?" His expression hardened. "Or is it all an act?"

"An act?" Her voice caught. "Why?"

"A good question." He glanced at the three warriors who still stood at the rack. "She was the one in the temple who tended the body. See what you can find out."

With horror, she realized what they intended. As Ji took her arm, she panicked. "No! I have nothing to tell you. I swear it!"

"They always say that," Yargazon told her. "And they always lie."

"It's true!" She struggled frantically as the interrogators laid her out on the rack. "How could I know *anything?*"

"You tell me." He watched while they untied her arms and pulled them out onto the frame. Their lack of remorse chilled her; they worked with efficiency and showed no sign of humanity. She could have been an animal rather than a human being. The worst of it was, she *did* know things they would want—the existence of the dragon powder, and that one of their targets had escaped and was even now headed to Quaaz to warn the Taka Mal army.

The manacles dug into her skin, hard and unyielding. As they closed the shackles around her ankles, another crushing thought came to her; she couldn't use her spells to attack, for she would be trapped in the blaze, as well, chained to the rack while the tent and everyone within it burned.

The interrogators stepped back. The nomads had moved away and were clustered by the entrance. Ginger stared at Yargazon, and he watched her with narrowed eyes, as if he had measured her behavior and found it wanting.

One of the warriors stepped out of view, behind the rack. A creak groaned, followed by the grate of gears turning. Ginger's arms jerked, and the chains stretched her out. At first it didn't hurt, but he kept cranking the wheel, stretching her farther, until she gasped. She felt as if she would be torn in two.

The general stood near her head. "You saw what happened to the last person we used this on. Better to tell me the truth now rather than make us do to you what we did to him."

"I don't know anything to tell you." She stared up at him. "How could I?"

He motioned to someone behind her—and the wheel creaked. She cried out as the rack stretched her limbs.

"Eventually it will dislocate your joints,"Yargazon said. "But if you cooperate, I will take you off."

"I am cooperating." She choked out the words. "I don't have anything to tell you. I swear."

"What did you see outside your temple the night the miners brought in the body?"

"I was in the temple. I didn't see anything outside."

"What did the miners tell you they saw?"

"Nothing."When Yargazon lifted his hand to the soldier behind the rack, Ginger said, "I swear it! They said *nothing*."

"Nothing?" His voice cut like a knife. "You expect me to believe they found a dead man and said they saw nothing?"

She strained to recall what Harjan and the others had told her. "They thought he had been attacked."

"By who?"

"They didn't say. We didn't know—*no!*" She groaned as the wheel turned. "It's *true*. They had no idea who killed him."

"You're lying,"Yargazon said. "What did they see? Who did they tell? What did you see?"

"Nothing, I swear," she said, desperate. "What could we see? It was dark. They found a body. They brought it to me. That was all."

The general motioned to another of the interrogators, and the man went to the table where several objects glinted. She couldn't discern what they were, but he picked something long. As he came back into the torchlight, she saw what he held: a cat-o-nine tails.

"No. Please," she pleaded. "I have nothing to tell you."

"Not that one," Yargazon told him. "It leaves scars."

Ginger hoped that meant he didn't want her limbs dislocated, either. It wasn't much help; they could cause her a lot of pain before the effects became permanent. But she would take anything that might help her hold out longer.

The man exchanged the whip for a leather belt. Yargazon gestured to the warrior behind the rack, the wheel scraped—and Ginger screamed.

So they interrogated her. Yargazon kept up a relentless stream of questions: what did she know, what had they seen, what was the army doing, who were their contacts, what was she hiding. He asked about everyone his men had seen at the temple, the Dragon's Claw, or the village. At first she thought he was looking for something specific, but she soon realized he was fishing for anything he could force out of her.

And she talked.

It poured out of her, between her screams and sobs, details of her life, her service at the temple, even how she cooked her supper and cleaned the fountain. She told them every detail of her trial and why they accused her of witchery—except the most important fact, that their accusations were partly true, she *could* do spells.

When they asked about Darz, she said she had married a village man who rescued her from the stake. She described every meal she had supposedly cooked for him during her last nine days in the temple. She told them he was a farmer, that he lost his temper when he drank, and how he had been a respected member of the village before he threw it away to save her from burning alive. And she knew the general couldn't care less.

She didn't tell them about the powder. She claimed an earthquake toppled the Dragon's Claw. In an excruciating irony, they accepted her lies and thought her truths were false. Yargazon obviously had no patience with those who believed in sun dragons, witchery, or spells.

Never once did he ask her if Darz was alive. Somehow she kept from saying it, though so many times she barely stopped the words from spilling out with all the others. When she came close, when the revelations were mixed up in what she was saying, she switched into long descriptions of the most boring facts she could recall, the soap she used to clean floors, how hard it was to keep mice from eating the tallow candles, how the squash crops this year came in too early and tasted bad.

And the sun went down.

She knew when the night descended because power roiled within her. But even if she gained enough reprieve from the agony to focus a spell, she had no shape. It was too dark to see anything except the general and the man with the leather belt.

Yargazon leaned over her and spoke in a deceptively gentle voice, a sharp contrast to his questions. "Tell me what I need to know. Then this will all be over. All you have to do is tell me the truth."

She wanted to blurt it all out, give him *anything,* anything to stop the agony. She could feel her joints straining, ready to break. Bruises and welts covered her body. The shackles cut into her, and blood seeped over her skin, mixing with her sweat. His words were too much. She almost *believed* him: if she would just tell him everything, he would stop the pain. But she knew he was lying, that if she revealed she had held back, they would intensify their efforts. Gods forgive her, she didn't know how much longer she could keep her secrets.

"Sir?" The voice came from across the tent.

Yargazon straightened up and turned toward the entrance. "You're early," he said, beckoning to someone.

Footsteps crunched and another officer appeared, a gangly man with a black mustache. "We're ready to leave," he said.

The general nodded with approval. "You should make Quaaz easily by tomorrow." They were speaking quietly, but with Yargazon so near the rack, Ginger could hear.

"My messenger arrived from Quaaz at sunset," the man said. "He says our people are positioned and ready within the palace. We expect them to move at noon tomorrow."

"Good." Yargazon rubbed the back of his neck. "We march in the morning, both the cavalry and foot troops. We should arrive in the late afternoon. By then, the assassinations must be done."

"They will, sir." The man started to speak, then stopped.

"What is it?" Yargazon asked.

"It's the queen, sir. She would make a valuable hostage."

"So she would." Yargazon exhaled. "More than that. It would be fitting to have her as my prisoner. It's an abomination she ever ascended the throne." He stood thinking. Then he shook his head. "We can't risk it. As long as she lives, she might escape and rally her people. Look what a symbol the atajazid offers to ours, though he is only seven. No, she must die, and all her heirs. No one with a claim to the Topaz Throne can be left alive when the atajazid takes it as his own."

"But you still want her Aronsdale consort alive?"

Yargazon nodded. "He's not native to Taka Mal. Many people object to his being here. But he is related to King Cobalt. We can use him as a hostage in bargaining with the Misted Cliffs."

Chills wracked Ginger's body. She couldn't believe Jazid would turn on Taka Mal and murder the royal family. It was an ugly plan— but effective. No one at the palace would expect it. The queen was probably hosting highly-ranked officers from Jazid even now, offering them sanctuary from execution in their own country. They would be well-placed to betray their benefactors. They could kill the queen and her baby, and gods only knew what they would do to her Aronsdale consort. The addition of the Taka Mal army to theirs would double the Jazid forces. They could attack the conquering army in Jazid with renewed strength to take back its throne for their boy king.

One of the interrogators walked over to the general. As the man with the mustache saluted and left, Yargazon turned to the warrior. "Is there a problem?"

"Sir, I don't think she knows anything, except how to scrub floors and cook the damn pumpkins. She's just a girl. If she had anything to tell us, she would have already broken."

Yargazon looked past him at Ginger. "She seems too slow even to think for herself."

"It will do permanent damage if we pull her much longer."

Please, Ginger prayed to the dragon and the sunset. *I know you can't or won't interfere with our lives. But I entreat you. Make them stop.* She didn't know why she tried; even if the Dragon-Sun or the Sunset could have helped, they were gone from the sky. The night was the time of Jazid's Shadow Dragon.

The general walked to the rack and stood with his hands clasped behind his back as he considered Ginger. His gaze had a dark hunger that terrified her.

"Very well," he said. "Take her down and clean her up. Have someone bring her to my tent. I will be in a meeting, so leave a guard with her."

"We'll take care of it, sir."

Yargazon inclined his head. Without another glance at any of them, he strode from the tent. When he went beyond the torchlight, Ginger could no longer see him, but the canvas crackled and metal somewhere rattled. Distorted shadows swung back and swung forth in the torchlight.

As they released her from the manacles, tears ran down her face. She could barely move. They pulled away the scraps of her tunic and bathed her with tepid water from a basin they brought out of the shadows. One of them pulled a soldier's tunic over her head, and another brushed her hair. The third gave her a tin of water and waited while she drank not one, but four cups. She tried not to think of what waited for her in Yargazon's tent. She sat on the rack, neither looking at them nor responding to their ministrations. Instead, she turned her concentration inward to the power seething within her. She let it build, but it had no focus. Without a shape, she could do no spells, and it was too dark to see anything but the rack, which was misshapen.

When they finished, one of the men said, "Can you walk?"

She didn't think she could move. Her skeleton felt as if it would fall apart. She had to force herself to stand up. The tent tilted around her and the edge of the rack rushed up—

Someone caught her as she fell. He kept his hand under her arm, holding her upright until her vertigo passed. When she inhaled, trying to steady herself, another man took her other arm. With two of them holding her up, she stepped toward the entrance. Another step. Another—

And she saw it.

The ring was iron and as wide across as her outstretched hand. She couldn't see what it was hanging from, only that it was slowly swinging back and forth by the entrance, probably disturbed when Yargazon had left. She stared at it—and the power roiling within her suddenly had a focus.

She envisioned flames.

The spell exploded unlike any other she had done. Driven by her agony, it erupted from every wall of the tent, every surface, every object within, even from the ground under her feet, though the packed dirt had nothing to burn. The world *blazed*.

Her interrogators caught fire. They shouted and dropped her arms, beating at their flaming clothes. Except it wasn't just their clothes; fire engulfed them until they became living torches. One of the warriors threw himself on the ground and rolled back and forth. Another stumbled into a table piled high with scrolls. Fire roared across it, destroying the record of secrets the interrogators had wrested from their victims. The third man staggered back and fell across the burning rack.

Their cries pierced the night. The spell flared wildly through Ginger, and she felt a backlash as if it were happening to her. But it *wasn't*: she was the only person or thing in the tent that wasn't burning.

Ginger lurched into a run. She could barely stay on her feet, but the desire to be alive and free were even greater than her pain. She raced out of the blazing tent and darted behind a spur of rock, leaving behind the roar of flames and the screams of the monsters who had tortured her.

People were shouting and running across the camp. Ruddy light from the torches in front of the general's pavilion backlit them, but she doubted they could see her behind the rocks. The first place they would go was the tent. She crept away from the inferno, staying low behind the boulders.

When Ginger had put the overhang between herself and the tent, she took off in a limping run, down a slope toward where she had seen the horses. Shouts rang out behind her, but they were about the fire. She had no doubt it was too late for them to salvage the scrolls. She couldn't bring back the Taka Mal officers who had died at Yargazon's hand, but she had at least ensured Jazid would never have use of what they knew.

The calls receded as she ran from the camp. The rocky ground cut her feet, but she didn't care; nothing could stop her from leaving this place. As she approached the corral, she tried to summon a spell to calm the horses. She had no shape, so she felt the front of the tunic until she found a round button. It was too small to give her any real power, but she managed enough to keep the horses from trumpeting her presence to the camp.

With her joints and her battered muscles protesting, she climbed up on the corral fence. The surge of desperation that had fueled her race from the tent had taken its toll, and now she could barely keep moving.

"Closer, sweetings," she murmured to a horse. He nickered and wandered over, then nuzzled at her hand.

"I've nothing to give you," she whispered, trickling her spell over the animal. Her every joint seemed to protest as she climbed onto its back, and the rough hair of its coat scraped her thighs. She had no bridle or riding blanket, nothing to hold onto but its mane. It smelled of oats and mud and horse.

The animal shuffled and shook its head. Her spell was fading; if she didn't leave soon, the horses might become agitated and draw attention. Right now, the roar of flames and the calls of the people battling it masked her small sounds, but it wouldn't be long before they realized she wasn't in the tent.

"Come on," she urged. Using pressure from her knees, she coaxed the animal toward the gate. Too late, she realized she should have opened the corral first. She hated the thought of getting off, but she had no choice; even if she had known how to jump a fence, she doubted they had enough room to gather speed.

At the gate, she laboriously slid to the fence and then to the ground. When she opened the gate, the horse walked out. Another followed and nibbled the sparse grass poking out of the rocky ground.

"No," she whispered. If any horses wandered into the camp, it could alert Yargazon's men to what she had done. She herded the second animal back inside and closed the gate. The one she had chosen neighed, and she prayed no one heard. If anyone was approaching, though, they were doing it more quietly than her ears could detect. She climbed back on the fence and clenched her teeth as splinters jabbed her feet. The horse stamped when she pulled herself onto his back, and she strained to hold her wan spell of comfort. With shouts from the camp ringing in her ears, she prodded the horse into motion and headed north.

Dragon-Sun, Ginger thought. *I know these dark hours aren't your time. But I entreat you. If you truly find favor in me, help me keep this precious freedom.*

She rode northward, based on the stars. Although the moon gave some light, it wasn't enough to risk letting the horse run full out over the rocky terrain. It was a steady mount, and it accepted her presence, which probably meant it was a pack animal rather than a war steed. A charger might not have let her ride him even with a spell of soothing.

As they sped up, wind ruffled the horse's mane, and a chill cut through her tunic. She could have formed a warmth spell, but she needed to conserve her strength. The silence of the night surrounded them, broken only by the clicks of sand-chirpers. So far, she heard no pursuit. So far.

Her spell finally died. Mercifully, the horse continued without it. As the pound of her heart eased, she sagged in her seat. She hurt so much. She had drained her resources, but she managed a tiny spell that eased the distress in her joints.

An oddity registered on her mind. The air was clammy. In the desert, especially during summer, this much moisture never thickened the air. Puzzled, she lifted her head to look around.

Fog covered the land.

Ginger slowed the horse, and it neighed as if to protest the unearthly mist. Although the sky overhead was clear and stars shone like crystals, on the ground, a luminescent fog swirled in the moonlight. A tendril curled around them, and the horse balked, then stamped his feet and backed up. She offered him another spell, calming him enough so he didn't bolt, but he stepped restlessly. The mist hid the land, and it was rising, already at her elbows. She could barely see the horse beneath her.

"This isn't natural," she muttered. Streamers swirled around her face, cool on her skin, and the world turned white. The horse was growing even more agitated; if he bolted now, with the ground hidden, he could stumble and snap his leg.

"It's all right," Ginger said, letting him walk. Within moments, though, he stopped. He neighed in protest, yet when she prodded him, he refused to go. The *mist* was holding them in place. It curled more thickly around her waist and under her arms. When she pushed at it, her hand slid along a huge coil wider than her body.

A scaled coil.

It lifted her off the horse and swung her high into the air. Below her, the fog boiled—and solidified into a figure on the ground. It was huge, longer than a caravan of twenty wagons and higher than the spire of a clock tower. Gigantic wings that could span half of Sky Flames unfurled from its back and covered the land in impenetrable mist. Two silver eyes larger than her head glowed in its elongated snout. Its mammoth tail was even longer than the creature, and its coil gripped her body. It held her by the thinnest portion at the end, yet even that was thick enough to cover her torso.

The Shadow Dragon opened his mouth and roared white flames.

Shadows

The dragon covered the land.

Ginger's mount had bolted and was racing south, beyond the body of the dragon. The horse looked tiny from up here, where the dragon had hoisted her into the air, though he remained on the ground. When she realized just how high he was lifting her, she squeezed her eyes shut.

Cold air blew past her face. She opened her eyes—and found herself staring into one of the dragon's eyes. The silver orb had a slitted black pupil that either reflected the stars or else had stars within it. It also reflected her terrified face. His head was longer than Ginger's body, and fangs thicker than her leg glinted in his mouth. Smoke curled from his nostrils.

He swung her closer.

Priestess. The thought reverberated in her mind.

Why do you capture me, Shadow Dragon?

You called me.

I called the Dragon-Sun!

The sun cannot hear you at night.

She bit her lip. *What will you do with me?*

I have not decided. He turned his head and studied her with his other eye. The smoke from his nostrils wafted around her, acrid and hot. You are a favorite of my enemy.

Ginger felt a strange calm. She was frightened, yes, but she had survived so much these past days that fear no longer had power over her. *I am no enemy of yours,* she thought to the dragon. *I think I am not so favored by the sun, either, given what he has allowed to happen.*

We cannot affect the events of humanity, Ginger-Sun, even when those we favor suffer.

Dryly she thought, *Yet here you are, affecting events.* Her escape, to be precise.

When a holder of power calls us with enough strength and enough need, we can manifest in the world of humans.

A holder of power? What is that?

One who wields a power of fire or shadows. Such humans are rare. I know of only one in the last two hundred years.

Who?

You.

I am no power. Lately I can barely keep myself alive.

You are strong. If you were not, you would be neither free nor coherent now.

She wasn't convinced she *was* coherent. Maybe what happened in Yargazon's camp had taxed her mind until it snapped. *I didn't call on the sun. He came to the earth of his own volition.*

You indeed called him, when your people sought to burn you. He descended and asked you to be his wife. You refused him. Why?

I serve the Dragon-Sun gladly, she thought. *It is my honor. But in matters of the heart, I had given my word to a human man. A man like me. How could I be the consort of a fire dragon?*

I do not know, he thought. We can rarely manifest.

Why?

It unbalances nature for the sun to leave the sky or the night to become a void. When I formed, it left nothing where shadows had lain. The balance must restore itself.

This was a power she neither wanted nor could fathom. She might be able to call forth the dragons, but she had no say over what they chose to do. *I didn't know.*

You are a force, Ginger-Sun, one we cannot control. He scrutinized her with one eye. I must decide how I will respond.

She feared he meant to end her life so she could no longer summon them. His tail rested against her hips, and she felt the powerful muscles in the coil. He could easily crush her.

The dragon's great wings lifted into the air and swept down, creating an immense gale that blew Ginger's hair back from her body. Arching his neck, he breathed white flame into the sky. The coil of his tail tightened—and he leapt off the earth.

"Gods above," she whispered as they soared into the sky. Then she clamped her mouth shut, lest she invoke another deity in the pantheon her husband claimed didn't exist.

The ground fell away with heart-stopping speed. The dragon swung her through the air in huge, slow arcs as his tail swept back and forth. Freezing air rushed past her bared skin.

Shadow Dragon! Don't drop me!

I will not.

The ground passed below with dizzying speed. His wings beat the air in great arcs, their span so large she couldn't see far enough to discern where they ended and the night began.

It's a long way down, she thought.

I must fly. He curled his tail forward until she was near his head. **I can waste no time, for when the sun rises, I will become shadows again.**

Where are we going?

That depends on whether or not I see what I seek in time.

What do you seek?

If we find it, you will know.

Will you let me live?

Yes, Ginger-Sun. A sense of surprise at her question came with his thoughts. **I saw what they did to you, and how you resisted. You have bravery. Goodness. It is fitting you are favored by the sun.** His eye blinked slowly. **But take care in calling us, for it harms nature. This does not please us.**

I'll be careful.

Good. He swung her back in a majestic curve until his tail was once more behind him.

She wasn't certain how long they flew, but he didn't slow down until the horizon had reddened with the first tints of dawn. As the light increased, the dragon became translucent. She braced her hands against his tail to reassure herself of its solidity.

They landed in a desolate landscape of ragged natural terraces, the debris of failed mountains. She barely felt the jolt when his massive tail set her down. He didn't unwind the coil; instead, it faded into the pre-dawn light.

Shadow Dragon, wait! She ran alongside his disappearing form until she reached his head. The dawn sky shone through his body. *You've taken me far from the Jazid army. Thank you.*

It was not far enough. His thoughts receded. The Dragon-Sun gave him to you, and I have tried to return you, but I can do no more....

His body vanished, and she was by herself in the predawn flush of day. Her own power swirled within her, but it would soon fade as well, when the Dragon-Sun rose.

"Goodbye," she said. His last thought reverberated in her mind: *The Dragon-Sun gave him to you...* It sounded like he meant Darz. Right now she would give a great deal to see her puzzle of a husband.

Ginger shivered, alone in the vast landscape with no horse or supplies. Rock formations rose before her in huge steps. She trudged up one, her pace slowed by her bare feet. She had tough soles, but walking on floors and hiking in the desert were very different matters. By the time she reached the top, the sky blazed red and gold, presaging the sun. She needed a vantage point where she could survey the land for a good route north. She limped around a spear of rock, looked out—and gulped.

A group of Jazid cavalrymen had surrounded a man in the rough clothes of a Taka Mal commoner. They were playing with him like cats with a mouse, galloping in circles around him, most of the time just out of his reach. The Jazidians screamed their bloodcurdling cries and lunged in to slash at the man while he turned his horse in a circle, trying to defend himself on all sides. They probably hadn't been at it long, given the early hour, but the fight would be over soon, with ten against one. Metal clanged as blades struck. He fought with uncommon expertise, but she doubted he could hold them off much longer.

The Taka Mal man suddenly reared his horse, silhouetted against the sunrise—just as Ginger had seen him silhouetted against the flames of a blazing plaza.

Darz! She almost shouted, then stopped herself. It would do

neither of them any good if the warriors captured her. The sun would rise any moment, but until then power thrummed within her. The button on her tunic was no good; she needed a stronger shape.

Ginger squinted in the predawn light. The Jazidians wore helmets topped with tetrahedral points. She focused, but they were too far away, and she couldn't see the shapes well enough to awaken a spell. She headed down the ridge, keeping in the shadows of jutting slabs. Rocks stabbed her feet. At the bottom, she crouched behind a pile of boulders and concentrated on the helmets. She saw Darz's face, the determination and the fear. He knew he was near death. The Jazidians were tightening their circles, drawing in closer. He kept on fighting, his lips drawn back in a snarl.

Ginger focused again. Her spell caught—and slipped. She wasn't close enough! But she could go no farther without being seen, and she had little doubt what would happen if they caught her out here. It would only make them kill Darz faster, so they could get to her sooner. Ji's rough voice grated in her memory: *Men die and women suffer.*

Not today, she thought. But she had no time! The sky was lightening. She focused harder on the helmets, harder, harder—

The spell caught.

Flames erupted from the men attacking Darz. The spell was neither as large nor as intense as the one she had created in the tent. But it was enough. With shouts of alarm, they turned their attention to themselves. Several jumped off their horses and rolled on the ground, and the others beat at the flames or yanked off the impossibly burning armor.

The instant they let up their attack, Darz wheeled around and took off, galloping south at a hard pace.

Ginger ran out from behind the boulders. "Darz," she shouted. "Here!"

His head jerked, and she knew the moment he saw her; it was as if a spark jumped between them. Veering toward her, he leaned off his horse, his expression fierce. As he reached down, she grabbed his arm. In the same instant she jumped for his horse, he heaved her upward. She scrambled awkwardly as she vaulted up behind him.

"Hang on!" Darz shouted.

Ginger grabbed him around the waist and held on tight, her front pressed against his back. "We have to get to Quaaz!" she called. It was hard to talk with Grayrider running so hard, but Darz must have heard, because he veered north. Grayrider's hooves thundered on the hard ground.

They soon left the Jazid soldiers behind. Eventually, when no sign of pursuit showed, Darz let the horse slow to a stop. In silence, he helped Ginger down, his face so fierce it frightened her. Then he had them remount so she was in front of him. As they set off at a slower pace, he wrapped his arms around her and buried his face in her hair.

"Gods almighty," he said in a low growl. "I thought I'd never see you again."

His intensity unsettled her. "You came alone?" Surely the merchants hadn't stranded him in the desert.

"No one in the caravan would help." Anger crackled in his voice. "They thought you ran off with Cook. They were furious, both at losing the people who made their food and at me, for bringing you with the caravan. I told them you would never do such a thing, but they didn't believe it."

"You said that?" she asked. "I wasn't even sure you liked having me around."

"Be sure," he said gruffly. "I knew the nomads had you. I've seen how they operate. When they choose a victim, they'll dog her forever. They savor the chase."

"They had a buyer." She hated the words as much now as when Ji had spoken them. "General Yargazon."

"*Dusk* Yargazon? You mean the General of the Army for the Atajazid D'az Ozar?"

"Yes, him. Except they didn't use all those titles." She shuddered with the memory. "They just called him the general."

"He's the prince's regent." Darz spoke grimly. "Right now he's probably the most dangerous man in Jazid. He escaped execution-ers from the Misted Cliffs and snuck the prince out as well. Rumor claims he intends to put the boy back on the Onyx Throne."

Her voice cracked. "Not until he takes the Topaz Throne."

"Good gods, Ginger, what happened?"

She told him everything. Even before she finished, he was pushing Grayrider to go faster. When she said assassins planned to murder the queen at noon, he urged the horse into a gallop, and Ginger could no longer speak. They swept across the land. She kept silent about how much she hurt; her discomfort was nothing compared to the danger faced by their queen.

The sun climbed in the sky, and Darz soon had to let Grayrider slow down, lest he tire the horse so much, they couldn't reach Quaazar. After a few hours, he reined to a stop.

Darz rubbed Grayrider's lathered neck. "I know a water hole where we can rest."

Ginger could hear how much that cost him, having to stop. But if their horse died, they would never reach Quaaz in time.

The water hole was a pond fed by a spring and sheltered by

enough of an overhang that the sun didn't dry it up. While Darz tended Grayrider, Ginger lay in the shade and closed her eyes. The relief from riding was bliss, but it wasn't enough. She was going to clatter apart in a pile of bones and skin.

"Ginger," Darz said.

She opened her eyes. He was crouched next to her.

"I'm sorry," she said. "I should be stronger."

"You've more strength than two of those Jazid monsters combined." He laid his palm on her cheek. "You need a doctor."

She had never known a real doctor; they were people in tales from the cities. She smiled wanly. "Not too many out here."

"No." He looked miserable. "I'm afraid not."

"When we get to Quaaz, please don't turn me out."

"Good gods, why would I do that!" Then he winced. "Sorry. Too loud."

"It's all right."

"Why do you keep thinking I'm going to turn you out?"

"All those men looking at me, touching me…"

"I would like to kill them all," he said flatly. "Slowly. Agonizingly. Make them scream the way you screamed. But I have no intention of losing you, the treasure I found hidden in a mining town." He shook his head. "I can't imagine how you held out against Yargazon's interrogators. They're notorious. Never would I have believed he'd turn them against our people."

"They thought I was too stupid to understand what they were saying." It took so much energy to speak.

He sat next to her, one leg bent, his elbow resting on his knee. "If you had told them about me, they would be scouring these lands now, searching." Softly he added, "You saved my life, Ginger-Sun. Again. In more ways than you can imagine."

She looked up at him. "What about those men you were fighting?"

"They found me just before you showed up. When I refused to turn back, they attacked." He pushed his hand through his disheveled hair. "It seemed crazy they would threaten a Taka Mal traveler in his own country. Now it makes sense. They don't want anyone to find Yargazon hiding an army on the border. Killing a solitary traveler here is easy. They could have left my body in the desert, and no one would have ever known."

She wondered how many other travelers had met their death that way. "Do you think Yargazon can take the Topaz Throne?"

"Not if we can reach Quaaz in time." He stood up and offered her hand. "We should go."

She slowly sat up. "You can ride faster without my weight tiring Grayrider. You should go on by yourself." She didn't want to be alone in the middle of the desert, but she wanted even less for the queen to die. "Send someone back for me."

Darz looked at her with a strange expression, as if she had suggested he cut off his head. He pulled her to her feet, then drew her over to Grayrider. She limped at his side, uncertain how to take his silence. When they reached the horse, Darz stopped and regarded Ginger with that fierce expression of his, as if his eyes could swallow her. Then he offered his hands, cupped together, for her to mount the horse.

"Darz?"

He spoke softly. "I could no more go on without you than I could cut out my heart."

Something happened inside of her then, as if a stiff, rusty bolt had released in her heart. Until this moment, she hadn't realized how much she had locked away her feelings. She touched his cheek with the tips of her fingers. Then she put her foot in his cupped hands, and he helped her up onto Grayrider.

Within moments, they were riding, speeding against time to stop the warlords of a deposed child-king from conquering their land.

The
Topaz Sword

It was nearly noon when Darz reached the outskirts of Quaaz. Ginger thought they were riding through a town, the crowds were so thick. But they hadn't even reached Quaaz yet; these were just travelers going to the city. Darz let Grayrider walk to rest the horse, but Ginger felt his impatience as if it were a tangible presence. They rode past adults and children on foot or in oxen-drawn carts. People ignored them or watched with mild curiosity and then returned to their business.

They soon reached a wall taller than any other human-built barrier Ginger had ever seen, with crenellations along its top. Two great towers flanked the gate. Darz took an audible breath—and snapped his quirt against Grayrider's flank. The horse surged into a gallop and surged past the lines of people and animals entering the city. Gatekeepers were stopping everyone and asking questions. Darz raced straight past them, and people scattered out of his way.

"Hey!" The shout came from behind them. "You there! Stop! *Sentinels, get them!*"

Darz kept going, and within moments they were deep in the teeming streets of Quaaz. Ginger didn't know whether to gasp at his audacity or gulp. They might end up as prisoners of the queen's guard instead of rescuing her.

Buildings clustered on both sides of the street and people leaned out high windows, calling to those in other windows. Pedestrians crowded the streets, shopkeepers called out their wares, carts bumped along, and children ran everywhere. Ginger had thought J'Hiza was big, but compared to this place, it was a tiny hamlet in the middle of nowhere. These streets went on forever, in every direction, each as crowded as the last.

Darz knew the city well. They had to slow down, lest they trample someone, but he maneuvered through the crowds faster than Ginger would have thought possible. People yelled at him when Grayrider bumped them, but no one otherwise paid attention. They were just two more in the multitudes who thronged Quaaz.

Darz immersed them so well in a maze of crooked lanes, she soon had no idea where they were relative to the gate where they had entered. If they were lucky, the same was true for the sentinels following them.

The Topaz Palace rose above the city. Ginger had heard about the golden-yellow stone that gave the structure its name, but until she saw its towers glowing with their golden onion bulbs, she had never known how radiantly beautiful a building could be in the sunlight.

As they neared the palace, the city changed. Streets became wider and less crowded. They clattered across plazas with fountains. The houses set back from the road were hidden by gates and vine-covered fences abloom with sun-snaps and fire-lily vines.

Finally they galloped into a huge plaza where a reflecting pool stretched out to the palace itself. Darz gave Grayrider his head, and they raced alongside the water. Guards on foot were running toward them, coming around from the other side, and also two riders in gold dragon helmets and red and gold uniforms. They bellowed warnings, but Darz kept going, ignoring them all.

"Darz!" Ginger shouted for him to hear. "You have to stop! They'll think *you're* attacking!"

"They'll recognize me." He said something else, what sounded like, "I hope."

By the time they arrived at the courtyard in front of the palace, the men on foot had almost reached them. They yelled for Darz to stop, yet no one drew his sword. Ginger sincerely hoped that continued, that when Darz dismounted, they didn't skewer him first and demand to know what he was doing afterward.

Except Darz didn't dismount.

The two great double doors of the palace were open, and a man in a sunrise-plumed helmet stood in the entrance with his curved sword drawn. When Darz rode straight at him, Ginger groaned. Her husband was mad! Or perhaps everyone here was mad, for she couldn't understand why the doors were open.

As Darz galloped by the man, he shouted what sounded like, "Get spear caster!" Then they were inside and pounding across a courtyard with a circular fountain. The soaring arches of a colonnade surrounded it, and topaz mosaics covered the walls, arches and pillars. Darz thundered under an arch and into the hall beyond. Ginger had given up being nervous; this was so far outside her experience, she had no referent to absorb it all.

They galloped down the gleaming halls, and tiles cracked under Grayrider's hooves. People scattered out of the way, servants and soldiers and clerks. From their shocked looks, she gathered they didn't think this was normal, either.

At the end of an especially wide corridor, two gigantic doors stood ajar. Darz clattered past them and into a large hall with stained-glass windows. A carpet stretched from the doors all the way to a dais at the far end, where two thrones stood side by side, plated in gold and encrusted with gems.

As Darz galloped down the hall, a tall man with silver hair ran into the far end, near the dais. He dazzled Ginger, and she couldn't take in his full appearance, only his brilliant red-and-gold uniform and the huge curved sword at his side. Then she realized the sash that slanted across his chest bore disks enameled in sunrise colors. She recognized them from descriptions in the history scrolls; he had on the dress uniform of a Taka Mal general. She had read only of ranks as high as four disks; if he had five, he must truly be formidable, perhaps even the General of the Army, the man in command of the entire military.

"Darz, we're in trouble," she said. If he heard, he gave no sign. He brought Grayrider to such an abrupt stop at the dais, the horse reared up above the general. Ginger clutched its mane and prayed Darz didn't end up killing the commander of Her Majesty's armed forces.

As Grayrider came down, the general shouted at Darz, "What the flaming hell are you doing?"

"Where is Vizarana?" Darz demanded.

Ginger expected the general to call for guards. Instead he said, "In the Sunset Garden. Why?"

"Who is with her?" Urgency crackled in Darz's voice.

"The Jazid envoy. She and Drummer took him to the lake."

"Both of them?" Darz shouted at him. "Not the baby, too?"

"Yes, actually." The general frowned at him. "We've been entertaining the diplomats from the Jazid army."

"Diplomats, hell," Darz said. "How many Jazidians are with her? And how many guards?"

"Just one Jazid officer. Major Tarcol," the general said, his face puzzled. "And two of our palace guards."

"Listen to me," Darz said. "Yargazon has an army that may be marching on Quaaz. His Shadow Assassins exist, Spearcaster. They've been murdering our officers. I want you to put *anyone* here who has anything to do with Jazid under guard. They aren't to go near Vizarana. And send a full contingent of palace sentinels to the Sunrise Garden. *Now.*"

With that, he wheeled Grayrider around and took off. He didn't even pause to let Ginger off the horse. She was too shocked to protest. What she had just seen, Darz giving orders to a general— no, she couldn't absorb the implications, not yet.

He raced through the palace and under an arch into a huge garden. Trellises curved everywhere, heavy with red pyramid-blossoms. He raced down yellow gravel paths between flower beds of snap-lions. Fire-opal blossoms blazed on bushes sculpted to resemble gold-wing hawks in flight.

Beyond the flowers, a hill of impossibly succulent grass sloped to a lake. It dizzied Ginger; she had never seen so much green in one place. Sunlight glanced off the lake as if it were a gigantic mirror. As her mind adjusted, she realized people were running under the trees near the shore. It was more than the four General Spearcaster had described. A group of large men in the dark clothes worn by Jazidians were attacking a woman in a green silk tunic and trousers and a slender man with impossibly *yellow* hair. The woman held a baby in her arms. Two beleaguered Taka Mal guards were trying to hold off the attackers, but they were woefully outnumbered.

Grayrider's hooves tore up the grass as Darz sped toward the group. One of the taller men caught the woman and wrenched her to a stop. Two other men grabbed the man with yellow hair. The Taka Mal guards were fighting three of the Jazidians, their swords flashing, but they couldn't break through to the woman. When the man who had caught her tried to take the baby, the man with yellow hair went berserk. He fought furiously against his captors with his fists, but he was obviously outmatched in size, strength, and training.

"Gods almighty." Darz drew his sword and shouted in his booming voice, "Get the flaming hell off her!"

The fighters spun around, and the woman twisted away from the man who had caught her. She lunged into a run, cradling the child against her chest, and raced up the slope toward Darz. She shouted something, not "Help me!" but what sounded like, *"Help Drummer!"*

Darz bore down on them all with his sword held high. The Jazidians regrouped to face him, their blades glinting, and the Taka Mal soldiers ran to the man with yellow hair. Then Darz was in the midst of the group, slashing at the Jazidians from horseback. He faced six of them, but they were on foot, which gave him an advantage. And he was *angry*. Ginger didn't think he even realized she was still on the horse. He clenched her around the waist with one arm while wielding his sword with the other, and she held her breath, praying his rage didn't incinerate her along with the warriors.

What must have looked like an easy kill to the assassins suddenly wasn't so simple. Darz swung at one of them, and the man parried with a straight rather than curved blade. Metal swords clanged as the swords hit. Darz struck again, and this time he knocked the weapon out of the man's hand. It arced through the air and landed in the grass.

To Ginger, time seemed to slow, as if they moved through invisible molasses. Darz's blade descended again, painfully bright in the sun. The assassin raised his arms to ward it off, and his face clenched into a snarl. Then the sword hit, cleaving the man through his arm and from his left shoulder to his right side. Blood shot into the air, splattering Darz's horse. Ginger screamed, and it echoed in her ears. Until that moment, she hadn't truly comprehended what it meant that her husband was a warrior.

Everything jolted back to normal speed, and she realized other riders had joined them, the sentinels Darz had called for. It was too many people, too many voices, too much happening. The assassin Darz had killed lay on the ground in his own blood.

Several sentinels dismounted and joined the Taka Mal guards protecting the man with yellow hair. Two of the assassins were crumpled on the grass, and the sentinels were taking the others prisoner. The woman with the baby was trying to reach the man with the yellow hair, but people had surrounded her, talking, hovering, enclosing her and the child in a protective cocoon. Ginger stared at her, knowing she had seen the face before. Her head was swimming. That woman…her face…it was on the gold hexa-coin of Taka Mal.

"Ah, gods," Ginger whispered. She swayed and started to topple off the horse.

Darz put his arms around her, still holding his bloodied sword. He leaned over, his forehead against the back of her head. "Don't fall, Ginger-Sun."

"Sire," a man said. "We have them all. Four are alive."

Darz's head lifted. "Lock them in the north tower. And have Spearcaster and Firaz meet me in the conference room."

Ginger struggled to get her bearings. The yellow-haired man and the woman were together now, the man with his arms around the woman and her baby, the three of them surrounded by guards. Yellow hair. How could it be? The only person she knew without dark hair was herself, and hers was the color of fire. It was easier to wonder at his hair than to absorb the truth, that she was looking at the queen of Taka Mal and her Aronsdale consort.

It finally registered on Ginger's dazed mind that a sentinel on a large bay horse had come over to them. He was the one who had spoken to Darz. She couldn't take it all in, but she didn't want to pass out, not in front of all these people.

The sentinel was watching Ginger. To Darz, he said, "Do you or your guest need any medical help?"

"I'm fine," Darz said. "But, yes, bring a doctor." Holding Ginger, he spoke in a low voice. "I couldn't let go of her. The assassins—they tried to murder all the heirs."

"Yes, sir." The sentinel didn't seem to know how to respond. Ginger was glad she wasn't the only confused person here.

After the guard went for the doctor, a man on a sleek black charger rode up to them. He must not have been in the royal party entertaining Jazid diplomats, because he didn't have on a dress uniform; he wore "only" the day uniform of a Taka Mal general, with four rather than five disks to indicate his rank.

This second general peered at Darz. "Where have you been? We've been searching for you for over a tenday."

"It's a long story." Darz sounded exhausted. "Firaz, would Yargazon really do it, ride on Taka Mal?"

"We've sent scouts out to see what they can find." He was staring at Ginger. "Who is this beautiful creature?"

"Do not call my wife a creature," Darz said sharply.

Ginger hadn't been fully aware of just how many people were around them, all talking, until everyone went silent. The queen turned from her discussion to look. Although she still had the shawl that had wrapped her baby, her husband held the child protectively cradled in his arms.

"Your wife?" Firaz's brow furrowed. "I don't recall any negotiations about you taking a wife."

"I did the damn negotiations myself," Darz growled.

"I see." Firaz didn't look as if he saw at all.

Darz reached into the travel bags and rummaged until he found the scrolls. "These are the documents. She and I both signed them."

A memory rushed back to Ginger: Darz, trying to rewrite his name on the scrolls and smudging it instead. Making it look like *Baz.* And he had added *Ar'Quaaz.* It was an arcane way to say "of the city of Quaaz." Except it had one other meaning, even rarer and more antique: *Of the House of Quaaz.* No one used it, of course, because Taka Mal had almost none of the ancient highborn houses remaining except the Zanterians—

And the Quaazeras.

He had written his true name on that scroll that night, at the same time he wrote that she and their children would be his full heirs. Baz Goldstone Quaazera. Gods help her, she had married a member of the royal family.

General Firaz had unrolled one of the scrolls and was studying it. "Damn thing looks in order."

The queen spoke from where she stood with her consort. Her

voice was husky and rich. "Baz, it would behoove you to provide your wife with more clothes than the undertunic of a Jazid soldier."

Ginger shivered and crossed her arms, painfully aware of her clothes. The undertunic was opaque instead of translucent, but she was still sitting in front of all these impossibly important people with her arms and legs bare, and nothing but a light shift covering her.

Vizarana walked over to them, flanked by guards. The image on the hexa-coins hadn't exaggerated her beauty. Black curls cascaded over her shoulders. At the moment, her very large eyes were also very angry. She frowned at Darz. "If this lovely young woman is your wife, perhaps you might treat her in a more hospitable manner?"

As soon as Darz inhaled, Ginger knew that, saints help them, he was going to shout at the queen of Taka Mal. Before he managed a word, though, Vizarana frowned with an expression that looked exactly like his when he was irate. "Don't yell at me, Baz."

"I was saving your damn life," he growled.

Her face gentled. "And I thank you with the deepest gratitude, dear cousin."

Cousin. Ah, no. Vizarana was the one he was supposed to have married. Except she wed the Aronsdale prince instead. Her "skinny" husband was the lithe young man who stood watching them while he held his child as if he would protect her from a thousand assassins.

General Firaz was scanning the scroll. "Baz, this says you married her twelve days ago."

"That's right." Darz's hair rustled as he turned his head behind her. Pinwheels danced in her vision.

Firaz had a strange expression. "Then it is possible she may be with child?"

Saints above! Ginger's face flamed. Why would he bring up such a private matter? She probably wasn't pregnant, but it was a matter between Darz and her, not Darz and her and his generals.

"I know," Darz said. Incredibly, his voice was uneven. He had faced death at least three times in the past few days without a flinch, yet at the mention of the slight chance he might have impregnated his wife, his voice shook. Ginger thought perhaps she understood men even less than she had realized.

In a low voice, she said, "It happens, you know."

Darz spoke softly. "Aye, Ginger-Sun. Yargazon sought to murder Vizarana's heirs, never knowing he had as his prisoner the woman who might carry the child third in line to the Topaz Throne, after Vizarana's child and myself."

And then, finally, she understood. All of it. Why the Dragon-Sun had tested her fidelity to Darz, and why the Shadow Dragon implied the sun had chosen Darz for her, though he favored her for himself. *If you want him, you may have him.* The sun had given her the Quaazera prince, the man of highest rank and title in all Taka Mal, the human embodiment of the Dragon-Sun.

It was too much. She sagged in Darz's arms. She wanted to say *Take me home,* but she had no idea what place to call home. She needed somewhere safe, away from all these staring, stunned people, where she could curl into a ball and nurse her injuries.

"Baz," the queen said. "I think you better let her down."

Darz, or Baz as they called him, spoke gruffly. "Firaz, I'll meet you and Spearcaster in the conference room in twenty minutes." He waved his hand. "Take the sentinels."

The general nodded and brought his horse around, calling out orders. Many of the sentinels left with him, but six stayed to guard the royal family. One of the sentinels helped Ginger dismount. Acutely self-conscious, she held down the hem of her tunic as she eased off the horse. When Ginger was standing on the ground, Vizarana motioned the sentinel away and took Ginger's arm, offering her support. Ginger could do little more than stare at Vizarana's wild curls and fiercely beautiful eyes.

Belatedly, Ginger realized what she was doing. "Your Majesty, forgive me," she rasped, and started to drop to her knees. Next to her, Darz jumped down from the horse.

"Don't do that." Vizarana caught her elbow and drew her back up. She started to lay her shawl over Ginger's shoulders, but then she stopped.

"Saints above," the queen said. "What happened to you?"

Darz put his arms around Ginger, and she leaned her head into his chest, grateful for the support. So tired. She was so tired. Every muscle in her body hurt.

"Dusk Yargazon racked her," he said grimly.

Vizarana's stunning voice turned icy. "I see."

Spots danced in Ginger's vision. Her legs felt odd, as if they no longer contained bones. They melted under her. With a sigh, she slid out of Darz's hold and crumpled to the ground.

21

Sky Colors

Time flowed. Hours. Days. Ginger didn't know. She lay on a soft mattress enveloped by covers. Sometimes a woman hovered over the bed, tending her. Another woman came, older, gentle. She fed Ginger soup from a yellow glazed bowl. Other times Vizarana was there, speaking in her distinctive voice. Guards came in and out of sight. But most of the time Ginger escaped into sleep.

The next time she awoke, the bed had turned hard. Gritty. Lifting her head, she peered around.

She was lying in the desert.

Bewildered, Ginger slowly sat up. She felt as if she were moving in a thick syrup. Whoever had brought her here had left her with nothing, not even water. A chill cut through her shift. She shivered and rubbed her hands on her arms. Surely she would have awoken when they carried her out here. Unless they drugged her. Did they find her marriage to Darz that abhorrent? Although he wouldn't be the first Quaazera prince to wed a priestess, it was unusual. They might tell him she died while he was away dealing with Yargazon. But that didn't fit; they had seemed solicitous rather than hostile.

She recognized nothing here and saw no sign of the city or the travelers who thronged to it. Orange ground spread to the horizon, with jagged red rocks. No life showed, not even the virtually indestructible sand-grass. The day had dimmed as if it were overcast, yet the sun burned low on the horizon in a cloudless sky. The light had a red cast, and the desert was dark even where rays of the setting sun touched the earth.

Ginger climbed to her feet and looked around the stark plain. She rubbed her hands on her arms, seeking warmth. The last molten sliver of the sun vanished below the horizon, and the desert reddened even more. The color wasn't in the sky, it filled the air. The luminous hues swirled into a pillar—

And took on human form.

The woman was twice as tall as Ginger, and the layered drapes of her gown glowed like a sunset. Her hair rippled and streamed until it was difficult to tell where it ended and the air began.

Ginger went down on one knee and bowed her head. *You honor me, Lady Sunset.*

Rise, child. Her voice was like whiskey that had aged for centuries, millennia, eons. It held the promise of beginnings but also the fading of life.

Ginger rose to her feet. *I am privileged by your presence. But I did not call you.*

You have always called me, Ginger-Sun. She extended her hand, and a fire opal glowed on her palm. **With this.**

Did you give me the spells? Hope stirred in Ginger. Would she finally understand the source of her power? *Then I will always honor them.*

If you use them in honor of me, I am pleased. She closed her hand around the opal, and its light shone through her fingers. But the gifts do not come from me. They descend from Your Aronsdale grandfather.

Gifts? *I fear they are a curse.*

They are what you make of them. Be wise. Her thoughts flowed. Understand the price they exact. The illness you suffer now is as much from the violent use of your power as from what you endured by Yargazon's hand.

Ginger had felt the backlash of her spells. *The darkness is within me.*

To know light, you must know shadows. They cannot exist without each other.

Ginger spoke the fear that had always been with her, even more since she had created the inferno in Sky Flames. *The power makes me less.*

Why?

Because I'm capable of terrible acts.

You can choose to reject such acts, except when to do otherwise would be a greater evil. Her ageless gaze never wavered, though her body rippled with light. To do what is right though you are capable of great wrong is a more powerful good than to do what is right because you can do nothing else.

I don't know if I can always choose what is right.

You have said it yourself: If the dragon always smoothed your path, it would weaken you. You choose. That demands more of you, but in doing so, you become more. Remember this.

I will remember. She spread her hands out from her body. *But why, if I celebrate the sun, do my spells come only in the hours of shadow?*

Perhaps it is for you to bring light into the dark. Her thoughts rippled. So it is that I set you a task.

A task?

Bring light to my daughters, Ginger-Sun. You have come within the highest circles of the land. If you can make a difference in the constrained lives of my daughters, I charge you with that task.

As it is your will, it will be mine. She wasn't sure how she could better the lives of other women, but she would try.

The colors of Sunset's body faded. If your need is ever again great, call on us. I cannot promise we will come; The balance must reassert itself. But we will try....

The light disappeared, and Ginger was alone in the desert. The sky overhead had deepened into twilight, and stars sparkled like a dust of diamonds.

"Wait!" She turned in a circle, searching the barren land. "Don't leave me here."

Only the keening wind answered her.

"Wait!" Ginger sat bolt upright. Voluminous bedcovers fell down to her waist. She was staring at a candle burning in a porcelain holder at the foot of her bed. The rest of the room was in shadow. The window opposite showed the twilight sky with a glitter of early stars.

The pounding of her heart slowed. Maybe she had dreamed the Sunset. Taking a breath, she pushed her hand through her hair.

Orange sand scattered across the sheets.

Across the room, the door swung inward. A woman bustled in bearing a tray with a steaming bowl, and another woman followed, holding a candle. With a start, Ginger realized the light bearer was the queen.

"You're awake," Vizarana said. She motioned for the other woman to set the tray on the nightstand. The smell of leek and saffron soup wafted enticingly around Ginger.

After the maid left, Vizarana sat in the chair by the bed and set her candle on the tray. "Are you hungry?"

"In a bit," Ginger said. "I'm a little groggy." In truth, she was too self-conscious to eat in front of the queen. Vizarana was twice her age, with a matured beauty that came as much from her strength as any arrangement of features. In her presence, Ginger felt callow. Rather than the constraining garb favored by highborn women, the queen wore a red tunic and a pair of Zanterian riding trousers dyed a rich crimson. Gleaming crimson balls dangled from her ears, and a matching necklace glinted around her throat. Her black hair spilled wildly about her shoulders. In the gold sheath on her belt, a dagger with a topaz in its hilt glinted. She looked like a barbarian warrior more than a stateswoman.

"My honor at your presence, Your Majesty," Ginger said.

"And mine at yours," Vizarana said. "But you don't have to call me 'Your Majesty.' We're cousins, now. Jade will do."

Jade. Not even Vizarana, but her private name. "Thank you. Please call me Ginger."

The queen nodded, accepting the name. "How do you feel?"

"Muzzy," she admitted. Her mind was clearing, though, and filling with questions. "Do you know what happened with General Yargazon? Is Darz all right?"

Jade tilted her head. "Who is Darz?"

"Well, he told me his name was Darz. You all call him Baz."

"Ah." Jade drew one of her feet up onto the chair and rested her elbow on her bent knee, a feat few other women of highborn status in Taka Mal could have managed, given their constraining garb.

"It's a mess," Jade said. "Thank the saints we had your warning. Yargazon had brought his army to within only an hour of the city when Baz met him with ours." A fierce satisfaction showed in her gaze. "Yargazon was quite shocked to see my cousin alive and well. Alive, well—and furious."

Ginger crumpled the covers in her hand. "Did they fight?"

Jade let out a long breath. "It seems that for today at least, we are spared a war. Had their plan succeeded, it would have been different. Who would have led our army? General Spearcaster, yes, but with the loss of the royal family, and Jazid descending with no warning, we would have been vulnerable." She pulled her hand through her hair, drawing curls back from her face. "As it was, the forces were evenly matched and ours far better prepared than Yargazon expected. Or so I'm assuming. He claims he had no intention of attacking, that he had learned of the assassination plot and was coming to defend us. He says you made up the entire story about his intention to betray Taka Mal."

Anger swept over Ginger. "He's lying!"

Jade raised her hand, palm out in the traditional gesture of calm. "We know, Ginger-Sun. A great deal of evidence supports what you've said." Her voice hardened. "Including the murder attempt against my cousin and heir. It also explains the disappearance of several of my top officers." Grief showed on her expressive face. "Your description of Colonel Aroch was devastatingly accurate. Nor would he have ever willingly told you that information about my covert agents. You couldn't have known unless you were present where it was forced out of him."

With a sinking sensation, Ginger realized who she meant. "The colonel was the man they interrogated before me?"

"Yes, we think so." She rubbed her eyes, then let her arm drop. "I've known Aroch for years. To think of what he went through—

and that they attacked Baz, my closest kin—" She took a deep breath. Then she said, simply, "Yargazon has made an enemy."

Ginger suspected the queen was far more dangerous than Yargazon realized, perhaps more than he could even comprehend. But Ginger had also sensed the power simmering within him. She could well believe Darz's claim that he was one of the most dangerous men alive. "General Yargazon won't give up."

"I know." Jade thumped her fist on her knee. "It was a wickedly effective ploy. If he had succeeded, he would have doubled the size of his army and put the boy atajazid on a throne the Misted Cliffs doesn't control. Even failing, he creates a threat to the Misted Cliffs that weakens their hold in Jazid. Cobalt has already overextended his forces trying to secure their country. Now he must contend with a threat to Taka Mal, as well, which means he either must extend his forces further or risk losing sway in the desert. He is bound by kinship, too, because of Drummer, my husband." She shook her head. "I know people see Cobalt as evil. But Yargazon is the one I fear."

"I can see why." Those few words barely touched Ginger's feelings on that matter.

Jade regarded her for a moment.

"What is it?" Ginger asked.

"Yargazon doesn't deny he bought you as a pleasure slave. In fact, he insists we return you to him."

"What? *No.* You cannot!"

"Ah, Ginger-Sun. We would never do such."

Ginger took a shaky breath. She saw something on Jade's face she hadn't seen for a long time, not from the elders or the nomads or the interrogators. Compassion. Lately, the only people who had shown it to her were Darz, Heath, the miners and Jalla. And Kindle, who could be a good person when he wasn't drinking or trying to blow up people.

Jade spoke quietly. "Dusk Yargazon is no fool. He is well aware that abducting the wife of the General of the Queen's Army would be an act of war."

"Baz commands the entire army?" She knew she shouldn't be surprised, given what she had seen. But still.

Jade smiled wryly. "I take it he neglected to mention that fact, too."

"Among a few others."

"Don't be angry with him. He was protecting himself."

"Against me?"

"Actually, I think he did trust you. But none of the people around you. He was also worried what you might reveal if you were captured." She inclined her head. "You have our deepest gratitude, Ginger-Sun. To go through what you did and never reveal that Baz was alive—I will forever be indebted to you."

"I don't think I could have held out much longer."

"Many would have broken sooner."

She thought back to what Darz had told her so many days ago. *It seems I'm on leave whether I want to be or not.* "Darz—I mean Baz, said he had been going to Taza Qu."

Jade spoke in a voice heavy with grief. "I was the one who wanted him to take some time. He lost someone close to him in the Battle of the Rocklands, both a mentor and a friend, another of my generals. I knew Baz needed to mourn. But after he vanished—" She closed her eyes for a moment, then opened them. "I blame myself. If I had let him stay on duty, the assassins wouldn't have found him."

"He's the one who chose to slip away from his guards that morning." Ginger understood much better now why Darz had been so adamant she never go anywhere by herself.

"It wouldn't have mattered if I hadn't urged him to go."

Ginger spoke in a quiet voice. "And you and your baby would be dead now, and your consort a Jazid prisoner."

Jade stared at her for a long moment. Then she murmured, "Aye, that's true."

"General Yargazon is not someone I wish to meet again," Ginger said, one of the great understatements of her life.

"The doctor and midwife tell me—well, they don't think you were forced." Jade spoke awkwardly. "But neither was certain, with all the riding you did."

"I wasn't." Ginger crumpled the sheet in her fists. "He hadn't gotten around to it yet."

Jade leaned forward. "Know this, Ginger-Sun. No matter what anyone has said in your village or anywhere else, you have nothing to feel shame for." Then she said, "But if he did force you, we *must* know."

Her face was burning. "He didn't."

"Baz says you had your menses on the trip with the caravan."

"He *told* you that?" What a thing to discuss with the queen.

"I'm sorry." Jade looked as if she meant it. "But Yargazon says he slept with you, and that if you have a child, it will be his."

Ginger stared at her. "That's horrible!"

"Baz used less repeatable language," Jade said wryly. "But if you give birth in nine months or less, Yargazon is going to claim he sired the child who stands third in line to my throne."

"I can't believe this," Ginger said. "He's telling you he raped your cousin's wife and therefore he has a claim to the throne? That's crazy."

"Apparently Baz had a similar reaction." Jade's smile had no humor in it, only an edge like a honed knife. "Firaz tells me they literally had to hold Baz back from trying to kill Yargazon and starting a war right there."

Ginger scowled. "Then why isn't Yargazon in a dungeon?"

"Unfortunately, his encampment straddles the border. He claims he was in Jazid when the nomads brought you to him." Her gaze darkened. "And in Jazid, it is legal to buy women."

"Except for the 'small' matter that I'm already married."

"I'm afraid niceties like marriage and consent have little to do with this." Jade shook her head. "It wasn't so long ago Taka Mal had similar laws. They've changed over the years, and I've made progress. But it takes time. I can't just throw around decrees. Too much, too fast, and the people will reject my authority. It's iffy enough already having a woman on the Topaz Throne." She looked as if she had eaten a sour fruit. "According to Jazid custom, what happened to you is acceptable, and according to their justice system, it's legal."

"But surely he can't take me back."

"Not while you're on Taka Mal soil." Grimly, Jade added, "Assuming proof exists that he had anything to do with your disappearance." She gave Ginger a look of apology. "My husband and I always have guards, everywhere, even in our home. I'm afraid the same will have to hold for you." After a pause, she added, "Eventually you get used to it."

It sounded like a relief to Ginger, after all that had happened. Hesitant, she said, "I thought you all would object to me as a consort for Baz."

"Oh, my generals like you, just from what Baz has told them." She gave an affectionate snort. "Hell, they're men. They liked you the moment they laid eyes on you. They see a gorgeous woman, they stop thinking."

Ginger couldn't help but smile, imagining how Darz would respond to *that* statement. Definitely loud. "Even so."

Jade's grin flashed, so much like Darz. "I've *never* seen my cousin so smitten. General Firaz says he can't understand why you put up with Baz, but he thinks having a priestess for a wife will be good for my cousin."

Ginger wasn't sure they understood. "He told you, didn't he, that I don't come from a noble or royal line?"

Jade shrugged. "Neither does Drummer. A priestess is considered a highborn woman, but Drummer's connections are all by marriage. His father is an orchard keeper." Wryly she added, "You should have heard my generals complain about *that*."

"Drummer?" Ginger asked. "You mean your husband? The man with yellow hair?"

Jade made an exasperated noise. "Why is that the first thing people always say about him? Firaz even gave it as a reason I shouldn't marry him. A lot of people in Aronsdale have yellow hair." She paused, considering Ginger. "Or red-gold."

"My grandfather was from Aronsdale."

Jade started to speak, paused, started again, then stopped and scratched her chin.

"What is it?" Ginger asked.

"Baz showed me the opal you carry."

Gods only knew what would happen if the queen thought she was a witch. "It's a good luck charm." Ginger smiled, trying to deflect the conversation. "It must work. I met Baz."

Jade snorted. "You call that good luck? Not for your ears, I'd wager."

She couldn't help but laugh. "He does have a robust voice."

"That's a diplomatic way to put it." Jade's smile changed into something harder to read. Curiosity perhaps. "Drummer has such a charm, also. His is a gold cube."

Ginger recalled one of her earliest conversations with Darz, when he described the Battle of the Rocklands: *Some say this dragon in the sky was no more than a trick of light and air created by the queen's consort.* Was Jade trying to tell her something, but holding back just as Ginger would hesitate?

Ginger spoke carefully. "If Prince Drummer was a commoner, how did he end up related to the king of the Misted Cliffs?"

"It's convoluted," Jade admitted. "Drummer's sister married Muller Dawnfield, the cousin of the king of Aronsdale. Later, the king of Harsdown tried to conquer Aronsdale. The Aronsdale king defeated him and ended up in control of Harsdown. He sent his cousin Muller to be sovereign there. Cobalt was the son of the deposed king of Harsdown. It took Cobalt years, but he raised an army to take back Harsdown. To stop the war, Muller's daughter agreed to marry him. So Cobalt doesn't get the throne of Harsdown, but his son will. Cobalt's wife is Drummer's niece."

The lives of royal families sounded a lot less pleasant and a lot more complicated than Ginger had ever imagined. "Goodness."

"I don't think much of that was involved," Jade said dryly.

"But King Muller married a commoner, yes? Drummer's sister." Jade met her gaze. "That's right."

"They do that in Aronsdale, I've heard." She hesitated. "People say it is because the royals seek mages to be their brides."

"So they say."

Ginger didn't know how to ask if it were true. "Does it bother Prince Drummer that people think his sister is a mage?" *Or Drummer himself?*

"I don't think so." Jade shrugged. "People say all sorts of things about royal families. It's the mystique, you know."

"I guess so." She doubted Jade would say more. Ginger didn't blame her, having almost died at the stake for just the rumor of such abilities. She rubbed her eyes. "It must be late."

"Ach!" Jade sounded just like Darz. "I shouldn't keep you awake."

She thought of what had happened before the queen came in to see her. "Did you see the sunset tonight?"

"Wasn't that odd? I've never seen one with *no* colors."

Ginger's pulse jumped. "Yes. I wonder why it happened."

Jade shrugged. "My astronomers say the sky had less dust than usual. It seemed the same as usual to me, but they know more about such things."

No colors. A chill went through Ginger, and she brushed at the orange sand scattered on the quilt. Another thought pulled her, too. She spoke shyly, still unsure of her place here. "Is Baz back at the palace?"

"He's been in council with my other generals." Jade picked up the candle and rose to her feet. "I'm going to join them. I'll tell him you awoke."

"Thank you."

Jade went to the door. But then she paused. Turning back, she said, "Sometime, perhaps you would like to discuss Aronsdale with Drummer. He might be able to help you learn more about your grandfather's heritage."

Her pulse leapt. Her grandfather's greatest heritage to her was her mage gifts. "I would like that."

"I'll tell him." With that, the queen departed, leaving one flickering candle. Ginger lay down, worn out, while her thoughts roiled....

She woke into darkness and rolled against Darz. Fast asleep, he gave a snort of a snore and settled deeper into the mattress.

"I'm glad you're here," she murmured. "Even if you do snore too loud."

Apparently he wasn't as deep in slumber as she thought, for he chuckled and turned onto his back. He pulled her into his arms so she was lying with her head in the curve where his arm met his shoulder. "Light of the moon, priestess."

A memory jumped into her mind: his sword cleaving the assassin in two. She didn't know if she would ever reconcile these parts of his personality, the man who touched her with such gentleness and the killer who fought so savagely.

"I'm not really a priestess anymore," she said. "I have no temple."

"Jade is going to ask if you'll serve in the palace temple. We don't have anyone." He yawned. "She's trying to figure how to phrase it so it doesn't sound as if she's taking advantage of your coming here."

"I think you just took care of that."

"Oh! Damn. I'm an idiot."

She kissed his cheek. "But a handsome one."

"You're supposed to say, 'No, you're not an idiot,'" he told her. "Or 'I would be happy to serve in your temple.'"

She settled more into the curve of his arm. "It would be my honor to serve as priestess for the royal family."

"Ginger!"

"Hmm?"

"I'm going to rue the day I ever introduced you to Jade," he growled. "You treat me just like she does."

Ginger liked being compared to the queen. But then her good mood receded. "She's the one you were supposed to marry, isn't she?"

"Yes. But she's too much like my sister." He rubbed his hand over her shoulder. "I'm glad I didn't."

"She's gorgeous."

He hmmphed. "She's impossible. She wouldn't have married me anyway. She was afraid I was after her throne."

Ginger didn't ask if that were true. For him to say anything but "no" could be treason. She had no doubt he was loyal to his cousin. But she could see another reason they never married; it would have been a constant struggle for power. She wondered if they realized they had chosen similar life-mates, a companion who was gentle where they were fierce, someone younger, vulnerable, in need of their protection, a spouse who was like water to their fire. It didn't matter that Vizarana was female and Darz male; their Quaazera heritage outweighed all the rest.

"You said her name was Lima," Ginger said.

"I couldn't tell you her real name." He grinned. "Don't tell her I said Lima. She'll kill me. I used to call her Lima Bean when we were children. She hated it."

"I won't tell." Ginger paused, puzzled. "You also said she and Drummer married for love."

"They did." Grudgingly, he added, "The treaty business was a good idea. But she didn't come up with it until after she proposed to him."

That really woke Ginger up. "*She* asked him?"

Darz snorted. "He's a damn minstrel, for flaming sake. An acrobat who's never wielded a sword in his life. It would have been an insult and presumption beyond redemption for him to ask the queen of Taka Mal to marry him."

"It all sounds so romantic."

"Ach! Why do women *say* that? It wasn't romantic. It was maddening and damn near got that boy killed three times over."

"He's hardly a boy."

"He's too young for her," Darz groused. Then he sighed, and the tension in his arms eased. "But for some reason, Jade loves him. He makes her happy. So I can live with it."

"Good…" She closed her eyes.

He turned on his side. "Don't go to sleep, Ginger-Sun."

"Darz—"

"I know," he muttered. "'Behave, Baz. She's been through a lot. And don't make a baby for at least three months.'"

"They told you not to touch me for three months?"

"Let's just say it was strongly suggested."

"I need time, but not that much." Given the way her body was reacting to him, she suspected it wouldn't be long at all. "We can figure some other way to avoid pregnancy for three months."

His voice lightened. "I like that idea better."

She smiled, pleased. "You're a prince."

"Yes, I know," he grumbled. "I assure you, it doesn't mean I'm a nice person."

"You try to hide it. But you don't very well."

He groused more, holding her, but she could tell he was pleased.

He fell silent, and she thought he had gone to sleep. Then he asked, "Are you awake?"

Drowsing, she didn't have the energy to answer. After she had been quiet for some time, her breathing deep and regular, he murmured, "I think I'm in love with you, Ginger-Sun."

Softly she said, "Then I am a lucky woman indeed, to have my feelings returned."

"Ach! I thought you were asleep!"

"Mmm… Light of the moon, my loud husband."

He laughed and lowered his voice. "Light always, wife."

For the first time since the night the miners had brought Baz into the temple, she felt safe.

Epilogue

Ginger wandered the exquisite wings of the Topaz Palace and marveled at its beauty, the mosaics, the arched windows, the detailed carvings in the woodwork. In one hall, life-sized portraits of the Quaazeras stared at her, fierce men and lushly beautiful women. Her two guards followed at a discreet distance, close enough to protect her, but far enough away that she didn't feel as if they were treading on her heels.

She found the temple in the woods near the lake. It was much like the one in Sky Flames, with inverted terraces for a roof, an airy main room, smaller chambers around the periphery, and the glowing RayLight Chamber in its center. Its size was the same, too, though the temple in Sky Flames had been for an entire village, whereas this one served only the palace.

The craftsmanship astonished her: porcelain vases, engraved arches that resembled frozen lace, lush tapestries on the walls—it was incredible. The basin of the fountain was wider across than two men were tall. Sculpted fire-lily statues opened in the center, and water cascaded out of the blossoms. The sunwood furniture was set with brocade cushions in sunrise colors. It was also covered with dust. She would need to do a lot of cleaning to make the temple presentable, but such a fine place was well worth the effort.

Nor would she be hindered in her work. Instead of a wrap, the maids had offered her an astounding choice of garments, all acceptable for a priestess, they assured her. The yellow skirt they suggested she wear fit low on her hips and hung to her ankles, so full that when she spun around, it swirled in a circle. The yellow silk bodice sparkled with topazes. It covered most of her torso, but left her abdomen bare, and also her lower arms. In Sky Flames, even before she had trouble with the elders, such apparel would have convinced them they needed to lock her up forever. More than so much else, these clothes made her aware of her new freedom.

She sat on the ledge of the fountain, pensive. Although she would gladly serve here, it reminded her of all she had lost. She couldn't imagine returning to Sky Flames even now, when she could ride into the village as consort to the Quaazera prince, with a full company of the army. She could never again see the village without remembering the betrayals of the elders or reliving the terror of flames roaring around her at the stake.

She had written her brother to let him know she was all right, that matters had worked out better than anyone could have expected. She hoped he and Harjan would visit her. Along with that letter, the queen sent a retinue for Kindle, to bring him to Quaaz so he could work with the army on the powder. Whether or not anything would come of this "gunpowder," Ginger had no idea. Nor did she think she would ever feel comfortable around Kindle. But he had a lot of good in him, if he could learn to control his temper. And he was an excellent choice to investigate the powder; he had always had a knack for making things work, and he seemed fascinated with the challenge.

Darz wanted to heave the elders and Dirk into a dungeon. But Ginger had checked the legal archives; they hadn't broken any laws. Although no one was burned at the stake anymore, the antiquated law remained part of Taka Mal's legal code. She knew Darz would have them arrested if she asked. She didn't. Given her new status, they wouldn't get a fair trial; if she let them be convicted that way, it was no better than what they had done to her. She wanted to face them, to *make* them see the wrong they had done. She didn't want them executed; she wanted them to suffer guilt for the rest of their godforsaken lives.

Until she could handle the anger burning within her—and control it—she couldn't see them. She had to deal with the darkness in herself before she faced it in others. She wasn't ready yet. But the time would come. Then she and Darz would go to Sky Flames.

"I forget how serene it is here," a man said.

She jumped up and whirled around. A few feet away, Drummer Headwind stood watching her, his yellow hair gleaming in the light slanting through a stained-glass window. Even without moving, he had an extraordinary grace. He wasn't as tall as a Taka Mal man, barely taller than Ginger herself, and he had a lithe build rather than the bulk she was used to seeing in men. His eyes were *blue*. The extraordinary color looked unreal. His face was handsome, but in a way that made the word *beautiful* or even *pretty* seem more apt. He looked neither fierce nor deadly. By Taka Mal standards, he wasn't at all masculine, but she could see why the queen found him compelling. He was uncommonly pleasing to look upon.

She suddenly realized she was gawking at the prince consort. Mortified, she dropped to one knee and bent her head. "My honor at your presence, Your Majesty."

Footsteps sounded on the stone floor. Then Drummer was down on his knees, peering at her. "Did you drop something?"

"Goodness! You shouldn't be on the floor. I haven't swept it yet." She scrambled back to her feet.

Drummer rose in a fluid motion and smiled, a dazzling flash of white teeth. "Neither should you be on the floor. And Ginger-Sun, you needn't sweep the temple. You have maids to do all that. Acolytes, too, someday."

"Oh." She put one palm against her cheek. She was used to doing everything herself. "It's gracious of you to visit."

He motioned to the fountain. "Would you sit with me?"

"I would be honored."

They settled on the ledge while their guards stood at the temple entrances. The fountain burbled next to them.

Drummer regarded her with a kind gaze, "I'm just a minstrel. Don't kneel to me."

She spoke softly. "There is much to get used to here."

"It takes awhile." He pushed his hand through his shining hair. *Like the sun*. He had sky eyes and sun hair. "But a person adapts," he said. More to himself, it seemed, he added, "Eventually."

From his tone, she suspected he was still adjusting. It had to be hard for him, immersed in a culture where he was considered strange and exotic; a place where few people were inclined to trust him; where strength, height and military prowess were far more valued in men than an ability to sing. She couldn't imagine how he dealt with the royal court after he had spent his life wandering as a minstrel.

She had at least learned the protocols in the temple, so she could serve all who came to her.

In the same instant Ginger said, "Queen Vizarana thought you might—" Drummer said, "Jade said you—" They both stopped, and she laughed self-consciously.

"Go ahead," he said.

"It's just, well—the queen thought you might help me learn about my Aronsdale ancestry."

He nodded, seemingly relaxed, but his shoulder muscles were tensed beneath his shirt. "If you would like."

She took the opal out of a pocket in her skirt and held her hand open with the pyramid on her palm. "My grandfather gave this to me. He said someday I would want to go to Aronsdale." She regarded Drummer with an apologetic look. "I have never so wished. But I would like to know—to—" She stopped, afraid to say more.

"About this?" he asked. A golden radiance formed around the pyramid, sparkling with points of light.

"Oh!" She stared at the light. "That's beautiful."

"It doesn't frighten you?"

"But why would it—" Ginger stopped, realizing what she was about to say. Drummer had made the light while their guards were here. The soldiers were too far away to hear her and Drummer, or see her hand clearly, so they might think she had a candle, but no guarantee of that existed. She felt as if she were standing on the edge of a cliff with no idea what lay below.

She leapt.

"How can you make light with my opal?" she asked. "Don't you have to use your own? I've only used this rock, except a few times when I was—" She almost said *desperate,* then stopped. She didn't want him to ask her why. "When I was trying especially hard."

His shoulders relaxed, and he exhaled. Perhaps he had feared her reaction as much as she feared his. The light faded around her opal.

"It's the shape," he said. "The more sides it has, the greater the power it gives you. And three-dimensional shapes are stronger than those with two dimensions." He nodded at her opal. "That's a good shape, a strong one."

"It's the most sides I've ever used." The circle and ring were two dimensions.

He didn't seem surprised. "Each mage has a maximum shape."

"And colors, too?"

"Yes! That's right." He beamed at her. "Colors determine the type of spell. Red creates heat and flame. Orange is for physical comfort. Yellow soothes. Green is for sensing emotions, and blue is for healing."

He knew! Someone existed who understood. But green and blue? "I've never done emotion or healing spells."

"Every mage has different talents. From what Baz told me, yours are the hot colors."

Hope unfolded within her. "Will you teach me?"

He gave her a rueful look. "I'm no expert. But I'll try. We can learn together."

"I would like that."

"Like *what?*" a rumbling voice demanded.

Ginger didn't jump this time, though this new voice was, on the surface, far more threatening than Drummer's musical words. She looked up at the scowling warlord who stood a few paces away. The contrast between him and Drummer was so acute, they seemed like

different species. Darz towered, his broad shoulders and heavy mus-
culature evident. He wore his day uniform, a dark red shirt with five
enameled disks on the chest and brown trousers with heavy boots.
His black hair was tousled as if he had been riding, and his eyes
blazed. It was only noon, yet already the shadow of a beard darkened
his face. Even when he wasn't angry, he looked fierce, as if he were
ready to skewer someone.

Ginger rose to her feet. "Light of the morning, husband."

He stalked over to them and glared at Drummer. "You better not
be singing to her."

Drummer also stood. "A pleasant day to you, too, Baz." He didn't
sound exactly thrilled.

"It was lovely to talk to you," Ginger told Drummer. Then she
took Darz's arm. "Perhaps you will join us?"

Darz's smile quirked at Drummer. "She might civilize me yet, eh?"

Drummer gave a startled laugh. He had the tact to refrain from
answering.

The three of them talked for a bit, and Ginger watched Darz and
Drummer, fascinated. Although they behaved as if they didn't like
each other, she didn't believe them. They were so unalike, they
would probably never see the world in the same way, but she had a
feeling they had come to terms with their differences more than
either was willing to admit. It made her smile, but she refrained from
any comments that would embarrass them.

Eventually Drummer returned to the palace, and Ginger and
Darz strolled outside, where the gardens drowsed in the heat of
midday. So much green life: grass and flowers and vines and trees.
It cooled the air. More eloquently than all the jewels and gold in the
palace, the copious water here spoke of the great Quaazera wealth.

They stopped at a wooden bridge that arched over a creek. Trees heavy with red-box vines drooped over the water, and sun-dragons grew in profusion on the banks, mixed with exotic blue skybells the Aronsdale queen had sent as a wedding gift for Jade and Drummer. The perfume of flowers drifted on the air. Gold-wings trilled, and butterflies with red and gold wings floated over the blossoms. The creek gurgled, part of it routed to the temple and the rest flowing to the lake. They stood at the rail where they could see that body of water, which mirrored the endless blue sky.

"It's so lovely," Ginger said.

"Aye." Darz sounded subdued. "So much in our world is ugly and harsh. A place like this seems ephemeral, as if we could lose it tomorrow to war or treachery or violence."

His pensive tone surprised Ginger. "The Topaz Palace has stood here for over six centuries. The House of Quaazera has ruled even longer."

He smiled at her. "How do you know all that?"

"I read history scrolls."

"We have many in the temple."

"I can catalogue them for you." The prospect appealed to her, and with help in the temple, she would even have time.

Darz kissed her. "I'm glad you're here, Ginger-Sun."

"I'm honored."

"I don't want you to be honored." His grin flashed. "I want you to be madly, passionately enthralled by your irresistible husband."

A laugh bubbled within her. "That, too. Especially by his modesty."

"Well, he tries." He moved behind her and put his arms around her waist. "If you'll be patient with him."

"Always," she murmured. In truth, she liked him exactly the way he was, grumbling, snoring loud voice, and all.

They stood together, gazing at the lake that gave life to the desert much as a lonely warlord and priestess had given life to each other.

Don't miss the first novel in the new Heart of Stone trilogy by
C.E. Murphy!

Because daylight can kill more than vampires....

Jogging through Central Park, Margrit Knight hadn't planned to encounter a dying woman, a mysterious stranger and an entry into a world she'd never dreamed of. But she could hardly deny what she'd seen...and touched.

Alban, one of the fabled Old Races who have hidden their existence for centuries, reveals himself to Margrit so that she can direct the police away from him and find the real killer.

As the dead pile up, Margrit must race the sunrise to clear Alban's name and keep them both alive....

Heart of Stone
coming in November 2007!

LUNA™

Available wherever trade paperbacks are sold!

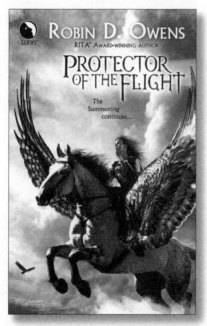